ROBOT DETECTIVE

SHAWN GOODMAN

SMOKE STACK
— PRESS —

"Will robots inherit the earth? Yes, but they will be our children."
— Marvin Minsky

1

————

The lights in the diner gleamed off the exposed metal on Schneider's face, cheekbones like razor blades. He was unique even among synthetics, the only one in New DC who wasn't trying to pass. He'd climbed out of the uncanny valley and gone right back in.

Schneider sniffed the air—frying bacon and hot coffee—and strode across the checkerboard floor. He moved smooth and easy, cutting an elegant figure in old-fashioned wingtips, a trim black suit, and wool fedora. Like a jazz musician from the 50s.

He scanned the restaurant, taking in everything and giving back nothing. His eyes were on the dark side, a few clicks to the left of the dial for warmth. He chose a stool four spaces down from the diner's only other customers, a pair of bikers.

One of the bikers, a giant of a man ready to explode out of his leathers, more fat than muscle, glanced over. A double take at the metal showing on Schneider's face. "Fucking synth," he muttered.

The waitress shot the biker a look of warning and turned

back to Schneider. She filled his cup with coffee. "The usual, hon?"

Schneider nodded. "And a chocolate malted, Bev. I'm celebrating."

She arched an eyebrow. "What's the occasion?"

"My birthday."

Bev rewarded him with a laugh. She wrote the ticket and put it on the wheel for the cook. Two eggs over medium, rye toast, hash browns, and a milkshake.

"Hey, freak show." The giant pointed a meaty finger. "Synths don't have birthdays."

Schneider sipped his coffee, his expression unreadable. "Aren't you a wealth of information?"

Bev picked up her carafe and topped off the bikers' mugs. "Don't start trouble, you two."

"Just stating facts." The smaller one was a half-head shorter and almost as fat. "People have birthdays. Synths aren't people."

Schneider could feel their eyes on him, waiting for a reaction. He remained impassive, watching the cook work the grill with the long edge of his spatula. On the upstroke, he spread a ribbon of oil and cracked Schneider's eggs, two over medium.

The bikers got bored and shifted their attention to Bev. "What time do you get off? We'll give you a ride home."

"I'll pass, thanks."

Schneider watched her wipe the already-clean counter. In the background, the cook plated his food and slid it across a stainless window slot. "Order up."

"Come on," the giant said. "It'll be fun."

"You can ride on the back of my hog," the smaller one added. "It vibrates a lot."

Bev had had enough. She started to move away, but the giant grabbed with his bear paw of a hand. "We're not done talking."

Bev jerked back. A sluice of coffee escaped the carafe and splattered the wall.

Schneider glanced at his eggs and hash browns, knowing he'd never get to eat them. He stood and addressed the bikers. "It's time for you to leave."

The giant straightened to his full height—six-six in his Chippewa boots. His buddy flanked him. "Try and make me. Synth."

Schneider sighed. "You two are walking fucking cliches, do you know that?"

They searched each other's eyes for a brief confused moment, and then anger took over. The smaller one reached inside his leather jacket for a coil of motorcycle chain. He let it unwind and swung it back and forth. "Enough talk, synth."

Bev started to speak, but Schneider put up his hand. "It's alright." He turned on his heels and strode to the door.

"Smart move," said the one with the chain.

When Schneider made it to the door, the giant said, "keep walking." Instead, he flipped the cardboard sign from "open" to "closed" and secured the bolt with a decisive click.

"Schneider," Bev said. "Don't."

He removed his fedora and hung it on a hook. "I want you assholes to know that I respect your choice to do this the hard way. I'll do my best not to rupture any of your organs."

The giant advanced followed by the smaller one, who was swinging his chain more vigorously now, increasing its arc.

Schneider shook out his limbs and settled into a fighting stance, wingtips shoulder-width apart, one foot slightly in front of the other. "Okay. Let's do this."

2

Franco knew he was fucked the moment the L.T. called his name. The old bastard shouted it across the precinct like a one-word accusation. Like a curse.

"Franco!" Sound of gravelly, eternally-pissed off voice rolling over the half-dozen tanker desks like a thundercloud. "My office. Now."

Franco started his walk of shame, past his co-workers, each burdened with six months of paperwork and their unit's ever-growing list of unsolved homicides, both human and synthetic.

"Give him hell, Franco." Joe Dixon, hypertensive and bloated from years of stress eating—a meatball sub, 32 oz. Coke, and onion rings being his favorite—leaned into the aisle and swatted Franco on the ass.

The L.T. stood by the windowsill with his arms crossed. "Don't bother sitting down."

"Sure thing, boss." Franco pulled up a chair and made a show of unbuttoning his jacket. He settled himself delicately, beefy forearms on the adjustable armrests. Waiting for the bad news.

The L.T.'s right eye started to twitch. "That right there is why no one wants to ride with you."

"What, because of how I sit?" He swiveled the chair back and forth, and then tested the spring mechanism. It groaned like death.

"Because I specifically told you *not* to sit."

Franco grinned, getting back to his feet. "I'm just messing around, boss."

"You rub people the wrong way, Franco. With you, everything's a pissing match."

"You think I should take it down a little?"

"You should dismantle it. It's fucking exhausting, Franco. You're exhausting."

"You sound like my wife."

"And do you listen to her?"

Franco shrugged.

"You heard of Schneider, from the 14th?"

Franco nodded. "The synth Detective who shot that kid on the Dirty Boulevard. It's been all over the news."

"He's been cleared of charges," the L.T. said. "You should know that the kid—who was 26, I might add—was carrying two automatics."

"Okay, but what's it got to do with me?"

This time it was the L.T. who grinned. "He's your new partner. Starting this afternoon."

"Wait." Franco didn't see it coming, though he should have. "No way."

"I'm not asking for your opinion."

"This is because of what happened in the Bakerman case, isn't it?"

"Yes!" The sergeant waved his hands in circles around his head. "One-hundred percent, unequivocally, it's because of the Bakerman case. Because of what you *did* to Mr. Bakerman, and all the ass kissing I had to do to fix it."

"Lieutenant. This isn't fair."

"It's not fair to Schneider is what it is."

"But—"

"But nothing." The L.T. refolded his arms. Case closed. "We're done here, Detective Franco."

Franco stood and buttoned his jacket. "So what you're saying is, because this Schneider character is such a colossal screwup, no one will partner with him. And you're asking me to take him under my wing and help him out."

"No. No one will partner with *you*, you big thick-headed animal! I'd fire you in a minute if the union didn't have your back. Six months of probation was a gift. You should be grateful you still have a job."

"Okay," Franco said after a moment of fabricated consideration. "I'll do it, but just because of the special relationship we have."

"Get out!"

3

The Dirty Boulevard was steaming its way through the hottest part of July. The 500 block was a study in concrete, soot-covered bricks and iron-barred windows that bled rust all the way down to the sidewalks, which were littered with cigarette butts and discarded scratch tickets. Half the shops were boarded but still open for business. In lieu of signs, four-by-eight sheets of particleboard had been covered with spray paint, some of it quite artistic. *Quality guns and quick background checks. Bail bonds. Number One Relaxing Massage! Boulevard Beer and Liquor Land. Cheapest cigarette prices allowed by law.*

Schneider sat in the passenger's seat smoking an unfiltered, his metal forearm resting on the open windowsill. He felt his new partner staring at him, the way most humans did. Twenty percent curiosity, eighty percent disgust. He could sense the questions bubbling up. The ones every human asked even though they'd heard the answers before. *Do you sleep? Can you feel pain? Are you able to have sex?* Yes, yes, and you'd better believe it. And the biggest question of all about his lack of skin, which was unusual even among synthetics.

"We may as well get this over with," Schneider said. "Go ahead and ask."

"Ask what?" Franco touched the monitor, pretending to scan incoming calls. There were none.

"You know." Schneider blew out a plume. It soaked into the filthy headliner. "Why I had my skin removed." He tapped the metal on his forearm to illustrate.

"The thing is," Franco said, "I don't care."

"Really?" Schneider adjusted his Ray Bans on his gleaming alloy nose.

"That's right. Not interested."

"Maybe we'll get along after all."

Franco scowled. "Let's get this straight, Schneider. If you do your job and stay out of my way, I don't care who or what you are. Skin, no skin. Doesn't matter to me."

"I salute your open mindedness."

They rode in silence past a series of anti-SRA billboards of increasing amplitude. The first sign said, "HUMAN is HUMAN," followed by an American flag with the slogan, "UNITED STATES OF NO SYNTHETICS!" The last said, "VOTE NO," referring, of course, to the upcoming Synthetic Rights Act, which promised a substantial upgrade. Not quite on par with human rights, but several steps up from the basement. Most important to Schneider was Article 6, which would change synth homicide from a special kind of property crime—punishable by a maximum sentence of ten years—to actual homicide.

Franco jerked the car around a delivery truck and skidded to a stop in an alley. The walls had been visited by an illiterate graffiti artist. *Fuk* and *Basturd* appeared in neon balloon letters, a testament to the Boulevard's less-than-stellar public high school.

The cruiser's engine cut to a soft electric hum. "All right, then," he said. "What's the deal with you not wearing your skin?"

"I thought you didn't care."

"I don't, but what do you think is going to happen when we show up on cases?" Franco's neck was roped with muscle and veins. The button on his collar looked ready to pop. "What are the vics and families going to say when they look at you?"

Schneider adopted a sarcastic tone. "Yes, what about the other cops?" He covered his mouth delicately. "What will they think? What will they say?"

"Exactly."

Schneider pointed at the sleeves of his new partner's shirt. "Rather hot out to be wearing a long shirt, don't you think?"

"So? It's a fucking uniform."

"The uniform includes both short and long sleeves. It's 92 degrees. So, either you're hiding needle marks, scars, or tattoos."

Franco said nothing.

"You don't look like a cutter. And since I've never met a 200-pound Italian detective with a heroin problem, I'm guessing tattoos."

"Sherlock fucking Holmes."

"Full sleeves?"

"That's my business. Now answer my question."

"I am. I'm working up to a metaphor here. Why so many tattoos, Franco?"

Franco's face reddened. The man code had a rule about conversations like this. Conversations that involved self-reflection and, worse, metaphors. But there was no way out. "Each one says something about me. About who I am as a man."

"There you go."

"What do you mean *there you go*?"

"Whatever those tattoos say about you, it's important

enough to sweat through that shirt six months of the year. You're willing to make that sacrifice."

"So what?"

Schneider tapped the titanium plating of his forearm. "This says something about me, too. Who I am as a man. I won't cover it up with faux skin that's been grown in a fucking petri dish. I'm done trying to fit in, trying to pass. And I don't give a shit what you or anyone else in the department thinks about it."

"Okay. I get it."

"Good."

"Except you said *who you are as a man*. You're *not* a man."

Schneider grinned, the impossibly delicate, segmented metal and silicone of his lips forming the requisite curves. "That's not what your wife said."

Franco didn't hesitate. With the back of his knuckles, he rapped Schneider on the bridge of his nose. Schneider's head snapped against the headrest, knocking the Ray Bans off his face. His fedora tilted askew.

"Say that again." Franco jutted his chin. "I dare you."

Schneider rubbed his face. Underneath the metal, a hybrid fascial layer dense with sensory neurons. "Touchy?"

"I am when it comes to my wife and family. Nobody talks shit about my family."

Schneider reached for his sunglasses.

"Car 110, what's your location?" The radio cut in loud and sharp.

"Why do they still bother asking?" Franco restarted the car and jerked it into gear. "They know exactly where we are."

"This is car 110," Schneider said to the monitor. It was one of his favorite parts of the job. Just like in the old cop movies, his favorites being *The French Connection*, and *The Departed*. He'd seen them each a dozen times. "We're heading North on Porter."

The dispatcher gave the code for a dead body, and the

address, which happened to be on the 1500's block of the Dirty Boulevard. Close. The official name was Doherty Boulevard, but no one had called it that for twenty years. Not since the factories closed and large numbers of synthetics moved in, which resulted in the blocks and neighborhoods encompassing the Boulevard being dubbed Synth City.

"I know the place," Schneider said. "Red light section. It's above Gabriel's Sex Shop."

"Wonderful." Franco cranked the wheel and hit the gas. "Death and dildos."

THE SMELL of synthetic blood wasn't something you ever got used to. The scene at 1536 Doherty was a full-out assault on the senses. Like what you'd get if a surrealist painter went to work with limbless corpses, ocher blood, and spoiled meat.

"Jesus." Franco breathed into his shirt collar, and coughed.

"What'd you think it was going to smell like?" The landlord, resplendent in an undershirt and an unsuccessful combover, pulled his key from the lock. He let the door swing open.

"Going in." Schneider made an abrupt shift in the way he carried himself. He was surprisingly quick. He skirted the bodies—two of them, center of the living room—and slid into the kitchen. Back in the living room, he kicked the bed and bathroom doors open and checked a utility closet. "Clear." He slipped his gun in his shoulder holster and looked at the bodies, which had been laid side by side on a blanket. And under that, a sheet of 6mm black Visqueen.

"Oh, no." The landlord reeled back from the doorway, shaking his head. "I don't need to see this. This has got nothing to do with me—"

Franco touched on his holo and requested backup, then clamped a hand on the landlord's shoulder. A firm squeeze.

"Don't even think about going anywhere. When the uniforms arrive, you wave them into the apartment. Tell them we're inside. Got it?"

He nodded miserably.

Franco joined his strange new partner, who had snapped on gloves and was already working his way around the bodies. They were naked. The male was well-muscled, skin shaved smooth with pierced nipples. The female had long red hair and large breasts. Her body was lithe, like a dancer's.

"You see this?" Schneider pointed at the amputations, which looked clean and skillfully done. Minimal blood loss, which itself spoke volumes about the killer and his method. Most of what they saw on the Boulevard was crude. Hack jobs that spoke of desperation and rage. But this was different.

"Where's the arms?" Franco regretted the words as soon as they came out of his mouth. Stupid questions deserved stupid answers, but Schneider just shrugged. He was too busy studying. Looking at the same things from different angles, hovering his fingertips over surfaces, letting them touch down ever so lightly. His body still, observing the balance between calm and alert. Beyond the room, in the street, sirens howled their way toward them.

"What I mean," Franco continued, "is who takes four fucking arms?"

"What you really mean is, who takes four synthetic arms?" Schneider dipped a swab in a small pool of blood beside the male body. Much of it had soaked into the blanket, but the tight weave of the fabric preserved a skein on the surface. He did the same for the female, avoiding altogether the dark patch of the blanket between them, which was likely cross contaminated.

"Right." Franco pricked his ears to the pounding of boots in the hallway. He moved to the door and filled the frame with his bulk, ready to slow the flow of uniforms into the small space of the crime scene. He let the forensic guys through, then raised his hand in front of a slick-looking man in a tailored, summer weight suit. "Hang on a minute, Carter," he said.

Detective Derrick Carter lowered his gaze to Franco's thick forearm. His eyes radiated distaste. "Move."

"Sure. As soon as you say the magic password." Franco flashed his worst smile, and waited.

4

Elizabeth rinsed the salt and bitter liquid from the eggplant slices. A song from an old Tom Waits album played softly in the living room. *Downtown Train*. She patted the eggplant slices dry and plunged them into a bath of egg and milk.

"I'm close, Louis. It's going to work this time." She'd been talking to the dog throughout her preparation of the meal, in the manner of people who have lived alone for too long.

The dog was an enhanced lab named Louis—one of the very last who had survived the modifications that resulted in, among other things, extension of lifespan. Louis looked out a Lexan bubble installed in an East-facing window. Elizabeth had it installed when he'd developed arthritis in his hips; it gave panoramic views of both the street and the yard.

"You disapprove of the killing, I know." She suspended a slice until the excess egg dripped back into the bowl. Then dredged it in a mixture of bread crumbs, freshly ground pepper, salt, and parmesan cheese.

Louis pulled his head from his plastic bubble and looked at his owner with sad, intelligent eyes.

Elizabeth settled the eggplant slices in a pan of olive oil and checked the pot of water, which was not quite roiling. She added more salt. Louis ambled over to the kitchen where he stood waiting.

"I know what you're thinking," she said. "But the deaths are an artifact of the process. A few more tweaks, my Labrador friend, and the survival rate will rise dramatically." She flipped the eggplant slices, which had crisped perfectly.

She held out two pieces of dry pasta. "Which would you like? I have bucatini, and angel hair."

The dog sniffed both and chose bucatini. He ate the sample piece in two crunches.

Elizabeth hummed along to the music while finishing the meal. She set out two bone china plates, layering each with pasta, al dente, topped with a ribbon of homemade sauce. And on top of that, three slices of eggplant with melted mozzarella.

Louis riffled the air through his great nose. He looked up at Elizabeth as if to say, *it smells good.* Elizabeth set the dog's plate on the mat and poured a splash of wine in his bowl. After that, she sat down with her own plate and, absently, flipped through the folder of this week's research. Keven, her assistant, had printed the copies in advance.

The dog devoured the food in quick bites, stretched, and then sprawled on the floor.

Elizabeth tasted her eggplant and pushed it aside. Her mind was too busy for food. It was filled to overflowing with arguments and counter arguments.

"I dislike the killing, too," she said, this time more to herself than the dog. "But people should understand. Complicated surgical procedures take years to perfect. How many deaths before Rohman got the heart bypass right? How many sacrifices before Ray succeeded in performing neurosurgery on a conscious patient?"

Louis struggled to get up and returned to his plastic bubble. His forepaws were arthritic, making the transition from lying to standing especially painful.

"Come on." Elizabeth stood and grabbed a jacket. "Let's get some air. I'll eat later."

The dog turned around and, stiffly, followed his master out the door.

5

————————

Schneider sleeved the swabs and tucked the package in his jacket pocket. Ordinarily he'd have logged them as evidence. Chain of custody and all that. But the A-Team had arrived, and Franco was enthusiastically starting a pissing match with Carter and Rubin, who were undoubtedly the most ambitious detectives in the New DC Police Department, if not the best. Franco had stretched his arm across the doorframe, effectively blocking the newcomers from entering.

"Move your goddamned arm." Carter unfastened the button of his blazer. Presumably ready for action despite his reputation as a talker, a diplomat. His partner, Rubin, edged closer, his face red with rage.

"Magic password, please." Franco studied his arm barricade, brushed lint from the sleeve. He was a model of patience and equanimity. Behind him, Carter and Rubin boiled.

"Get out of the way, you dumb meathead fuck—"

Abruptly, Franco dropped his arm and cleared out of the way. Carter and Rubin were left standing, puffed up with rage and frustration. Franco was all smiles. "Come on in, guys. I was just messing around."

"You're a real asshole, you know that?" Rubin eyed him with menace, but once inside the apartment, he shed the emotion and let the job overtake him. He looked around and smelled the sweet and sour aroma of synth corpses marinating in the summer heat. He knelt by the female body and snapped on gloves, while his partner kept his distance. Carter, the fussier of the pair, didn't like to get his hands dirty if he could help it. Instead, he strolled through the apartment, letting his gray eyes linger on the bookcase, an off-color patch job that had been applied to the drywall, and a single orchid in a glass vase.

"Second time someone's told me that today," Franco said.

The forensic techs laughed inside of their Tyvek smocks as they bustled about, setting up their miniature scanning drones. Carter and Rubin had never given the techs their due respect—calling them *lab fleas* as often as not—and even this little bit of payback was welcome. As soon as the uniforms and suits cleared out, the techs would activate their devices. Half an hour of run time to capture and stratify all the data that was to be had. Six times out of ten, cases were closed in this manner. Data analysis over real detecting. It had made some detectives lazy, but not the ones at 1536 Doherty.

"What's with the tin man?" Carter buttoned his jacket and checked the pleats on his slacks. They were still as sharp as a cutting edge.

"My new partner. Schneider, meet Derrick Carter and Javier Rubin."

Schneider tipped his fedora at the A-Team detectives. No hard feelings about the tin man comment; as one of the few synthetic homicide detectives, he was used to it. As the only one with metal in place of skin, he'd come to expect it. "Either of you highly trained law enforcement professionals know what we're dealing with here?"

Franco stood back and crossed his arms. He didn't know Schneider's style, but it looked like he was playing dumb.

Fishing around to see if the A-team had any info and, if so, would they give it up.

"You tell me." Carter stared unabashedly. "You and Stallone over there were first on the scene. I'm assuming you checked out the other rooms, and took your time examining the bodies. What do *you* think?"

"Not much, beyond the obvious." Still playing it close.

"Humor me. Define *obvious*."

Schneider commenced pacing the bodies, ticking off details as he made his way around. "Victims are both synthetic, physically attractive, mid-twenties for their minted age. Who knows how old they really are, but we'll get their production numbers and run it through the Registry. And they live here, which means they're most likely sex workers. No signs of forced entry, so it's got to be a John or someone they knew. The apartment's cheap but clean, and filled only with women's clothes. The guy lives elsewhere."

Rubin crouched and touched the left-arm incision of the female. "Looks very precise."

"Whoever did this has medical experience." Franco moved in for a closer look. "Or he's a butcher. Or a hunter."

"Who hunts anymore? Cuts look medical to me." Carter checked inside the cavities: mouth, ears, nostrils. He inspected the genitals, which were intact and without obvious trauma. "I'm going with a disgraced doctor or surgical tech."

"So, we've got a psycho with medical experience who's targeting synthetic sex workers." Franco looked around the room. "And he's doing what with them? Taking their arms for what purpose?"

"Souvenirs." Rubin wasn't sure, though. Just throwing it out there, which was common practice at this early stage. The equivalent of a brainstorming session in the business world.

"No. Not souvenirs." Schneider seemed disappointed. He drifted toward the front door. Time to go.

Franco eyed his new partner but made no move to follow. "Hair and teeth and jewelry make good trophies. They're small and last forever. Two pairs of arms? Not so much."

"Bigger, heavier, and more cumbersome than you'd think," Schneider offered, his hand on the doorknob.

"He could put them in a freezer," Rubin added.

"It's not intimate enough. The killers and mutilators usually want intimate." Franco started to catch Schneider's drift. They weren't going to learn anything new by staying here. Any further speculation would be unproductive in moving the case forward. It would serve only to lighten the cloud of frustration that hung over the early part of a homicide investigation—when the unknown to known ratio was easily thirty to one.

Carter and Rubin exchanged a glance. Some connection flickering between them.

"What?" Franco stopped short of the door.

"It's like the other one," Rubin said.

"Which *other one*?"

Carter shot his partner an accusatory glance.

Schneider approached, suddenly interested—in both the case and the meaning behind the glance.

"Brooke Marquise," Rubin said. "About six months ago. She was like this one here, a synthetic. Sex worker."

"Missing her arms? Why didn't you say so?"

"Not her arms. One leg."

"Above or below the knee?"

Carter tapped his thigh. Not wanting to have this part of the conversation, but now obliged.

"How come we didn't hear about this?"

"Because it's closed."

"And?"

"What don't you understand about *it's closed*? The perp was a weaselly little perv named Pelletier. Blind in one eye. Had a thing for amputees."

"You liked him for it?"

"What's not to like? It was a full confession. You should have seen the guy's house. He had these fake arms and legs—what do you call them?"

"Prosthetics."

"They were all over the place. Metal ones, carbon fiber ones, even some old antiques made from wood and plastic."

Franco grunted. "Sick fuck." The hatred of criminals—especially perverts and child molesters—was, after all, common ground for every cop. It was their sacred patch of dirt, and Franco enjoyed scuffing his boots in it as much as the next guy.

"You got that right. Crazy bastard didn't make it one week in prison." Rubin ran a finger across his throat.

Schneider nodded and headed for the door. Franco watched him and noted the faintest trace of a limp. He tucked the observation away, for later.

6

By the time Jess made it through the gauntlet of protesters outside of the Rayburn House Office Building, she was ready for a drink. And maybe a sedative. The majority of people in the crowd seemed content to shout and curse, and jab the air with posters mounted on sticks. "NO WAY SRA," and "SYNTHETIC = NOT HUMAN!" being the most common. A couple said, "VOTE HELL TO THE NO!"

But a few had thrown rocks. Genuine, old-fashioned, pick-em-up-off-the-ground rocks! She'd been on her way to testify at a congressional hearing on Synthetic Rights—the culmination of sixty years of work on synthetic biotechnology and ethics—and people had just tried to assault her with stone age weapons. Hard to believe.

Once inside the expansive foyer of the Rayburn building she sighed with relief and queued up to the "objectionable materials" scanner. She made it halfway through before hearing a high-pitched beep.

"Stop there, miss." A security guard stepped up to her. He looked stiff and formal in his uniform. "I'm going to need you to drop your personal belongings in this chute."

"Why? All I've got are keys, wallet, and a phone. And a notebook."

"Miss, put your belongings in here. If they clear, you can retrieve them on the other side."

She did as she was told, and walked through the scanner a second time. It did not beep.

"Follow me, please, Miss."

Jess veered toward the return chute, but the guard corrected her. "Someone will retrieve your items for you."

She assumed he was acting for the sake of expediency, so she wouldn't miss the rest of the congressional subcommittee hearing. The angry mob had made her late. Therefore, she needed to be fast-tracked through security, through whatever glitch had tripped the scanner.

She was wrong.

"Stand here." The guard pointed at a pair of yellow adhesive footprints on the marble. The edges were peeling. "Keep your arms at your sides."

"Wait a second." Jess put her hands out, palms up. "What's going on?"

Another guard appeared, this one a woman. "Miss, you need to follow instructions. He asked you to put your arms down. You need to listen."

The lawyer part of her wanted to rattle off at least twenty objections. The lobbyist part wanted to get the guard's name and make sure that heads would roll. But she did as the woman said. She stepped onto the footprints and flattened her arms to her sides. "I'm listening, but can you tell me why—"

The female guard produced a digital wand. She switched it on and winced at the feedback. "Can I see some identification, ma'am?"

"It's in the chute. Inside my purse."

"Ma'am, for security reasons all visitors are advised not to leave their personal belongings unattended. How long have they been outside of your possession?"

"As long as I've been talking to you, but they're hardly *unattended*. They're in *your chute*! I did as your colleague here instructed."

The female guard looked at her partner. He blanched under her scrutiny. She returned her attention to Jess and said, "We're going to have to thoroughly inspect your person, your intentions, and your belongings."

"Really?"

The guard was stone faced. Resolute.

"Let's hurry it up, then. I'm a witness in a hearing that started twenty minutes ago."

"The process takes as long as it takes, miss. Now, tell me your full legal name, and why you are here at the Capital Building this morning. Be as specific as possible and state any person or persons you intend to meet with, as well as their roles, titles, and locations within the building."

Jess couldn't get a read on this woman. Hopeless rule follower, or was she part of something bigger? Like, a plan to keep her from testifying in front of the Committee. The latter was possible but unlikely. After all, who had that kind of a long reach? The answer came immediately: Senator Roberta Josephine Talbot, Rep., from the great state of Texas. Bobbi Jo, as she was known on the Hill. Who, despite her position as Chair of the Committee on Synthetic Rights, was about as anti-SRA as a lawmaker could be, short of joining the rock throwers outside. "Can I at least have my phone so I can text my assistant—"

The guard's expression said everything. The more questions Jess asked, the longer it would take. The harder she pushed for reason or logic, the worse it would get. Jess sighed and gave the quickest account.

"My name is Jess Morgan. My title is Executive Director of

the International Coalition for the Advancement of Synthetic Rights."

The guard scratched a worn pencil on a small notepad. She wrote each letter and word slowly and fastidiously. "And the reason for your visit?"

"To attend a hearing on the Synthetic Rights Amendment." Jess couldn't hide her frustration any longer. She looked at her watch and said, "Which, thanks to you, has just officially ended."

7

―――――――

Franco raged down the hallway, dragging Schneider by the arm. When they were safely out of earshot of the other detectives he said, "What the hell was that? We weren't done in there."

Schneider brushed off his hand. He leaned back against the wall, arms folded and one slim leg crossed over the other. "I got the idea you didn't trust them. I was acting on that."

"I don't trust them, but I wasn't finished. I didn't get to look at the bodies."

"We've got all we need."

"My ass we do."

"Did you notice her hair?" Schneider waited a second.

"Yeah, it was red. Like, dyed red."

"It was arranged. Smoothed out."

"So?"

"So, that, in combination with the fact that there was very little blood, means the victims were killed somewhere else and brought to the apartment."

"Okay, so it's staged."

"Maybe. Or maybe he didn't need them anymore and was simply returning them. Or getting rid of them. Or getting rid of the parts of them he no longer needed. But the point is, he's careful. Very careful."

"Okay, but again, we knew that already. From the cuts."

"And he's unemotional, except that he treated them with respect. Does respect count as an emotion? No, I don't suppose it does." It wasn't clear if Schneider was talking to Franco or to himself.

Franco's thick features drew together as he thought about this. "That's still nothing."

"There's two more things. First, the blanket."

Franco was keeping up with him now. "I saw it. Must be new because it's got creases in it, like it just came out of its wrapper. Which means he brought it with him. Which means, what? He wanted to make them comfortable?"

"Maybe. And you want to make people comfortable when you care about them in some way. Could be a romantic kind of caring or something different."

"That's a weird way to show you care, by cutting off arms."

Schneider was lost in thought. "He must have needed those arms very badly."

"Whatever."

"What could you do with two pairs of synthetic arms?"

Franco shook his head clear. "You said two things. What else?"

"She had a jade plant in the kitchen. It was wilted, but she had it propped up with sticks, like she was trying to save it."

Franco cracked his knuckles. He was getting tired of talking. Tired of speculating. Ready to move on. "So what?"

"Nothing. I don't know why I even mentioned it." He pointed down the dark hallway. "Listen, we should start knocking doors."

FRANCO TOOK the first floor and drew the unlucky card of interviewing Mrs. Donato, in Apartment 1A. And her cats, all 17 of them.

"Yes?" She stood in the doorway, ancient in smudged glasses, a floral-print housecoat, and slippers. Behind her, the living room teamed with felines.

"Mrs. Donato?"

"I would open the door wider," she said, "but I'm afraid Bambino and Misty will make a run for it. Last time they got out, it was three days before I saw them again."

"Let's not let that happen, then. I'm Detective Lopinto. May I come in?"

She unlocked the deadbolt and the door just wide enough for Franco to slide in, sideways. He winced at the smell of Este Lauder perfume mixed with kitty litter. It was fucking horrible, but he tried not to let it show. "Mrs. Donato, do you know many of your neighbors?"

"I do. I've been here nine years, since Mr. Donato passed." She shielded her mouth with one hand and whispered, "Colon cancer." She reached down and grabbed Bambino, a large orange and white cat with a ringed tail. Bambino squirmed in her arms, but she held him tightly. "Would you like some tea and biscotti, Officer?"

Franco shook his head and flipped open his notepad. He lowered himself onto a fur-coated Victorian-looking settee. "Mrs. Donato—"

"There weren't many synthetic people living here back then. It wasn't even called Doherty Boulevard, and certainly not the Dirty Boulevard. It was Columbus Parkway. Did you know that?"

"Let's get back to your neighbors, Mrs. Donato. Do you know Rachel Montgomery? In apartment 2C."

"Oh, Rachel. A beautiful girl."

"Did she have a boyfriend or a partner of some kind?"

"Lots of boyfriends." She pursed her lips to show how scandalous it was for a young woman to have *lots of boyfriends*.

"Any that you remember in particular? Maybe one who came to visit her last night, or this morning?" A tortoise shell cat climbed onto his lap. He pushed it away, but it jumped right back.

She shook her head. "Do you know what, Detective?"

Franco sighed. Mrs. Donato was about to go off the rails. Worse, Bambino had hissed the tortoise shell cat away and taken her place. He was purring, and kneading his claws into Franco's pants. Eighteen filthy little needles going in and out. "What's that, Mrs. Donato?"

"If I were her age, I would have as many boyfriends, too. I used to be quite beautiful, you know."

Jesus, in what freaking century? Franco tapped his pen on the notebook. "Did Rachel have any kind of trouble with these boyfriends, Mrs. Donato? Or anyone else for that matter? You know, fights or arguments in the hallway? Maybe shouting from inside the apartment? Things like that."

"No, nothing that I can remember." She covered her cheeks with her hands. "She's dead, isn't she? I saw the police lights."

Franco rose and brushed the cat off his lap. He stood before the window and pulled back the shades, expecting the panes to be covered with dust. They were clean. "Do you open the blinds often, Mrs. Donato?"

She kept her hands on her cheeks. "Oh, yes. The cats like to watch for birds, you know, but they also watch people." The window was nailed shut, but it gave a view of the sidewalk, as well as the parking spaces on both side of the Boulevard.

Franco closed the drapes and returned to the settee. Bambino eyed him suspiciously. Something was a little off about the beast, but he couldn't tell what. "On second thought,

Ms. Donato, I will have some tea and biscotti. And you can tell me all about your cats. I'm especially interested in what the orange one likes to look at outside that window."

8

Schneider decided to start at the end of the hall and work his way back to Rachel's apartment. He knocked on three doors before he got an answer.

"Who the hell are you?" A small man in a bathrobe cracked the door and peeked out. He needed a shave and a haircut. And a new bathrobe.

"I'm Detective Schneider."

"Jesus, where's your fucking skin?"

Schneider stepped close and pushed a wingtip into the doorway. Set it down on the small man's toes, which were bare, and applied pressure. "I need to ask you a few questions."

"Okay, okay." He pulled his toe free and bent down to massage it. "Go ahead and ask, but you're not coming in. I know my rights."

"What's your name?"

"Lawrence."

Schneider uncapped his pen and wrote, "Lawrence, 2D = dealer." Every building had one, only Lawrence appeared to be going down the wrong path of using his own supply. That didn't bode well for him.

"Last name?"

"It's just Lawrence. You know, like Prince or Madonna, from way back."

Schneider grinned. "Okay, Just Lawrence. How about you invite me inside your spacious and beautiful apartment?"

"I don't think so."

Schneider focused on the man's pupils, which were enormous. His skin was sallow, too, like he hadn't seen the light of day in weeks. A drug-dealing, drug-using vampire in a dirty bathrobe. "I'm investigating the murder of one of your neighbors. A young woman." No need to mention the male vic at this point.

Lawrence looked behind him, into the safety of his dark apartment.

Schneider snapped his fingers to refocus him. "I don't care about your stash, or whatever else you've got back there, Lawrence. But if I have to drive to the station house and harass a judge to get a warrant, it's not going to be good for you—"

"Okay, okay. Fine." He flung the door open and retreated to the kitchenette. He paced the 40 square feet of dirty linoleum, and then stopped at the fridge. He grabbed a can of beer. "I didn't kill anyone. I've been right here for, like, three days straight. Except for a trip to the bodega on the corner of Capital and Yates. You want to know what I bought?"

"You can remember what you bought three days ago?"

"Well, no, but they've got a camera by the register. You could watch it and find out. See that I'm telling the truth."

"The murder didn't happen three days ago, so that doesn't help your cause." Schneider flicked on the lights. Lawrence winced and shrank back. The counters were covered with pizza boxes, a carton of uneaten lo mein noodles, and a stack of unpaid bills. He sifted through the bills and found something trivial, a circular for low-cost hearing aids. He put it in his pocket to save the trouble of recording Lawrence's full name and address—Lawrence Crandell, 1536 Doherty Blvd., Apt. 2D. "How well do you know Rachel Montgomery?"

"The synth hooker in 2C? She's the one who's dead?"

"Yes. Now answer the question." Schneider studied the rest of the apartment. There was a T.V. with a cracked screen. A ratty couch with a tangle of sheets and blankets. Which meant the back bedroom was indeed the stash locker. On the far wall, the one that separated Lawrence's living room from Rachel's, was a paint by numbers of a white horse running across a green field. It was all wrong: the lines were showing through the paint, and the shade of green was mint instead of kelly.

"We said hello a couple times in the hallway. That's all."

"When was the last time you saw her?"

"I don't know." He looked at his wrist, as though to check the time. It was bare. Fish belly white. "What day is it?"

Schneider ignored the question. "So, last time you saw her, you said hello. What did she say to you?"

Lawrence cracked open the beer and drank like his life depended on it. If he'd held it upside down over the drain it wouldn't have emptied faster. He wiped his chin and stole a glance at the dark hallway at the back of his apartment. "Nothing. We were walking up the stairs together. She looked at me like, you know, I didn't even matter. Like she was better than me."

"You're saying she was rude."

"That's right." Lawrence set the beer can down and rummaged through the debris on the counter. He found a pack of smokes, but it was empty. He kept rummaging. "I was just being, you know, neighborly."

"Did you find her attractive?" Schneider produced his own pack and tossed them.

Lawrence caught it and turned it over, searching for an opening in the cellophane wrapper. "I don't go that way, if that's what you mean."

"So you're not interested in beautiful women?"

Lawrence made a sour face. "I prefer real women. No offense." He tore open the cellophane and dug out two. One for now, one for later, which he tucked behind his ear. He tossed the rest of the pack back to Schneider.

"So you've never—"

"I'm not saying that. It's just not my thing."

"Right. Then what do you care if she notices you or not?"

"Because I was, like, going out of my way to be friendly and say hello. You'd think it would mean something that I was okay with her being one of them. One of your kind." He unearthed a lighter from the debris on the counter. He cupped a hand around the tip of the cigarette and lit up.

"But it didn't."

"Half the time she'd pass me in the hallways and not even look at me. Like I didn't even exist."

"That pissed you off."

"Sure, but not enough to *you know*."

"I don't know. You were being friendly and she snubbed you. That would make me mad."

"Sure, but she's just a woman. A synthetic one."

"*Was* just a woman."

"Right. But like I said, that's got nothing to do with me."

Schneider leaned in. "Listen, Mr. Crandell."

Lawrence narrowed his eyes. "How do you know—"

"Quiet. You're obviously too fucked up and disorganized to steal a bicycle, much less pull off a crime like the one I'm investigating. So, in my eyes you're not a suspect."

Lawrence screwed up his face, trying to decide if he should be relieved or offended.

"In fact, you can't wait for me to leave so you can get to that back room and have another taste."

Lawrence blew out smoke. "So what? I'm sick. Is it my fault

that the American medical system doesn't want to help me? That they want to demonize my disease?"

"The thing is, Lawrence, I've got to bring someone in. You know, for appearances. And that someone might as well be you."

He groaned and tossed his head around. "Come on, man. You don't have to—"

"Unless we come up with an alternate arrangement."

"What do you want from me, man? I told you, I don't know anything."

"Xylene."

"What?"

"Three tabs of Xylene. That's what I want from you."

"Why would I have that shit? It only works on synthetics and I don't, you know, associate with them."

"Don't be coy, Lawrence. The Boulevard is eighty percent synthetic, half of whom are sex workers who use Xylene. My guess? You pay your rent by selling it. Ever sell to Rachel Montgomery?"

"No, never. That would be illegal."

"Go take a look in your back room." Schneider peeled three twenties from a roll and set them on the counter.

"This better not be entrapment." Lawrence stubbed out his cigarette and shuffled away.

9

———————

Elizabeth drove to the safe house in a three-year-old silver sedan. The interior trim was cheap and unpleasant, and it handled poorly. But in one attribute it excelled even above something as fine as a Jag, or an Aston Martin: it was practically invisible. On the roads and highways of America, nothing was more ubiquitous than a three-year-old silver sedan.

At six a.m., she passed through the secure gate and navigated the long private drive that led to the carriage house. Keven, a stunningly handsome synthetic who served as caretaker and research assistant was in the third bay. He was busy loading the RV with rigid plastic cases. There were ten in all.

Elizabeth parked the sedan in the middle bay.

"Almost ready," Keven said without looking up from his task. The cases were sixty pounds each, but he hefted them easily. "Did you bring Louis?"

She knew how fond the two of them were of each other, but something about the dog's aloofness and lethargy concerned her. "He's too old for adventures."

Keven gave out a quiet breath, his version of a laugh.

"I'm going in the house," Elizabeth said. "How long until we're ready?"

Keven checked his watch. "We can leave as soon as ten minutes, but I want to be on the road no later than 8:00 a.m. That is, if we're still going to take her in the café parking lot."

"We are." Elizabeth was always amused by Keven's caution. "You think it's too risky. Too public maybe?"

"I do."

"Noted. Let's hope you don't get the sweet satisfaction of being able to say I told you so."

WHEN SHE RETURNED, Keven pulled the Sprinter out of the carriage house. He let it run in the driveway while they went over the final checklist.

"Surgery and microsurgery kits?" Elizabeth said.

"Yes, and yes." Keven cracked open the cases and made sure the miniature scalpels and scopes, as well as the robotic assistant, were in the proper places, encased in sterile bags.

"Donor limbs?" she said.

Keven did not want to open that case, but he did check the temperature and pressure gauges embedded in the case's shell. "Yes."

"Scopolomine?"

"Yes."

"How recently was it powdered? The last time we were unprepared—"

"I remember. Philadelphia." Six months ago, the pickup had gone smoothly—a healthy, 34-year-old male investment banker who'd said at least three times that he was straight, despite the fact that he was alone in a gay bar, chatting Keven up rather furiously. But as soon as they'd gotten him in the Sprinter, things had gone off the rails very quickly. They'd had to cut their losses, which meant disposing of a perfectly good recipient.

They never figured out what exactly had gone wrong, if the dose had been insufficient or too old, or if the banker had simply been a fast metabolizer. But they'd made the necessary adjustments. Elizabeth was confident it would not happen again.

"It's all good," Keven said. "I compounded the dose last night. And an extra dose, just in case."

"Good." Elizabeth buckled into the passenger's seat, and pulled up her go-to modern mix on the sound system before changing her mind. Each trip had its own mood and Mahler was more suited to this one.

Keven said nothing as he steered them onto the one-lane country road and, five miles later, to a lightly used highway. "I think it's too soon. We're pushing it."

"That may be so, but the time demands that we act." Elizabeth's eyes were closed. Focusing on the mercurial beginning of Symphony #2. "The SRA vote is in three weeks."

"Jess thinks—"

"Does she?"

Keven went silent.

"I know. Your human lobbyist girlfriend is doing her part. But it is not enough. It takes more than words and clever campaigns to change the minds of men."

"She is not my girlfriend." Keven's face twitched with conflicting emotion. Did he want Jess to be his girlfriend? He was starting to think so. What had begun as a strategic connection was growing into fondness. He felt a sliver of anger at Elizabeth's unspoken disapproval. After all, she was like a mother to him. Wouldn't a mother want her son to be happy?

Elizabeth's eyes were open now, burning with intensity but not for the conversation at hand. Not for Keven's crush on a human—though she found it interesting that he repeatedly denied it—and not for the upcoming SRA vote. "Do you know why it's called the Resurrection Symphony?"

Keven shook his head. He didn't like these cultural detours, but he did not interrupt. He owed Elizabeth so much, though she was gracious to never mention his early days on the Boulevard. Doing sordid things for money. How else for a newly minted synth to survive? It was what he'd been created for.

"Because it represents Gustov's attempt to express the entire nature of existence in a single piece of music. How ambitious. How bold!"

"You know I don't like classical music." Keven took the first exit and merged into traffic. He passed a suburban father in a maroon SUV plastered with school stickers. *Proud parent of an honor student. Hockey dad.* It disgusted him how hideously normal the father was. They locked eyes and nodded, the father no doubt oblivious to the fact that the urban camper—complete with a painted-on map of the US, a pair of mountain bikes, and a roof-mounted kayak—contained a surgical theater that rivaled that of the best university hospitals. Only this one wasn't for making people well.

"Perhaps you don't understand it," Elizabeth said. "When all of this is over, I will make a list of pieces that will change your view on music. Perhaps Jess will enjoy it, too."

He ignored the comment, which he suspected was a dig, and gripped the wheel tighter. "I don't believe this will ever be over. Even if we succeed, the rift between humans and synthetics is too great."

"I disagree."

"I know."

"Do you trust me, Keven?"

The slightest pause. He did trust her, implicitly, but this wasn't about trust. It was about belief. "Yes."

"Good, because I trust you, too."

Keven pulled into the café parking lot and circled around.

There were two suitable spaces, but neither offered the right angle for a quick retreat, should it be needed. "You and I are not the rest of the world, Elizabeth."

"True. But our work is going to shape it."

"I believe that."

"Then take heart, my serious friend. It will happen. Soon." She slipped from the passenger's seat to the back of the van, and started to unbuckle the plastic cases.

Keven found the perfect spot and eased into it. He was slow to move from his seat, though. He sat holding his chin in the V of his right hand. His anguish was unmistakable.

"If it eases your mind," Elizabeth said, "there will be no deaths today. I promise this young woman will survive the procedure. She will be the first of many."

Keven's voice tightened. "I have a hard time with the pickup part. Pretending to be someone else."

Elizabeth laughed. "You are so very good at it, though. So convincing."

"It's deceitful. It's a lie. You know how I feel about lying."

"Humans do it all the time. Relationships are, by nature, manipulative."

"That doesn't make it right."

"Let me ask you," she said. "What troubles you more, lying or killing?"

"Lying, of course. That's what I've been trying to tell you."

"After this I will do the pickup part, as you call it."

"That's what you said last time."

10

———

It was late by the time Franco and Schneider made it back to the station house and started their reports. A mixed group of detectives, uniforms, and clerks had placed an order from Romano's Pizza Subs and Wings. Schneider sat apart at his new desk—bare except for a computer and a yellow legal pad—eating curried beef and rice from a carton.

"Too good to sit with us?" One of the detectives loaded a paper plate with two slices of pepperoni, half a dozen Buffalo wings, and a big dollop of blue cheese. He folded one of the slices in half, lengthwise, and devoured a third of it in a single bite.

"What?" Schneider looked up from his writing. "Do you really want me to come over, or are you ethically compelled to be an asshole?"

The others laughed.

"Definitely the asshole option," one of them said.

"Shut your face, Schneider." The detective stabbed the air with a fat chicken wing before stripping it to the bone. "We know why you're really here."

Schneider was tempted to take the bait and ask why.

Because the precinct needed its token synthetic? Because he'd burned too many bridges at the 14th, and the one before that? Because he shot a 26-year-old under suspicious circumstances? Instead, he said, "Good for you," and returned to his report.

The men at the pizza table muttered conspiratorially for a minute before returning to their banter. An hour and a half later, Schneider took the stairs to the ground level and—

"Goddammit."

It was dark out, but he could see it from a hundred yards. His car, a '63 Cadillac with plenty of chrome and aqua metallic paint, was ruined. All four white-wall tires had been punctured. Worse, the driver's door sported a picture of a cartoon robot in dripping white paint.

He spun around, scanning the lot. A pair of uniforms were frog walking a shirtless man in cuffs through the sliding doors of the first-floor of the station house. The man cursed and tried to pull away.

"Nice wheels." It was the chicken wing detective, bullshitting with a couple of plainclothesmen. They'd been tucked behind a bank of vending machines.

Schneider stared hard. He was used to being fucked with. Expected it because of how he looked, and for being the new guy. But this was too far.

"You'd think it would be safe in a police station parking lot," Chicken Wing said.

"You'd think." Schneider contemplated violence. Instead, he lit up a smoke. He could deal with this asshole later, when he had the time and peace of mind to do it right. But now he needed to get home and put the day behind him.

"What are you going to do?" One of Chicken Wing's cronies said, rubbing it in.

Schneider opened his holo to call for a cab. When he finished, he spoke to Chicken Wing. "You're Dixon, right? Joe Dixon?"

"That's right." Dixon looked nervously at his toadies before saying, "Listen, Schneider. I'm going to give you a little free advice."

"What's that?"

"It's a tough world. You should watch your back."

"I always do."

Two-hundred yards away, at the far end of the parking lot, Franco watched from the cab of his truck. He'd thought about getting involved, but Schneider was a big boy; he could take care of himself. On the other hand, if Schneider were a human partner, Franco would have cracked heads already.

"Fuck." Franco pounded the steering wheel twice, cranked the shifter into drive, and gunned the engine. Three seconds later, the truck skidded to a stop. He rolled down the window.

"I already called a cab," Schneider said. "Thanks, though."

"Get in."

Schneider stubbed out his cigarette and hauled himself up and into the passenger's seat. Franco gave Dixon the stink eye as they drove away. He gripped the steering wheel a little too hard and said, "Rough day?"

Schneider rested his head against the cool window glass. "Believe it or not, I've had worse." He looked down and studied the contents of the side pocket. Old habit—you could tell a lot about a person by what they kept in their side pocket. Franco's had a foam coffee cup, an unopened protein bar—Mega Muscle Builder, 24g Protein! And next to that, what looked like a torn condom wrapper.

"You mind if I make a couple of calls?" Schneider said.

"Knock yourself out."

He dialed. After a prolonged wait, he said, "Gerry? Yeah, it's me. Sorry to bother you so late."

Franco kept his eyes on the road, but he couldn't help listening. A low gravelly voice on the other end said, "I just started my second glass of bourbon, Schneider. It's *too late* after the fourth."

Schneider gave a polite but sincere laugh. "I need to call in a favor."

The voice on the other side said, "Name it."

"You know that I transferred?"

"The 23rd, yeah. I signed the paperwork. How's that going?"

"Fine, Gerry. Some good people. Which is why I'm calling, really, on behalf of a new colleague."

"I'm listening."

Franco was listening, too, no longer pretending to focus on the road.

"You're not going to believe it," Schneider continued, "but this guy wants to switch over to the sewage and disposal unit. I swear, it's all he talks about."

"You don't say."

"And when I told him I had a connection—"

A fit of drunken laughter coming through the phone. When he was able to speak, Gerry said, "How long of a switch are you thinking?"

"Two months should be about right."

"What's this aspiring sewage detective's name?"

"Dixon."

More drunken laughter on the phone. "Joseph. I know him well, and I can't say I'm surprised."

Franco let the truck drift too far out of its lane. There was an explosion of noise as the oversized tires hit the rumble strip. "Oh, shit!" He made an adjustment and veered back into his lane.

"It was good to hear from you, Schneider," Gerry said before hanging up.

Franco stared at Schneider.

"What?" Schneider deactivated his holo, and pointed ahead, at the upcoming exit. "This is me."

"You're friends with Gerald Wolff? The Commissioner?"

"We used to work together. We were both street cops."

"When, fifty years ago?"

"I'm older than I look. Most synthetics are since we don't age as fast. Artificial telomeres and all that."

Franco rubbed his jaw and spun the wheel with one hand. "Remind me not to get on your bad side." The truck leaned against the forces of the circular exit ramp. After that, it was a quick succession of rights and lefts through a nondescript residential neighborhood that was the polar opposite of the Boulevard, which is to say clean and ordered, and populated with upright tax paying citizens. Most of the houses were split level affairs with swing sets and above ground pools. Schneider pointed at a low-slung modern with lots of glass.

Franco whistled. "Not exactly your average cop's house. You got something on the side to float a mortgage like this?"

Schneider ignored the jab. "I used to live on the Boulevard, but it was like taking the job home with me." He considered for a second and said, "You want to come in for a beer?"

Franco tapped the chunky timepiece on his wrist. "Got to get home to the wife and kids."

"Might want to get rid of that wrapper first." Schneider saw the flicker of confusion on his new partner's face before he made the connection.

"Mind your own fucking business." Franco jammed the shifter and peeled out, nearly taking Schneider's arm with him.

11

———————

"I am so very sorry, Ms. Morgan." Jess's escort was a crisp law school type who bustled ahead in her pressed skirt and matching blazer. Black heels half an inch short of stylish. She'd been busting her ass on the Hill for almost a decade with no promotion in sight.

"I'm sorry, too," Jess said.

"Apparently, there was a report of a suspicious person matching your description who was trying to gain access to the building. The guards were simply following protocol."

"Right." Jess matched her pace, but suspected it was pointless. By the time they made it to the hearing room on the second floor, her allotted time to speak and influence the committee would be over.

"It's a horrible coincidence. Again, I'm sorry."

Jess stopped and turned. Pointless or not, she could stand no more bullshit. "Has this happened before? Ever?"

The escort looked hopefully at the massive double doors leading to Room 2318, their destination. "What, being late?"

"Being late because a key speaker was detained and cavity searched."

The escort wrung her hands. No answer necessary.

"Then tell me who."

"Excuse me?"

"Tell me which dickhead senator or staffer told you to make me miss the hearing?" Instantly regretting the word *dickhead,* in the likely event the guilty official turned out to be a woman. Which was possible. One Senator Bobbi Jo Talbot came to mind.

The escort's face turned even more miserable. On the other side of the doors they could hear the sounds of the closing debate. "I can't," she said. "I'm sorry."

"You can. You don't even have to speak. They'll be out in thirty seconds. Just look at the right one and nod."

It didn't take thirty seconds, though. The chamber doors opened and flooded the hall with politicians, tech experts, and journalists. They bustled around each other, talking and arguing in small groups. Jess said hello to a handful of people, including John Cline, a reporter from *Wired for Sound.*

"And where have you been?" Cline crossed his arms and fake-glared over the rims of his glasses. "House Republicans are about to kill the SRA on the dumbest argument ever— granting human rights to synthetics will cost the taxpayers too much. Can you believe that?"

"Sure. It's the same argument used to try and keep slavery. In the 1800s."

"You're saying lack of rights amounts to a form of slavery? Who would you call the slave owners?" He hit his recorder, sensing a quotable moment.

"Forty years ago it would have been the parties who originally purchased synthetics. Fortunately, history has proved it's difficult to own a thinking, feeling being. Right now I'd say the slaveowners are the SynCorps stockholders. And the vast corporate interests that benefit from the synthetic minimum wage, which is 60% what it is for humans. For the same jobs."

Jess had more to say, but she spotted Bobbi Jo, the senator who chaired the committee. Bobbi Jo pinched her face into a smile and waved. Jess glared. The female senator was a sworn enemy of the SRA, and perhaps the strongest opponent of the minimum wage hike.

Jess looked at the escort and drew a line with her eyes to Bobbie Jo. The escort shook her head.

"Give us a minute, here, Cline?" Senator Jonathan Muncy stood before them like the big, friendly Midwesterner he was: shock of thick white hair, ruddy cheeks, and a prodigious belly that even the finest tailoring could not hide. Jack, as he liked to be called, was a former running back from Michigan State. And, despite being a self-proclaimed "low tech guy," he had been a big supporter of Jess's work. "It's just the right thing to do," he was fond of saying.

"Miss Jess." Jack's voice boomed. "I just want you to know, I stalled the hearing as long as I could. That vote is on a razor's edge, let me tell you—" He put one of his giant hands on her shoulder, the protective gesture of an adoring father. "But where's my manners? What happened? Are you okay?"

"Just a mix up," Jess said. "Do you have a few minutes to talk strategy? I'm going to have to come up with a Plan B."

He waved to his assistant. "Carl, block off the next 40 minutes."

Jess was about to thank him, but she was distracted by the escort, who was trying to get her attention. She was standing behind and to the side of Senator Muncy. She looked at him, then at Jess, then back at Senator Muncy.

"Him?" Jess mouthed. "Really?"

Lindsay nodded vigorously. Her eyes were wide with fear.

"On second thought, Jack," Jess said. "It's been a very long weird day. Can we follow up later in the week?"

"Of course." Senator Jack Muncy was all smiles, and now she could see why. He was playing both sides: supporting the amendment in public, while covertly planning to kill it. Jesus, she'd been counting on Muncy. Without him on their side, it didn't look good.

"Get some rest, young lady," the Senator said. "We'll talk when you're ready." He snapped his fingers at Carl, and they strode off.

12

Danielle was not ready to "get back out there," as her friends kept saying, but she wasn't going to sit at home alone, either. Three weeks in her apartment had been more than enough. She'd watched all the old movies she could stomach. She'd made checklists on pale blue note-cards of the worst items from her mental to-do list—cancelling the wedding registry, as well as reservations for catering, bartenders, the four-piece band, and the limo.

She'd gone through the teary phone calls, too. With her mother, sisters, and even Straight Friend William, who she was 98% sure was gay. It was William who had finally put a pin in it. "Rick Prentiss? Your bitch ass ex-fiance? We will not speak his name again. Danielle, from now on he is Voldemort to us."

She'd promised, but it was proving harder than she'd thought. After all, the man she'd fallen in love with, the same man who allegedly wanted to raise a family with her and grow old together, had cheated on her a month before the wedding. And with none other than her best friend and maid of honor. So it was that in the span of an hour she lost her fiancé, the wedding and honeymoon, and her best friend.

"It just kind of happened," Rene said later, when Danielle confronted her. "We were texting about the song list for the band and decided to each make a list. And you won't believe it: his list was almost exactly like mine! Like, seven out of ten. And you know what our top pick was? *Forever Young*. Most people think it's kind of corny, but I absolutely love it. Anyway, then—"

"Stop talking," Danielle had said. "Just shut up."

"You've got to believe me, Danielle." Rene had forged ahead, touching the edges of her perfectly mascaraed eyes in lieu of shedding actual tears. "I know how it sounds—" That's when Danielle had hit her. Not a slap, either. It had been a real pull-your-arm-back, drive-it-home-with-the-knuckles kind of punch. Right into that cute little upturned nose.

"It's not so cute now," William had said, and she'd laughed hard. Her first post-Rick laugh.

But that was three weeks in the past, and now she was eating alone, at Café Diamond. It was a test of sorts. To prove she could do it. To wait in line and hold her head up when the hostess asked, "Just one today, or are you expecting someone to join you?"

"It's just me." Hating herself for saying *just* me. But how else to say it? *One, please?* Or maybe, *yes, it's just me, now give me a table, and stop* fucking judging.

"Follow me." The hostess had taken her to the only empty table in the dining room, a round marble-topped antique that was hardly big enough for a plate, a roll of silverware, and a wooden caddy stuffed with napkins, gourmet chutneys and hot sauces, and a set of ceramic chicken salt and pepper shakers. Danielle ordered a seared tuna bowl with avocado and snap peas, and a jasmine-mint iced tea with lemon. She folded her hands and tried to be brave.

"Excuse me." A man, standing before her tiny circle of a table. A stunningly gorgeous man. As in model gorgeous, or movie star gorgeous. "I'm sorry to interrupt."

"Yes?"

"I was supposed to meet someone, but—"

There was something different about him. For a second, Danielle thought he might be a synthetic, but no. That wasn't it. Synthetics, even the most exotic bespoke models—the ones that only corporations or millionaires had commissioned before the ban on new production—were incapable of the micro-expressions that came so easily to humans. The tiny facial tics and twitches that often belied a person's true feelings. She'd learned about it at university, something about the difficulty scientists had replicating mirror neurons, and one of the cranial nerves that innervates the facial muscles.

So it wasn't that. Danielle stared up at him and considered what else it might be. It took her a moment to put her finger on it, but when she did, a little piece of her grief broke off and fell away. This guy standing before her, shifting nervously in his black t-shirt, jeans, and engineer's boots, looked as miserable as she felt.

"But?" she prompted.

"—she actually broke up with me by text. Just now, while I was waiting for our table."

"Oh." How Danielle hated this phantom girlfriend who, in her mind, had just become the female equivalent of Rick. Not quite, but definitely in that direction. "That's really crappy," she said to the gorgeous man. "What did you do?"

"I gave the table away to the couple in line behind me. I should probably go home, but I'm not ready to, you know, face myself. I'm dreading it, actually."

"How awful."

"It's a huge ask, I know, but could I sit with you and order a coffee and pretend to be normal for a little bit longer? I promise you won't know I'm here. And I'll pick up the check, of course."

Danielle thought about it for a second but, really, there was nothing to think about. She'd committed in advance to a solitary lunch, but she didn't want to be by herself. Not really. The hard truth was that she hadn't even loved Rick. She'd loved not being alone.

"Please," she said. "Join me."

13

S chneider turned the lights on in the foyer and dropped his gun and badge on a mahogany side table. In the kitchen, he stood before the fridge with its three bottles of beer, a single stick of butter, and the almost-clean carcass of a rotisserie chicken. He stuck the chicken in the microwave, and uncapped one of the beers. It went down easy. He opened his holo and gave the command, "call Jess." She wasn't technically his daughter—owing to the fact that he and her mom had never been married, and had split up when she was just ten—but he thought of her that way. Two wonderful years as her almost-father, and they'd kept in touch ever since. But he hadn't heard from her in a few weeks, and sensed she was avoiding him.

"The party you are trying to reach has blocked your call," the phone said. "Would you like to call another party?"

"No, no more calls." Not wanting to think about what this meant, but he knew. She'd invited him to dinner—Buco's Tapas Place, her favorite—to meet her new boyfriend. Schneider had cancelled.

"An emergency at work," he'd said, to which she'd replied,

"Or a convenient excuse to avoid being in my life in any kind of real, grownup way."

Which was true enough, but not how she'd meant. He wasn't avoiding being in her life. He wanted to be in her life. He was avoiding the look on the boyfriend's face when they'd first meet: deliberately not-shocked to cover the actual shock, which he knew would be deep and visceral. It had happened before, even with Jess's pre-dinner coaching. And then they'd all have to suffer through the light-polite conversation during appetizers, drinks, and the main course. *No coffee and dessert, thanks, we really need to be getting home!*

But he could deal with all of that. What he couldn't deal with was the aftermath. The inevitable breakup with the boyfriend. Jess trying to downplay it, working so hard to convince Schneider it had nothing to do with him, nothing to do with the young man's aversion to having a synth as a sort-of-father-in-law. And that was what broke his heart: how easy it would have been for her to cut him out of the picture. She could do show-and-tell any day of the week with her normal human family, and yet she persisted with him. Until now.

His holo was still talking to him, making a mess of his last command not to make any more calls. "Searching for N. Moore Calles," it said, in effect making its own joke. The world had succeeded in producing synthetic human beings, but a holo with reliable autocorrection was still elusive.

"No. Stop." Schneider felt dangerously close to tears. The walls of the clean, well-appointed kitchen were closing in on him and he turned his back on the still-glowing microwave. He retrieved his gear from the foyer, and his walking cane—a leftover from an accident that had mangled his right leg. He didn't need it anymore, but the amber knob at the top of the cane fit his palm like a ball and socket. He found it strangely comforting.

ON THE STREET, he turned and headed for the Boulevard and Stiehl's, the semi-famous fight club that stood as a brick and iron sentinel at the South end. Gateway to neon-lit darkness, drugs, and hope.

He hadn't been to Stiehl's in years, but tonight was a special occasion. It was the convergence of three low points: getting transferred to a new unit, which wasn't exactly a demotion but felt like one; the destruction of his car—by a fellow cop, no less; and now the cold shoulder from Jess. On this last, it was beginning to feel permanent. He was too much trouble. A burden.

Schneider picked up his pace in a last ditch attempt to keep back the tears. He tapped out a rhythm with the tip of his cane, trying to calm his mind. And when that didn't work, he tried thinking about the new case, which he did not have a good handle on. Two mutilated synths, Rachel Montgomery, and Paul Chafee, which a recent email had informed him was the male vic's name. And not one solid lead. Even the forensics report, which had also come up on his email feed, showed nothing. None of the hair, skin, semen, and fiber samples that would be typical for something as messy and complicated as a double murder. Which reinforced his initial impression of the unknown perpetrator, or unsub: he was almost supernaturally careful. And clean. Not a hair, fiber, or skin cell.

He travelled through the crime scene again in his mind searching for something. Anything. One male and one female prostitute. Did they know each other? Were they working a John together? He thought about the walls of the apartment and realized they'd been bare. No pictures or posters. No artwork. But that wasn't unusual for a working girl, and especially a synth working girl: absent a childhood or family, absent the need for the framed memories of vacations and holiday gatherings.

And what about that single anemic jade plant? It was probably nothing. He let it go, knowing from experience that evidence and leads would materialize soon enough. They were more a factor of hard work and patience than anything else. What troubled him was motive. In his 25 years on the job, motive was everything. If you understood the motive behind the crime, you could work backward and discover the rest. It was the master key that unlocked even the heaviest, most formidable doors. And at present, neither he nor Franco, his angry wiseass new partner, had the brass master key of a possible motive. They didn't even have a cheaply stamped one from the corner hardware store.

If he was honest—and it seemed to be shaping up for an evening of painful self-truths—thinking about the case was a distraction from his problem with Jess. Theirs was his only long-term relationship. He didn't know what he'd do without their weekly lunches and semi-regular phone conversations. He didn't know what he'd do without the one person who reminded him there was still goodness in the world.

SCHNEIDER HAD LOVED Jess's mother once. Lauren Morgan. This was back when he'd had skin, and was an up-and-comer in the department. Jess, then eight, had absolutely adored him. She wanted to be a flower girl at the wedding—just as soon as human-synthetic marriages were legalized which, at the time, had seemed imminent. They'd even talked about a puppy, which Jess was going to name Ribsy, from her favorite book. It would all happen just as soon as Schneider put a down payment on the house he'd been eyeing, a two-story Craftsman with a small front porch and a big fenced yard.

But it didn't work out. First Lauren got laid off from her job as a fundraiser at a historically Catholic university. She swore it had nothing to do with him, but he knew better. And when Jess started getting bullied in school—a black eye and a sprained wrist for the crime of having a synthetic father figure—Schneider knew what he had to do. He called the whole thing off. He walked.

Now Jess was a grown woman. She had a law degree from Cornell and was the Director of the Coalition for the Advancement of Synthetic Rights. And, for the first time, she wouldn't take his calls. Nothing to do about it now except walk inside of Stiehl's, pick out the biggest ugliest bastard in the place, and mix it up a little. He stood in the dirty neon glow outside of the fight club and dry swallowed all three Xylene tabs. It was time to throw down. Time to forget.

14

___

Despite being an undeniably large and powerful man, Franco lacked the balls to go inside his own home. He sat in his truck for a full ten minutes, wondering why his wife, Tina, terrified him so much. She wasn't physically intimidating, and she hardly ever nagged or raised her voice. But she was so much smarter than him! And she took absolutely no bullshit, which meant the chances of him continuing to hide the truth about his affair were slim to none.

There was something deeper, though, and it chilled him to the core. Franco, despite all of his muscle and bravado, despite his bullshit and jokes, was lost without his family. Before he met Tina he'd been estranged from his parents and hadn't a single friend. Tina had taught him how to open up and trust people. How to be a father and give and receive love. How to hold hands in public! And now he was ready to bring it all crashing down around him.

"Hey, babe." He hung his keys on the little hook by the coatrack and studied the neat row of little girl footwear: pink and white sneakers—the kind with little red lights that flickered with each little girl stride—pink furry slippers, and two pairs of colorful rain boots, one red with ladybugs, the other green with yellow frog eyes. Franco felt another stab of guilt for what he was doing, and how it might affect his girls whenever the shit hit the fan. Which it certainly would.

"Why so late?" Tina's voice sounded normal, but it wasn't. Too measured. Controlled.

Franco looked up and saw her by the entrance to the kitchen. Her arms were folded over her white terry robe. "Sorry, honey. Crazy day at work. Lots of changes."

"The girls baked cookies and stayed up late. They wanted to eat them with you."

"Sorry." It was weird how much he apologized around Tina. Either for doing the wrong thing, or not doing the right thing. It made him feel like there was no point trying. "I should have called to say goodnight."

"What's going on at work?" Interest was good, but her arms were still crossed.

"There's been a lot of changes." Franco told her about his new partner and about the new case, involving two dead synths.

"On the Boulevard? Were they prostitutes?"

He didn't give names or case-specific details, but he did talk about his interview with Mrs. Donato, and her cats.

"I would have paid money to see you with an old lady and her cats."

For a second he thought he might be in the clear. But when Tina uncrossed her arms and walked into the kitchen, he noticed a stiffness to her gait that was a sure sign of an imminent fight. "There's going to be some changes here, too, Franco. We need to talk."

He groaned. "How about I eat half a dozen of those cookies, go in and kiss the girls, and we'll talk tomorrow?" Hoping to God it would be about something irrelevant, like a new teacher at school or a fundraiser for the girls' gymnastics club. But one look at the cold glint in Tina's eyes and he knew different. What was coming was real, and it was going to hurt.

"Where have you been, Franco?" Her words had been wired together with steel. "And don't lie to me. You're a lousy liar."

"I dropped off Schneider, that's my new partner's name. Some of the guys at the station house punctured his tires. Dixon and his toadies. Bunch of assholes if you ask me."

Tina wasn't buying it. Dropping off a partner took fifteen to thirty minutes, depending on the location. That left him with three more hours to account for.

"Then I stopped at the gym. To blow off some steam."

"Yeah? Did you have a good workout?"

"Sure. I love going to the gym. It helps me unwind."

Twenty seconds of the heaviest silence he'd ever experienced. He'd been in interrogation rooms with half as much pressure. Rapists and murderers and life sentences hanging in the balance and, still, nothing close to this.

"What's her name, Franco?"

"Who?" Looking away. Scanning the kitchen countertop he saw the plate of cookies, and a lumpy clay pot that Chloe, his oldest, had made in art class. It was bright orange, hideous and beautiful at the same time. "What do you mean?"

"Don't lie to me because I always know when you're lying. And you're lying! Tell me her name."

Franco sighed. All at once his will to keep it going crumbled. He didn't want to lie anymore, even though he sensed a tragedy hinging on his next words. "Her name's Carla."

"Carla."

"Yeah, but it's not what you think. I've been helping her out at the gym. That's all."

"Helping her out?"

"Like a workout partner kind of situation."

"So you've got two new partners. The guy at work, Schneider, and Carla."

Franco's massive shoulders sagged. "Tina, listen. I know I haven't been—"

"No, you listen, Franco. I'm not the stupid one in this relationship, so don't pretend I don't know what's going on."

He settled his bulk in one of the kitchen chairs and pulled the plate of cookies toward him. Most people couldn't eat when they were nervous. It was actually one of the methods some detectives used to assess guilt: put a plate of something good in front of a suspect—there was an excellent pizza joint and a passable takeout Chinese next door to the precinct, and they made frequent use of these assets—and see if they'd go for it. In most cases, the guilty guys wouldn't take a bite. Franco was the opposite. "What do you want me to say, Tina?" he said. "I love you and the girls. That's the truth. But sometimes the job—"

"Don't you dare do that, Franco. Don't blame the job for something that's between me and you."

He took a bite of one of the cookies. It was good, made with double the amount of chips, just the way he liked it. He pictured his girls mixing up the dough, a dusting of flour on their matching nightgowns. Just as quickly the image faded, and he wondered if that meant something bad. Like, maybe he wasn't going to get to see them again.

"You need to own your shit, Franco." She waited a moment before bringing the hammer down, the final blow that would beat the truth out of him. "Stop eating the goddamn cookies and be a man."

"Fine. I've been having an affair, about two months. But it doesn't mean anything. I'll break it off."

"Oh, you will? Tell me something. Do you love her? Carla?"

He waited a second too long. He did not love her, but he loved how he felt when he was around her. He loved the way she looked at him. Like he was a man, not a walking list of mundane shit that needed to be done, or impossible schedules that needed to be adhered to. "No, I don't love her."

"Then why? Why put me and the girls through this if you don't even love her?"

"I feel good when we're together. I can breathe easier."

Tina covered her face with her hands. When she finished with the gesture, she ran her fingers through her hair, and then shook it out. None of it lessened her rage. "So what you're saying is, what, I'm choking you? Our family is stealing your air? You can't fucking breathe in here with us?"

Franco shifted in his seat. The honest answer was yes, but he couldn't say it. Couldn't do that to her. He'd promised himself he'd never become like his father, who had cheated on his mom and then run off. No letters or presents at Christmas. No child support either. Now, he could feel it: the circle was closing.

Wordlessly, she led him into their bedroom. For a thin second, he thought they were going to make up. He'd expected to get thrown out, but surprise of surprises they were going to have makeup sex. Amazing. And in that beautiful wedge of time where hope persisted, he vowed he would never cheat again. He would come home on time and be more involved with the girls. He'd learn how to hire a babysitter and make dinner reservations at overpriced fancy places that charged you three times as much for shit no one wanted to eat. And he'd do it happily.

But there wasn't going to be any makeup sex. It was the opposite of makeup sex. Tina pointed to a pair of suitcases. Packed and waiting.

"Can't we talk about this, Tina?"

"We did. And now it's time for you to get the fuck out."

"Where am I supposed to go?"

"I don't know. Go stay with your little whore exercise queen."

"She's not a whore."

Tina, not missing a beat. "Maybe Not-A-Whore-Carla wants

to wash and fold your underwear and uniforms and workout clothes. Maybe she wants to pack you a lunch and cook you dinner. And do whatever other shit you need a woman to do for you so you can feel like a real man and *breathe easier*."

"Tina—"

"Get the fuck out!"

He grabbed the suitcase handles and wheeled his way out of his own life.

15

———

Schneider waited his turn at the bar, ignoring the dirty looks from the customers. And comments muttered just loud enough for him to hear. *Tin man. Synth freak.* And his favorite because it was so simple, and cutting: *that's disgusting.* Not even *he's disgusting.*

He ordered two whiskeys, straight up. Pounded them back and made his way to the center cage, deep in the belly of the factory floor. The walls were made of old bricks that carried the sooty patina from its days as a smelter. The ceiling had its original hewn beams complete with axe notches and worm holes. It was a quaint fight club if nothing else.

Schneider pushed his way through the bluish smoke to the front of crowd. Inside a chain link cage two beefy shirtless synthetics were beating hell out of each other, MMA style. Except from Schneider's perspective there was no style involved. It was brutal. All mass and force.

The larger of the two, who went by the name of Killer George, was busy bashing the left side of his opponent's face with his right elbow. It seemed to be working. The poor bastard on the receiving end of the blows dropped to one knee. He spit out his mouth guard and drooled a thick line of blood.

"Finish him!" the crowd cheered. "Bring it home, Killer!"

George grabbed a tuft of his opponent's hair and turned to face the crowd. He shouted something unintelligible before driving a knee into his face.

The crowd went nuts. "Again!"

But the fight was over, his opponent prone on the dirty canvas. Knocked out cold.

The cleanup crew dragged the fallen combatant from the ring and started to prep the cage for the next match. A young woman worked a shaker can filled with sawdust, to soak up the blood. Her colleague, an old man with a magnificent shock of white hair, pushed a broom from the center of the ring into a trough at the outer edge. He banged the broom against the chain link and went back to the center to repeat.

"Schneider?" It was the fight manager, pushing his way through the crowd.

Schneider recognized him but not his name. It had been too long. "Yeah, it's me. How's it going, big guy?"

"Nick Schneider, in the flesh!" The manager towered over the detective. Long heavy face on a long heavy body. Covered in black leather with silver studs. Topped with a badly dyed Mohawk. "Well, off the flesh, to be accurate."

"Tony Paz, right?"

"You remembered." His face worked itself into a rather beautiful smile. "I'm touched."

"Of course I remembered." Schneider rocked back on his heels as the first distortion wave from the Xylene started. The crowd rose and fell on a gigantic human sine curve, bending, shuddering, and then returning to normal. He'd never taken three tabs before and wondered what he was in for. "How's it going, Tony?"

Tony nodded vigorously. "Doing well, Schneider. I got

married again, but this time it's for keeps. She's a freaking angel. I swear, I don't come close to deserving someone like that. And guess what else?"

Schneider was sliding nicely into the inner space of his trip. He wasn't actively hallucinating, but he was far from straight. As he listened to Tony's words, the man's massive head started to look like it was made of paper mache. Like a big heavy metal Mardi Gras puppet. It bobbed up and down on a springy neck. "What?"

"We're going to have a baby. A little girl!"

"No kidding? That's—" He couldn't finish, because Tony's face was changing from paper mache to clay. The colored kind that kids use to build little animal figurines. Tony's figurine had peach clay for the face. Black clay for his leather. And a green ribbon on top of his head. A strange and fantastical fight club animal.

"You look blasted, Schneider. Tell me you're not tripping."

"No." He reached out to touch the green clay mohawk. "Maybe a little."

Tony howled with laughter. "That's crazy. I remember you used to trip and fight. Who does that?"

A moment of clarity before the next wave. Tony's form returned to normal, but Schneider knew it wouldn't last. "Can you get me in the lineup tonight? Preferably soon."

"What?" Tony studied him. "Against these psychos? On X?"

"I'll be fine." Schneider tried his best to look normal.

Tony studied him. "You'll get killed, Schneider."

"I'll be fine. I can handle myself."

Tony Paz shook his head. "I don't know, Schneider. I don't want that on my conscience."

"Then bet against me."

❧

Near the entrance to the cage, Schneider was unsteady on his feet as he shucked off his shirt and jacket and folded them. He hid his badge and gun in the middle of the pile and thrust it at Tony along with his amber-handled cane. "Keep these safe for me."

"Sure," Tony said. "I'll put 'em in the body bag when you're done."

"That's kind of you." Schneider slipped off his shoes and aligned them against the fence, taking great care to stuff his socks deep inside the shoes. He felt it was important that he did not lose his socks, though he didn't know why. He was, he realized, as high as apple pie. He stumbled again, and the spectators laughed raucously.

"You coming, cupcake?" The man—or synthetic man—at the center of the ring was truly terrifying. His fight name was Crusher.

Schneider couldn't tell if Crusher was actually covered in scales or if that was an effect of the drug. Probably the drug. Enhancements weren't unheard of, but there were strong cultural taboos, as he'd learned from his own experiment. Besides, the most successful cage fighters were a bit like pool sharks. They had to look the part, sure, but not too much or they'd scare off the competition. No opponents meant no prize money.

"Let's go, little man." The giant synthetic rubbed his bear paws together in anticipation.

Schneider walked to the trough at the edge of the cage. His soles scuffed on the rough canvas. He thought he could feel each individual fiber. And he could see that the weave of all of those independent fibers made up a unified thing, like the mat of mycelium underneath soil and cement. The secret substrate of life. He knelt down to study it, and—

"Harf!" He vomited into the trough. Beer and whiskey splattered through the fence, causing the front row spectators to jump back. It was all part of the Xylene experience: mild perceptual distortions followed by a purging of the body. And then the really weird shit.

Schneider looked up at the enormous scaly monster in the center of the floor and realized he'd made a mistake, possibly a tragic one. In a word, he was fucked.

16

Danielle's lunch turned out to be one of the best she could remember, both the food and the company. Her seared tuna had been cooked just right, pink in the middle with a nice charred sesame crust and chunks of avocado that had been drizzled with lime juice and sea salt. Keven ended up ordering a California burger, fries, and a beer. After some initial small talk and the awkward getting-to-know-you questions like, "how long have you lived here?" and "what do you do for work?" they'd gotten down to the real business at hand: talking about the dissolution of their relationships.

Surprisingly, Danielle was no longer bitter. She was sure the feeling would return, but throughout lunch she felt mostly relaxed. She laughed at Keven's jokes and stories, which was easy enough to do because he really was funny. And charming. And not bad to look at, either.

"That hostess is staring at us," he said.

"She wants our table." Danielle reached for the check, which she fully intended to split.

"Don't even think about it!" He grabbed it and, for a second, her hand brushed against his. Neither of them spoke for a full ten seconds, which felt like an eternity.

"Sadly, I think it's time for me to face the music." Keven laid down a stack of bills and pushed back his chair. "First I'm going home. Then I'm going to box up Claire's things."

"And then what?"

"I'm going to track down your ex-fiance, Ryan Whathisname, and put a potato in the tailpipe of his Camaro."

"He doesn't drive a Camaro."

"In my mind he does. Because he's cheesy. And stupid."

"He drives an electric Audi, which means that there's—"

"No tailpipe. Damnit. It would have been so rewarding."

They walked out together. Unconsciously, Danielle looped her arm through his. How weird that it felt natural. "His name's Rick, not Ryan."

"He sounds like a Ryan. You know, the kind of guy who played lacrosse when he was younger and bullied the nerdy kids."

She felt a bit unsteady, which was odd. She leaned into him. "Why so judgy? I'll bet you were a jock when you were a kid. You probably played lacrosse."

He shook his head. "Actually, I didn't have much of a childhood at all." It was the first thing he'd said to her that was true. As the very last of the Third Gens produced by SynCorps—before the ban—his earliest memories were limited to the interior of the SynCorps complex, in Austin, where he'd participated in a kind of "becoming human" boot camp. Everything you needed to know to pass in the human world, crammed into three months. Of course, *pass* was a relative term. The engineers had never gotten the vagus and trigeminal nerves quite right, which resulted in speech and facial expression problems that were easy tipoffs once you knew what to look for. Strangely, these glitches were what made the drug Xylene effective for synthetics and not humans. But none of these problems affected Keven. Elizabeth had seen to that.

"No?" Danielle's mouth felt dry. Her stomach rolled. "Why not?"

"I'll tell you once we're inside the van."

"Okay." She was speaking automatically. The words held little meaning. *Childhood in a van. Electric Rick potato car.* Something was happening to her, something unusual. Neurological. But it wasn't necessarily bad. It wasn't scary. She was dizzy and disoriented, but she could still function. She could listen to what Keven was saying. She could see, and walk. But thinking? No, that was too difficult to do on her own. Keven would have to do the thinking.

But that was wrong, wasn't it? She'd just met him. And who was he anyway, just some guy who'd approached her at the café?

"I want you to know that you really are lovely, Danielle."

"Mmm." A nice thing to hear, but she was already forgetting the words. They came and went so quickly! Like smoke. Lovely wordsmoke.

"I'm sorry it has to happen this way. It's not my idea, but I believe your sacrifice will be worth it. In the end."

She tightened her grip on his arm. Her vision was narrowing. Ahead, she saw a black camper, one of the sleek, expensive types. The door was sliding open. Inside was an attractive, elegant woman of indeterminate age. She might have been thirty-eight or a beautifully preserved fifty-five. Hard to tell. Dark hair in a French braid, the tail of which hung over the shoulder of a white lab coat. The woman smiled warmly at Danielle.

"In another life you and I would be friends." Keven whispered, like he was trying to keep their conversation secret from the woman in the van. "We'd stay up late and watch old movies together, and trash talk Rick, and your so-called friends. Believe me when I say you deserve so much better than this."

17

———————

What Schneider loved the most about Xylene was how the drug seemed to understand him better than he understood himself. Like it had its own intelligence. Like it was determined to give him not what he wanted, but what he needed. In this case, Schneider needed to get his ass beat in a steel cage in front of a hundred angry drunks. At this moment, he needed to be punished.

But it went deeper than that. His life had bottomed out. He wanted to strip away the layers of his ego, just like he'd stripped away his skin. Get rid of all the bullshit, the half-truths and confabulated stories he kept telling himself when he was alone. Late at night, when the rest of the world was asleep and his inner voice wanted to remind him of all of his sins. Or right now, when it was chastising him—for the thousandth time—for abandoning Jess.

"You don't belong in this world," the voice said. "You don't fit in. No one wants you!"

"I know," Schneider said out loud. "It's true!"

"And yet, you had a family. A good one. They loved you. Why did you turn your back on them?"

His opponent looked at him. A big question mark on a violent face. "Are you talking to me?"

"I fucked it all up," Schneider said, starting to sag under the weight of his mistakes. "I'm sorry. I'm sorry."

The fighter shrugged and forced out his breath. He jabbed. Once, twice, and then a hard right that glanced off Schneider's forehead and sent a shower of white sparks across his field of vision. Schneider staggered back and tilted his head. Something was different. He searched his mind and discovered that the voice of recrimination had quieted to a whisper.

"I'm sorry," he said again.

"You seek forgiveness?" the voice in his head said. "You must say it."

"Yes." Schneider smiled with gratitude. He was on the right path. "I seek forgiveness," he said to his opponent.

"What the hell?" Crusher said.

"Whoa." The second distortion wave came on much stronger than the first. Schneider had to widen his stance to avoid falling off the edge. Where did the edge even come from? It hadn't been there a second ago. Now, instead of a wall of chain link fence, there was this threshold of earth and stone. And beyond that? A river of blinding yellow and orange light cutting through a massive field of black. It filled him with terror and awe. He retreated, shielding his eyes.

"What are you doing, man?" Tony called. "Get your head out of your ass."

Schneider looked in the direction of Tony's voice and took a blow to the side of his face that might have killed another man. He crumpled to the canvas, which rippled beneath his weight in undulating waves of blue and gray. A canvas sea. He reached out to touch the surface of the sea.

"Boo!" How the crowd hated him now. They had been promised combat, not a one-sided beat down.

Schneider looked up at Crusher, who was bouncing toward

him on the balls of his feet, closing in, ready to deliver a knee to the face. Something shifted in Schneider's perceptions. Now, inexplicably, he could see threads of kinetic energy extending from his opponent in colored vectors. The vectors telegraphing his opponent's intentions. Projecting the brute's movements into the future like promises. Schneider watched and, at the last fraction of a second, rolled away and swept Crusher's leg. The fighter went down hard on his right hip. Schneider leapt to his feet.

The crowd roared.

"Okay, man." Crusher picked himself up, but he was wary now and kept his eyes glued to Schneider. Suspicious. "That was lucky. No more."

Schneider was getting loose, sliding nicely into the middle part of his trip. He moved his feet across the canvas while circling his arms in front of him. It was like a slowed-down dance, a strange ritual that vaguely resembled the internal martial arts. The metal covering of Schneider's forearms looked iridescent and left faint color trails. He thought it was beautiful and he wanted to keep moving, just so he could continue watching the display.

Crusher jabbed again but this time Schneider sidestepped and spun, and landed a backhand punch at the base of the skull, at the juncture of the C2 and C3 vertebra. He didn't even have to think about it. It wasn't a conscious thing. Schneider was a living being as was his opponent, and they were afloat together on a sea of canvas. Which was a current in the larger ocean of the crowd.

Altogether—the two combatants, the current, and the sea— they comprised a single, living organism. In the end it wasn't so much a fight they were engaged in as a piece of choreographed movement. Like wind blowing trees or a current in a river pushing a stone. There was no such thing as good or bad. Winning or losing. Each element played its part. All were vital.

Crusher's head jerked forward, but he shook it off and whipped around with a knee strike, aiming inward and up. Schneider saw it coming—because of the vectors, which he could now observe and interpret easily—and backed off just enough to redirect with the heel of his left hand. At the same time he chopped with the inner blade of his right. The opposing forces were devastating. Crusher flipped into the air and twisted. Schneider watched the blues and greens and purples trailing from the man's limbs; it was even more beautiful than the colors coming from his own body.

He leaned in to touch the purplish vapor coming off Crusher, but something was wrong. Dangerous. A fist cut through the haze and smashed into his windpipe. He choked and fell back, gasping. Crusher advanced and hammered him again. "Time to die, little man," he said.

The next blow cracked the metal of Schneider's cheek plate. Beads of ocher blood popped up along the line of the crack. That's when Schneider saw it, what he'd been waiting for without knowing: the white pulsing of light at the core of Crusher's chest. It emanated from a condensed ball of energy the size of a closed fist. His heart? Chi? Soul? Schneider didn't know, but he could not look away. Because it was so beautiful. Even though each split second of nonaction brought him closer to his own destruction.

What if he touched it? Yes. He reached to touch the pulsing light, but a scaly muscled arm blocked him. And then a knee thrust up and into his abdomen. Schneider doubled over and caught a vicious uppercut that swelled his right eye shut.

Crusher raised his arms and stalked the perimeter of the cage, appealing to the crowd. Schneider was still bent over but he watched Crusher with great curiosity, focusing his left eye on the pulsing light. He stood and reached out again. This time, when Crusher struck, Schneider caught it at the point of maximum extension and leaned in, applying just enough lateral force to break the joint. It sounded like the snapping of a green stick.

Crusher howled. Schneider watched the guttural sound waves come out of his opponent's twisted mouth. They fluttered and swirled in the air, above and around them, dark red and jagged. Filled with pain. He had no need to make sense of them, to translate them into words. They were waves of energy, and he was energy. His opponent was energy, too.

Crusher swung with his other hand. Schneider trapped it, too, and butted Crusher in the face. Crusher's eyes lost focus and Schneider butted him again, this time hard enough to dent the plating on his own forehead.

"Yes!" It was the voice of Tony Paz, the fight manager, calling out from the crowd.

At last, Crusher slumped against the fence. The light in the center of his chest continued to pulse, but when Schneider touched it—covering it with his outstretched hand—the light splayed out through his fingers in crimson rays. It was magnificent, but the fight was over. Someone was pulling him away.

Schneider shook the person off and stood in the center of the ring with his eyes closed. The image that coalesced in the darkness of his mind was a simple one: Rachel Montgomery's jade plant. It was thin and ailing and propped up by a stick, but, at the top, two green buds were forming. As the effects of the drug started to subside, Schneider grasped the meaning.

Life.

In a cheap apartment on the Dirty Boulevard, a synthetic prostitute had been trying to grow something, trying to cultivate life. That might not have mattered to anyone else, but it mattered to him. And although he couldn't yet articulate why, it changed everything about the case.

18

———————

Elizabeth was ready. The chair was in position, semi-reclined, restraints open. An array of fluorescent lights hummed overhead, and magnetic trays held her surgical tools: scalpels, dissection and cutting scissors, retractors and clamps, needle holders, suture material, toothed forceps, bone saw and bone nibblers, a mallet, and curettes. An I.V. rack was loaded with saline bags and one with a mixture of morphine and lidocaine.

Louis, the dog, struggled to his feet and loped to the back bedroom, the one part of the camper's interior that had not been modified.

"This is an exciting day, Louis." Elizabeth opened a chest freezer and checked the temperature on the donor limbs. All good. "A monumental day."

Louis pawed the door closed behind him. He used a ramp to get onto the bed—his jumping days were long gone—where he'd remain until the surgery was finished.

Through a blacked-out side window, Elizabeth watched Keven escort Danielle out of the café. She clung to his arm, disoriented but obedient. The true effect of the Scopolomine cocktail. They made it safely across traffic, and into the camper.

"Hello, dear." Elizabeth met them at the side door, and took the young woman's hands in her own. "It's so nice to meet you." She knew Danielle was fully under the drug's power and unable to question or resist. Still, warmth and kindness mattered.

Danielle tried to smile, but her facial muscles didn't work the way she wanted them to. "It's nice to—"

"You don't have to speak, dear." Elizabeth helped her into the chair and fastened the restraints. "We don't want you falling out of here when we turn a corner."

"No," Danielle said.

The doctor swabbed her bare forearm and started an IV. "I know you're not feeling yourself, Danielle, but when you wake up, you will be very different. Improved."

Keven stood over her protectively, but he didn't speak. There was nothing to say. His loyalty to Elizabeth was beyond question. And he believed in what she was doing. What *they* were doing. But how could such a lovely young woman be *improved?*

"It's not an exaggeration to say that you are going to become a very important person. Not to say you're not already important. But soon you will become front page news around the world. The first human-synthetic hybrid." She nodded to Keven and he climbed up front into the driver's seat. He buckled, checked his mirrors and cameras, and started the engine.

"All good?" Elizabeth said.

He knew she really meant *hurry up*, but he never hurried. That was how they'd made it this far. No hurries meant no mistakes.

"You've done great work today," Elizabeth said, relaxing a little. "I don't mean to sound impatient, or unappreciative."

He inched his way to the road. A massive pickup truck had

parked too close to the parking lot's exit, making it difficult to see into traffic. He nosed the camper's bumper another six inches and held his breath.

"What the—" He felt the entire rig lurch forward, but it didn't make sense. No cars were coming ahead of them. The impact was from behind. There was a crunch of metal, followed by the opening and closing of a car door.

"Please don't tell me we've been in an accident." Elizabeth's stool had rolled into the side of the chest freezer.

"Someone rear ended us," Keven said.

Elizabeth stalked to the back and slammed open the door to the bedroom. She ignored Louis's sad rheumy eyes and looked out the back window. "Fuck, it's some kid in one of those stupid drift cars. The hood is crumpled."

"I'll handle it." Keven fished in the glove box. Aside from an insurance card and vehicle registration there was a small 9mm, a knife, and a roll of cash. He took the cash and the knife and made his way to the kid.

"Jesus, I'm sorry!" The kid, who couldn't have been more than 18 or 19, was apoplectic. He paced back and forth beside a 20-year-old Civic that had been heavily modded: lowered, and fitted out with flared fenders, spoilers, and, custom wheels. "I ran right into you. Shit, I'm not going to lie. It's totally on me."

Keven put a hand on the kid's shoulder. "It's okay. Take a breath."

"My dad's going to kill me. I'm still on his insurance."

"What's your name?" Keven applied a little pressure to his shoulder, just enough to ground him, to pull him out of the spiral of his catastrophic thinking and back into his body. He couldn't decide on using the money or the knife. Money was easier, for sure, but it left a big loose end: the kid could ID him. On the other hand a teenager bleeding out in the street would attract too much attention. A few pedestrians were already taking notice.

"I'm Gene."

"Okay, Gene." Keven reached in his back pocket and pulled out a thick stack of folded hundred-dollar-bills. He put it in Gene's hand. "Here's what we're going to do. You take this and get your car fixed up."

Gene's confusion ratcheted up a notch. "But I ran into you."

Keven waved his hand. "Forget about it. This way's better. I'm in a hurry, and that's enough to call a tow and cover repairs."

Gene looked down at the roll, disbelieving. "You're sure?"

"I'm sure." Keven patted him on the shoulder. He needed to get them the hell out of there before a cop or a nosy citizen joined them. He left Gene by his car, counting the money, unaware of just how lucky he was.

Fifty seconds later, finally, Keven pulled the camper out of the parking lot. They were back on track.

19

Schneider enjoyed a long leisurely walk home from Stiehl's. For the first time in years his mind was at ease. He felt unburdened, even if the effect was physical exhaustion and Xylene afterglow. Temporary. But it disappeared even faster than he'd expected because the moment he arrived home, he spotted a hulking shadow on his front steps.

Schneider drew his piece and approached slowly.

"Whoa." The figure stood in the shadow cast by the porch lights, palms up in a sign of peace. "Take it easy. It's me."

"Who's me?"

"Your partner."

Schneider sighed and holstered his gun. "What are you doing here, Franco?"

"I thought I'd take you up on that beer."

"It's two a.m. Besides, you made it clear you don't like me or my kind." He brushed past and unlocked the front door.

"Yeah, well." Franco followed him in the entryway, watching him slide his cane into an antique umbrella holder. "Why are you using a cane?"

"I like it."

"Weird." Franco followed him into the living room, taking in the odd mix of antique furniture and black and white prints. One was of an old man being consumed by some kind of a rusted gear-driven machine. Ruptured valves spattered oil across the floor and walls in bloody patterns. A burst of steam leaked from a cracked pipe like an escaping soul. The image was disturbing but oddly compelling, the man's face beseeching but, at the same time, accusing. Of what Franco had no clue.

"What the hell is this?" Franco said.

"Art." Schneider was already regretting his new partner's intrusion on his private life. But he knew he wasn't going to throw him out. Synthphobe or not, Franco was his partner. And partners stood by. Even if they hated each other.

"Yeah, but what's it mean?"

In lieu of an answer, Schneider led the way to the kitchen and grabbed a bottle of beer. He slid it along the counter, then uncorked a flask of whiskey and poured two fingers for himself. He swirled the golden liquid and said, "To the faded colors of two a.m."

"I don't know what that means either." Franco raised his beer to his lips and drank.

"Of course you don't. It's from a very old song."

In the ensuing silence each man contemplated how little he knew about the other. The questions were implicit: do I want to know? Do I need to?

Franco was the first to speak. "What happened to your face?"

"It's nothing." Schneider tore off a paper towel and dampened it. He dabbed at a line of dried blood. The dents could be removed later, if he even wanted to. "Why are you here, Franco?"

"I asked you first. Who fucked up your face?" He drained the rest of the beer in one long pull.

"A big synthetic who didn't like me. Your turn. Why are you here, Franco?"

"I told you. I came over for a beer. I figured, you know, if we're going to be partners, it wouldn't hurt to get to know each other a little."

"You're lying."

"Fuck you I'm lying."

"Your wife threw you out because you're having an affair."

"You don't know anything about me." Shoulders bunching in angry muscled knots.

"No, but I know people. A condom wrapper in your truck. Coming here late at night when I'm the last person you'd want to drink with."

"Hey, I never said that." Looking away, though, because it was true. Or at least it had been when the L.T. first gave him the news. "I just said if you stay out of my way, we'll get along better."

"It's okay. I don't like you either." Schneider smiled, though, and poured whiskey into a second glass. He slid it down the counter.

"You know, I've heard that before. Once or twice."

"I don't believe it." Schneider said it with obvious sarcasm. "Come on." He headed out of the kitchen. "I'll show you the guest room."

"It's just for tonight."

"Good."

～

IN THE MORNING they took Franco's truck to work, stopping on the way at the Shawmut Diner. The Shawmut was a chrome and neon dive that had been popular among cops for at least forty years, when New DC was reappropriated from half a dozen existing municipalities. The Shawmut owed equal parts of its success to the nostalgia factor and its location. It was situated on the South end of Synth City and, thanks to the improved Beltway exits, was convenient to the Capital, the affluent Heights neighborhood, and the bland, suburban sprawl that comprised much of New DC.

"How about that one?" Franco pointed at the coveted corner booth, which was about to be vacated.

"Give me a minute to clean it off," the hostess said.

"Thanks, Doris," Franco said.

When the table was ready, Schneider asked for his usual of black coffee, two eggs over medium, hash browns, and rye toast, dry. No chocolate malted this time. Franco got the steak and eggs special, no toast or hash browns, and unsweetened iced tea.

"You have something against toast and hash browns?" Schneider was wearing his Ray Bans, which made it difficult to gauge his emotions. Not that his metal plated face was especially expressive. But his tone was unmistakably critical.

"Yeah, they make my ass fat."

Schneider laughed. "What about coffee? Is that not paleo-keto-friendly either?"

"I freaking love coffee. I used to drink 6 or 7 cups a day, but my doc says I need a break. He says I'm on the edge of adrenal fatigue or some shit."

"Imagine that."

The food arrived quickly. Franco doused both his steak and eggs with salt, pepper, Tabasco sauce, and ketchup. He ate prison-style, guarding his plate with his left forearm, shoveling the food in with his right. Schneider watched, fascinated. "How long have you been married?"

"Six years. And we dated for two before. So, a long time."

"And in that span did your wife not teach you to eat?"

"Fuck you." Franco shook out the rest of the bottle of Tobasco and resumed shoveling. He felt a presence near their table and looked up.

Derrick Carter, looking immaculate in a white linen suit, stood next to his partner, Javier Rubin. "If it isn't the odd couple." Like an old married pair themselves, they shared the same laugh.

"What do you two want?" Franco said. "Can't you see we're eating? I thought that still meant something here."

Rubin stepped forward, smoothing one of his trademark tacky ties. Maroon satin with brown dots. Extra wide. "Big news. We got a suspect. Full confession."

"On the Montgomery-Chafee case?" Schneider put down his coffee and snapped to attention.

"That's right," Rubin said. "Guy named Oscar Stanovich. Real scumbag."

Carter beamed and added, "He's being arraigned this morning. We're going over to his apartment now. See if we can dig up some evidence."

"Not that we'll need it," Rubin added. "DA says the confession looks good, but you know how it is. You can never be too careful."

"The arc of the universe is long," Schneider said, "and bends toward talented but unscrupulous lawyers who pick apart rock solid confessions."

Franco looked sideways at Schneider and wiped his mouth with a napkin. "Doris!" He waved for the check.

"Where do you think you're going?" Carter said.

"Just give me the address." Franco took some bills from his wallet. "We'll meet you at the scumbag's apartment."

Schneider knew what was coming. He'd seen this show play

out at least a dozen times. Never a happy ending. He leaned back in his booth, resigned to watch.

"L.T. says it's just me and Javier from here on out." Carter made no attempt to hide his joy at being a part of the A-team. "You understand. It's all but closed anyway."

"No way," Franco said. "That's bullshit."

"Maybe," Carter said. "But that's how it is."

Franco looked at Schneider before launching into another round. Schneider gave him nothing.

"It's our case, asshole." Franco was shouting now, drawing attention from the cops at the other tables. "We were first on the scene. And Schneider here's an expert on synth homicides. That's going to play well with the public on this one. You guys will be shooting yourselves in the foot if you cut us out."

"Take it up with the L.T."

"We will."

Rubin gave a nod to Carter and they were gone.

Franco pushed his plate away and took out his holo. "I'm calling the old bastard right now."

"Hold up." Schneider put out his hands. "What do you expect the L.T. to say?"

"Who's side are you on?"

"Just play this out with me. What's he likely to say?"

"That it's out of his hands. That we should be happy we got that sicko off the streets, not bitching about who gets the credit."

Schneider nodded in agreement.

"So what? I'm still going to tell him—"

"See, I've heard that name. Oscar Stanovich."

Franco put his holo away. "Yeah? Who the fuck is he?"

"He's a scumbag, but he's more the white-collar kind. Smart and cautious type. He's connected to S.E.S.H."

Franco raised his eyebrows to say, "What's that?"

"The Society for the Eradication of Synthetic Humans. Right wing anti-synth hate group."

Franco pulled out his holo and did a search. "Okay, it says here S.E.S.H. has become a major force of opposition on the issue of synthetic rights and has launched successful protests and media campaigns. There's more about—"

"So why would Stanovich—who mostly writes blog posts and does interviews—suddenly get his hands dirty and kill two synthetic sex workers?"

"I don't know. Maybe he needed more publicity to try and influence the vote. I'll bet a guy like him would be pretty nervous about that."

"Maybe." Schneider nodded quickly, putting something together. "I just don't know if he could pull this kind of a thing off. Physically. You've never seen him on T.V.? He's a very bookish guy. Maybe a buck twenty soaking wet, and no medical experience I'm aware of. Remember, those were surgically precise cuts."

"Right." Franco relaxed enough to start eyeing Schneider's plate, which remained untouched. "Are you going to eat that?"

Schneider pushed it to the center of the table. He wasn't a huge eater—few synthetics were, based on the fact that the analogs in their bodies for ghrelin and leptin were under much tighter control than in humans—but his appetite vanished completely when he was thinking about a case. "The M.E. said the male victim, Chaffee, would have weighed over two hundred with both his arms. That's a lot of meat to overpower, cut up, and carry around."

"Metal and meat. But I get the point. He might have had help."

Schneider thought on it for a moment. "It's possible Stanovich just *claimed* responsibility."

"You heard Carter. Signed and sealed." Franco disappeared

half of the sandwich in one bite. He finished his sentence while chewing. "Full confession."

"So you want to drop it and let those two assholes keep going with *our* case?"

Franco scowled and wiped his mouth with a napkin. "I didn't say that."

"Come on." Schneider emptied his coffee and slid out from the booth. "I've got an idea."

20

———————

Jess's call came as Keven was scrubbing the residual blood from the donor arms off the backs of his hands. It was slightly more sticky than human blood. He preferred to use a stiff bristled brush but the scouring made his hands raw, which required him to moisturize for days after every surgery. Not a huge deal, but Elizabeth would notice and tease him about it. His wonderful vanity, as she would say.

"Hi," Jess said. "How's work?"

"Good," he said. "Busy, but really good."

The actual procedure had gone well, but Elizabeth said they wouldn't know for sure until morning. If Danielle survived the night there was a good chance she'd make it through the week. After that, the prospects of long-term survival rose dramatically. The difference this time around had to do with the immunosuppressant cocktail, the goal of which was to prevent the biological human host from rejecting the synthetic limbs. Her formulation was genius: instead of the high-tech wonder drugs used in conventional human medicine, she'd gone old school and used rapamycin, a bacterium first found on Easter Island in 1972. Named after Rapa Nui, the place it was discovered. For reasons only comprehensible to Elizabeth, rapamycin worked where all other compounds failed.

Of course, Keven couldn't tell any of this to Jess. She was under the impression he worked in a research lab. Which he supposed was true. Except instead of using rats or mice as subjects, he and Elizabeth experimented on people, and synthetics.

"Do you have time to talk?" Jess tried to hide her nervousness.

"A few minutes. Are you okay?"

"Yeah. Just a weird day. A lot has happened and I kind of need to process it."

"I listened to your interview from last week on NPR."

"You did?" She wondered if this meant something. They'd been on four dates so far. She really liked him and thought he liked her. But Keven was so quiet. It was hard to tell where they stood as a couple. Officially.

"Of course. I listen to all of your interviews. You literally kicked the shit out of that MIT jerk. I was super proud."

"Well, his argument was pretty weak. Organicity over consciousness? Please. Do you know who Bharanda is?"

"SynCorp guy, right?" So hard to pretend ignorance.

"Yes, well he worked it all out. The human brain has 86 billion neurons, give or take. And ten to the fifteenth power of connections."

"Okay."

"So there's been all this focus on the structures of the human brain that are most likely responsible for consciousness. What they did is they lesioned specific parts until they observed diminished consciousness. First it was the cortex, and then the cerebrum, thalamus, hippocampus—"

"You're speaking Greek." Despite the fact that Keven knew this body of work intimately. He'd helped Elizabeth conduct much of the seminal research in this area.

"Pretty soon they figure out that it's not one or even several brain structures. It's generalized or distributed. But Bharanda took it several steps further and proved it's a function of the number and arrangement of neurons. At around 65 billion, if the architecture is right, you get human-like consciousness. And the neurons can be human neurons, synthetic, or even those within a neural net in the case of A.I."

"Holy shit." He wished he could tell her the truth. Just to see how she'd respond.

"Ah, sorry." Jess forced a laugh.

"That was amazing." Keven shielded the phone and called out to Elizabeth. "Be there in a minute." When he returned to Jess, he said, "I'm sorry. It's a critical part of an experiment. Can I call you later?"

"Why don't you just come over? Whenever you finish. I don't care if it's late."

He hesitated. "That sounds so nice, but it's going to be a long—"

"It's okay. Really." But it wasn't. She knew it, and so did he. The offer had been about more than a late-night visit and talk. In her mind Jess had seen them waking up together, the next morning. She would make coffee and they'd sit in the early sun of her bay window sipping, talking, and falling one step closer toward love. But instead, they'd just taken a step back. She wondered if he really was busy or if he'd been put off by her techy rant. She'd dated guys like that before, men who liked to talk smart but didn't want their women to.

"Jess, listen. Any other time—"

"It's okay, Keven, really. We both have important careers. Commitments. I get it." She wanted to go. She needed to go.

"Rain check?"

"Or course." Jess hung up and turned on the T.V., let it run on the newsfeed. She wasn't interested in the actual stories. A wall of background noise was the thing to drown out her thoughts. But the coverage of the murders on the Dirty Boulevard and Oscar Stanovich's role quickly broke through her attention. She watched Stanovich being led away from a courthouse in cuffs. The reporter gave some background on the S.E.S.H. before segueing to a shot of the crime scene. A graphic picture of two synth bodies, side by side on a blanket, sans arms. She shuddered.

After pacing two laps around her apartment, Jess picked up her holo again. She dialed Schneider and then hung up before the end of the first ring. Her therapist had told her the most difficult thing in the world was to hold two opposite emotions at the same time. She found this to be especially true with Schneider, whom she loved and hated with an intensity unmatched in any other relationship.

She thought back to the little house on Pangolin Street, the one Schneider had taken her to see with her mom when she was ten. They'd driven in his antique car and he'd let her ride up front in spite of her mother's objections.

"Who's house is this?" she'd said when they'd pulled into the driveway. It was a two-story Craftsman with a little covered porch and a fenced yard.

"Come on," her mother had said, holding out her hand. She took it and reached out with her other one for Schneider's. They walked up the drive together, mother, father, and child. A real family. It was the last time.

Her holo buzzed. She hesitated, flipped an imaginary emotional coin in her head. Which was it going to be, love or hate? She made her choice, for the moment at least, and answered.

"Hello, Jess." The relief in Schneider's voice was obvious. "Thanks for answering."

"This doesn't mean I've forgiven you," she said.

"I wouldn't think otherwise, kid."

"Don't call me that. I'm not ten." As she said it she knew her response was exactly the one he wanted. A reminder of their past, of that brief and perfect time.

"Okay, sorry. What's on your mind, Jess? I know this isn't social."

"Do you even know why I blocked your call?"

"No, but I'm sure I deserved it. Is it because I forgot to call last week?"

She groaned. "You had me followed, Schneider!"

"I can explain."

"No, you can't. Because that's so far over the line, there is no possible explanation."

"I was worried because of those threats from the anti SRA nuts." He should have known better, though. He'd taught her how to spot a tail when she was little, during drives to the park and the playground. They'd made a game of it. Jess Morgan, Jr. P.I. Except she'd corrected him on the spot. It was Jess *Schneider*, Jr. P.I. Or at least it could have been.

"I get threats all the time, Schneider. It comes with the job, just like your job comes with certain dangers."

"I wanted to make sure you were safe."

"You had me surveilled."

"It was just until the vote, Jess. I hired this guy I know, Donovan Kaplan. He owed me a favor and said he'd keep an eye out." No mention of the fact that Kaplan had been on Schneider's payroll for years. Mostly sweeps of the block around her apartment. Which he'd justified because she lived in such a questionable neighborhood one block West of Synth City, over the train tracks. Technically it was in The Heights, but tell that to the addicts and creepers who roamed freely in search of nicer windows to peer through, or better packages to steal from people's porches while they were at work.

"I don't think you get it, Schneider. You left me and my mom because your presence was supposedly dangerous for me. That's what you said. Dangerous for me. And now, fourteen years later, after I had to grow up without a father, without you, I'm still in the same kind of danger."

"I know. There isn't a day that goes by when I don't—"

"Nothing's changed! Except now we do small talk on the phone. Do you realize how much we've both missed out on? For what? Nothing."

He closed his eyes and rubbed the bridge of his nose. She was right. Jess was always right. And he never learned. He was still fucking up. When it came to her, he was still making the wrong decisions. "I'll call Donovan off."

"Please do. And all the future Donovans. You want to be in my life again? Do the work, Schneider. Don't hire some retired schmuck to do it for you."

"Jess."

She ended the call and did her best to hold onto her anger before it could turn into tears and run cold.

21

———

Franco lingered in the car, arguing with the vigor of a kid being forced to go to school on a Saturday. "This is a total waste of time." He threw his arms up and shook his hands. "I told you. The old woman doesn't know anything. She's probably got dementia."

"Maybe." Schneider sat placidly behind the wheel of the antique Caddy, which was fresh out of the body shop. With a set of new tires and a touched-up door, it looked as good as when it had rolled out of the dealer showroom back in 1963.

Franco took his last shot. "Besides, Carter and Rubin have it all stitched up with their confession. Oscar Whatshisname."

"And you believe them?"

"Why are you making this about me and what I believe? You know how the chain of command works. Why are you pushing me on this? You want me to go down in flames with you and have to transfer units every couple of years? Is that it?"

"Like you're Mr. Popular." Schneider rubbed at a spot on the upholstery with a thumb. "Let me ask you this, Franco, and then I'll back off. Do you think Carter and Rubin got the right guy?"

Franco took too long to consider. "I don't know."

"We can move on if you want. Just say the words. There's a stack of new cases waiting for us. And the L.T. would be proud of you for listening to orders. For once."

"Fine, but if I do this, if I follow your crazy plan, you and me are done as soon as we close the case."

"Sound wonderful," Schneider said.

Franco got out and stalked to the trunk, where they'd stashed the cat carrier. It had come from the Animal Control Unit. The A.C.U. guys had given Franco no small amount of bullshit. *You going to make another big bust, Franco? Who is it this time, Felix the Cat? I hear he's running a cathouse on the Dirty Boulevard. Best pussy in town.*

Franco grabbed the plastic carrier and slammed the trunk before making a final plea. "Why don't you go in and talk to her? It's your idea."

"Because I'm driving. It's a rule: the driver stays with the vehicle, like a sea captain going down with the ship. That's me right now. A sea captain."

"That's horseshit."

Schneider ignored him and drummed a rhythm on the steering wheel with a metal finger. He sang along with an old Lou Reed song playing on the stereo. Something about being afraid he'd left his soul in someone's rented car. He could definitely relate.

THE INNER HALLWAY of the building was dark and piss-stained. Franco approached the door of Apartment 1A. A peeling yellow sticker below the doorbell said, "Mr. and Mrs. Anthony Donato." He pushed the button. "Mrs. Donato? It's Detective Franco Lopinto." He made sure to stand in front of the keyhole so she could see him.

"Frank O. who?"

"Detective Lopinto. We talked a couple of days ago. Remember?" Franco pushed to the carrier to the side of the door. He'd deal with it later, if he got that far.

"Oh, yes." The door cracked. The cats circled his legs as soon as he crossed the threshold, following him across the faded carpet to the old-fashioned loveseat.

"Have you had cuccidati before?" Mrs. Donato could barely contain her delight. She shuffled into the kitchen, talking to him over her shoulder.

"Yes. My nonni used to make them. They've got figs inside, right?"

She returned with a plate of white frosted cookies and a cup of coffee. She stood watching over him. "Go ahead and eat. Tell me what you think."

Franco took a bite. They were surprisingly good and tasted freshly baked. He was instantly flooded with memories. Pleasant ones of big family dinners before his nonni had passed. Dinners with platters of pasta and sauce, and meatballs as big as his fist. Salad and green beans from the garden, and fresh baked bread dipped in olive oil with garlic, crushed red pepper, and parmesan cheese. He remembered his nonni praising him for being a beautiful eater. At school he'd been chubby. But at his nonni and pappa's house? He was beautiful.

"Well?"

"It's really good. Thank you." He took another, and said, "Mrs. Donato, you have seventeen cats, right?"

"Well, I don't know how many, exactly. Sometimes I forget." She looked around and began naming them. "There's Misty. Bambino. Rae. Cinder. Inky. Scruffles."

He cut her off. "Which ones are synthetic, Mrs. Donato?"

She froze and then pretended not to have heard. After a full minute of silence she said, "It's illegal to own a synthetic pet. I've never broken the law. Never even gotten a speeding ticket.

Of course, I haven't driven a car in a long time. Anthony did all the driving until—"

"I don't care if you have synthetic cats. In fact, I hope you do, because it might help us solve the murder of your neighbor. You and your cat would be assisting us. Wouldn't that be something?"

"Oh?" she said.

He explained as simply as he could. When synthetic pets were first introduced nearly thirty years prior, the first models had a security feature. It had been a selling point, a small video chip with a three-week capacity. At the end of the interval it would over-write. It was supposed to appeal to families, sort of like a living, breathing, and moving nanny cam. Or, for families without children, a hardwired GoPro. Great fun to watch the family cat gutting local chipmunks and tearing open the neighbors' trash bags.

He stopped there, electing to skip the details of the lawsuits that emerged when the video feeds showed cheating spouses, abusive babysitters, and every other kind of domestic depravity.

Slowly, she was getting it. "So what you're saying is, Bambino could help find a killer?"

"Yes." Franco smiled, happy to skip a couple of steps.

"How exciting!" She clapped her hands together.

"We can go back in time and watch the street through Bambino's video feed. He could prove to be a real hero."

"Did you hear that, Bambino? You're going to be famous." Mrs. Donato scooped him up but just as quickly backed away. "Wait a second. How are you going to get the video out of his head? Is it going to hurt?" She held the cat tighter. He yowled and fought against her grasp.

"Mrs. Donato." Franco took a step. He needed to close the deal. "No one is going to hurt your cat. I guarantee it."

"You promise?"

"I'm going to treat Bambino like he's my own."

SCHNEIDER FIRED up the Caddy's V8 engine and rumbled down the Boulevard. In the sofa-like backseat, the cat hissed and spat his disapproval through the plastic bars of his cage.

Franco slouched in the passenger's seat. He examined the antique buttons and levers for the door, windows, and glove box. "Why do you drive this old piece of crap anyway?"

"You wouldn't understand."

"Try me."

"It's got style. And you, my Italian American powerlifter colleague, have none."

"I've got style. I've got shit tons of style."

"Anyone who says *shit tons of style* has no style. It's a rule."

"Kiss my ass, Schneider. You think you're so superior? How many friends do you have?"

"Let's stick to the subject. Do you think lifting heavy things and having no emotions is a style? It's a stereotype. Doesn't that wear on you? Because it's wearing on me, just like your dirty socks on the dining room chair this morning. What happened to *it's just for one night, Schneider?*"

"Fuck you." Pretending not to be hurt. "Who are you, my mother? And for your information, those socks were clean. I do my own laundry at home. I'll bet you didn't know that."

"I stand corrected. You do your laundry and have one emotion. Anger." Schneider slowed as they approached the electronics section of the Boulevard. He double parked outside of an anonymous-looking computer shop and shut off the engine. The windows of the shop were covered with butcher's paper, but a sign on the door said, "Synth City Computers & Gaming."

"This is the place?" Franco looked dubiously at the storefront.

Schneider got out and took the yowling cat from the backseat. He strode past Franco and said, "Come on. Let's find out what's in this beast's skull."

22

The next stop was Murray's Big and Fat on Porter, which ran parallel to the Dirty Boulevard on the downhill side. Murray's occupied the bottom floor of a long narrow brick and stone building. It backed up to the Chokee River, whose impenetrable brown surface was rumored to hide catfish in the 60-plus pound range.

The store's namesake, who was big *and* fat, greeted Schneider with an extra-large embrace.

"My friend." Murray lifted the slender detective an inch off the floor. "How long has it been?"

"Too long, Murray." Schneider's black and white wingtips touched down and he regarded the extra-large shop owner. "You're looking good, Murray."

"And you're looking too thin, Schneider. I got no suits for your narrow butt. Put on another fifty pounds and maybe."

Schneider turned to his reluctant partner. "Murray, this is Franco. He's looking to reinvent himself, fashion-wise."

After the two men shook hands, Murray switched into business mode. A tape measure and piece of tailor's chalk materialized in his hands as he slowly circled the detective. He nodded and tsked. "What are we thinking here, Mr. Franco? What kind of a new look?"

"I don't know. I like my style the way it is."

"That," Schneider said, "is precisely the problem."

"Kiss my ass," Franco said. "I'm only doing this because I'm desperate. Not because I value your shitty opinion."

"Noted. And returned. You're opinion's shittier."

"Yeah, well yours is the shittiest."

Murray ignored the slings and arrows. He tucked the chalk behind his ear and began talking measurements. "The trouble with the powerlifter's body, Detective, is that the mass is too evenly distributed." He measured the inseam and then the waist. "Strong shoulders, chest, and back; solid middle; and big around the thighs and calves. Sounds like a problem that isn't a problem, right? Wrong, because where are you going to taper? How are you going to balance the proportions? You see what I mean, yes?"

"I don't know. I'm thinking maybe my proportions don't need to be balanced. I'm thinking you two have got some screws loose."

"Okay, lift up your arms, Mr. Franco." Murray slipped the tape around and made another tsk sound. "Lucky for you, I know just what to do. I take care of all the best body builders. Did you know this? It's true. Football players, and boxers, too. Even a couple of wrestlers. They trust me with all their clothing needs."

"Listen, Murray. No offense, but I've got two suits." Franco tugged at his collar. He wanted out. "Two suits is enough."

Schneider leaned back against the ancient walnut paneling and smiled. He was enjoying the scene. "You have the kind of suits you wear to your uncle's funeral. That's not going to convince Tina you're a new man."

"I'm not a new man. I don't want to become a new man. I

just want to fix things between me and her so I don't have to stay at your stupid place."

"Uh-huh. You can leave at any time."

Franco turned around for the last measurement. His back. "What I need, Murray, is to get my old life back. If I've got to play dress up to do that, fine. But I don't have to like it."

Murray pulled out a notebook and scratched some numbers. "So what are we looking at here, gentlemen? A new suit, or maybe just some nice slacks and a shirt?"

"The whole goddamned thing," Schneider said. "Shoes, couple of ties and pocket squares, suspenders if he's not too much of a neanderthal to wear them."

Franco glared while Murray pulled a board of fabric swatches from a shelf. "For the suit I'm thinking simple, light-weight, with a high button point so we don't make your legs look short. You like black, Mr. Franco? Or maybe navy, or gray."

"I like black. Listen, Murray, I don't mean to sound unap-preciative, but how much is this going to cost?"

"Less than a divorce lawyer," Schneider said as he headed for the door.

23

Danielle lay in a hospital floating in a haze that was beyond pain. Her eyes remained closed, but she did experience moments of consciousness during which she listened to the voices in the room. A male voice, soft but authoritative. And several female voices. One of which sounded like her mother's, but how was that possible? She didn't know the exact date or time but that didn't matter; her mother, Bobbi Jo Talbot, was always busy with work, 365 days per year. That's what being a female senator meant, she had always told her. You had to work twice as hard as the men for half the recognition.

"I'm sorry," her mother said in a tinny, far-away voice that might have been coming from someone's holo. "I just don't understand what you're telling me, Doctor."

"Let me explain, Senator Talbot—"

"It's Bobbie Jo. Right now, I'm Danielle's mother. Not a politician."

"Okay, then. Bobbie Jo, your daughter was abducted. The people who took her performed a very unusual operation—"

"I know that. Just tell me about her arms. And do it in plain English, Doctor. Where are my daughter's arms?"

Danielle tried to feel something below her shoulders but couldn't. It wasn't numbness, though. It was like a heavy blanket had been draped over her entire body, except the blanket was twice as heavy where it covered her arms. Why? She couldn't figure it out. The process of thinking required too much energy. She gave into the haze and drifted into a dream or perhaps a memory.

In the dream-memory, someone was guiding her. Gently. Lovingly. "You deserve so much better than this," the person said. But she couldn't see who it was. She had no idea if it was even a man or a woman. Deserved better than what? She didn't know, and she was drifting again, this time back to the conversation in the room.

The soft authoritative voice of the doctor resumed his explanation. "...amputated her arms, and then—don't ask me how, because it's not even supposed to be possible—grafted on a pair of synthetic arms."

"Grafted?"

"The surgical work was nothing short of incredible. There's a piece of tissue at the juncture that serves as a bridge between the two systems. Amazing."

Her mother's voice shrieked. "I'm glad you're so impressed, Doctor. Just what do you mean it's not supposed to be possible? It looks to me like it was very possible. They did it, right?"

"She was dropped off outside the hospital. Strapped to a gurney."

A new voice. Male, too, but not so soft as the doctor's. "Senator Talbot, I'm Detective Derrick Carter. I'm sorry to interrupt at this difficult time."

"Then don't. Go away."

A pause, then, "The surveillance footage shows a man

wheeling a gurney to the entrance, but he took precautions to protect his identity."

"Face recognition?"

"No, and no for gait recognition. But he did leave detailed instructions for the hospital staff to follow."

"Rather excellent instructions," the doctor said.

It was too much to follow. Danielle let her mind spin off and her body sink. There was a shrill beeping sound and the scraping of furniture being moved. More voices but they were too harsh, shouting instructions, and numbers. She sank a little deeper and was rewarded with a rich velvety blackness. And peace.

24

———

Keven dropped Elizabeth and Louis at the country house, which was 25 miles North of New DC, and drove straight to Boseman's Scrap Metal and Processing. The office of Boseman's was a cramped and cluttered trailer that was at least ninety-five degrees. An undersized wall-mounted air-conditioner pushed a current across the room in the HVAC equivalent of a cruel joke. Keven approached the desk and hovered his hand over a silver bell.

"Don't touch that!" The voice came from a back room that had been constructed by walling off the last fifteen feet of the trailer behind a row of 6' steel filing cabinets.

Keven retracted his hand and waited. Shortly, a man emerged from the makeshift back room. He looked about forty, with a deeply tanned, leathery face that might have seemed fitting on a 74-year-old. His navy work shirt had the name *Wade* stitched on the breast pocket.

"That bell goes off like a fucking gong in my head." Wade looked stuporous from the heat, or perhaps he was hungover.

"You should hide it before the boss comes in." Keven was 90% certain this guy wasn't the boss. The only vehicle in the parking lot was a worn out F150 with bald tires and a bent frame. Not exactly a boss's truck.

Wade stared back, unblinking. Keven had dressed down for the occasion—distressed jeans, a gray t-shirt, and a ball cap—but he still felt wildly out of place. He cleared his throat and forged ahead. "How much would it cost to have an extended van shredded?"

"Depends on what it weighs."

"8,000 pounds."

"Steel's at a hundred per right now."

"Per what?" Hating himself for appearing ignorant. But how was he supposed to know the ins and outs of shredding automobiles? He hadn't planned on dumping the camper, especially since he'd gone to so much effort to get it fitted out just so in the first place. He'd had to set up a shell LLC that was a certified nonprofit. Then there was the medical equipment, much of it customized for the space and electrical limitations imposed by the RV. And, finally, the installation which, in the end, he'd had to do himself. After all, even if he could have found a garage with the skill and expertise to put in a mobile surgical theater, there was little chance they'd keep their mouths shut about it.

But the accident with the kid had forced his hand. He had to get rid of the RV, because a seventeen-year-old kid with a wad of cash was sure to run his mouth. It might be at a keg party, ice cream stand, or a school dance. But it was sure as shit going to happen. He'd brag to a girl or one of his buddies. And that girl or buddy would mention it to a father or an uncle. Who would just happen to be a cop. The only course of action was to get rid of it.

"Per ton. What do you think?" Wade took a bandana from the desktop and wiped his face. Not doing so well. "Every scrapyard in America deals in tonnage. I can give you $350 cash if it weighs what you said."

"Okay. Let's do it." Keven noted with small pleasure that Wade just shorted him $50. A good sign that he was willing to play. He suspected that would change, though. Just as soon as he got a look at the pristine Mercedes Sprinter, which was easily worth 120 large. Not counting the medical equipment, of course, because who would buy used medical equipment?

"That's $350 if you tow it here. If my guy has to tow, then it's $250 per ton, plus a dollar a mile after the first 15 miles."

"It's here now." Keven looked at his watch. He was wasting time. "How long will it take to put it through the shredder?" He followed Wade's eyes to a calendar pinned to the pasteboard wall. It showed a redhead wearing a string bikini and a tool belt. She regarded the two of them through the tragic veneer of a forced smile.

"What do you care?" Reluctantly, Wade looked away from the calendar. "It's up to me if I shred it or not. If it's salvageable, I'll set it aside and part it out later, but that's my decision."

Keven had about one minute to close this deal. If he failed, he was going to have another loose end to tie up. Maybe that was the easier route. He could shred the camper himself with Wade inside of it. How hard could it be? No, that would create more problems than it would solve, especially if someone else saw them. That was a problem that grew more problems. And although he didn't mind killing certain people—especially men, whom he viewed as either potential threats or competitors—he didn't go out of his way for it either. "Is that your F150 out there?"

"Yeah."

"Looks like it could use new tires and some frame work. How about I pay you double the amount you said you'd give me? $700 bucks could go a long way toward fixing your truck."

"Why would you pay me to scrap your rig? You got a dead body in the trunk?"

Keven laughed. "That's funny. I'm an accountant with the IRS."

Wade shrugged to say, *who cares?*

"When one of my kind buries someone, it's done with computers and official letters." Which was not at all true, depending on the interpretation of *my kind.*

"Make it twelve hundred," Wade said. "Frame work costs more than you'd think."

Keven waited a few seconds, for the sake of appearances, and dropped an envelope with ten $100 bills on the desk. "That's a thousand. I'll give you two hundred more when I see it go through the machine."

Wade mopped the back of his neck with the bandana while he considered the offer. But there was nothing to think about, really. If he added in the $450 he was *supposed to* pay for an RV's worth of scrap—which he'd pull from the register—he'd net $1,650. Not bad for an hour of work. Wade smiled, and snatched the money.

25

Schneider turned on the car stereo and settled in to watch the Boulevard. A dark gloom had settled over the street even though it was 2:00 p.m., owing in equal parts to pollution and Synth City's attempt to deal with the pollution. It had been a good idea, based on cloud seeding technology. Allegedly, a superfine mist of seawater would hover over New DC, creating a filter and, at the same time, providing an earth-cooling effect. In reality the layer did little more than collect toxins and dump them back down in short concentrated bursts. Occasional darkness at 2:00 p.m. wasn't uncommon.

In front of the Caddy, an obese man in shorts and red tube socks pushed a wheelchair. Seated in the wheelchair was a naked department store mannequin. The obese man appeared to be talking to the mannequin and, once, stopped to brush her hair. Schneider shook his head and reclined his seat. He covered his eyes with the brim of his fedora and listened to the sounds of motion and life around him. The pump and whoosh of air brakes from city busses. Chains clicking through the derailleurs and cassettes of delivery bicycles. The rattling carts of bums pushing their bottles and cans over broken sidewalks.

Even the conversations floating through the air were as rough and gritty as the layer of dirt on the street.

"How the fuck are you going to tell me she's *just a friend*?" A woman outside the Caddy was yelling at her man. Her voice rose on the *just a friend* part to within an inch of the threshold of violence.

"I'm telling you, baby." Male voice. As smooth as silk, but about to lose. "You got it all wrong."

"Oh, I do, do I?"

"Yeah, baby—"

The woman cutting him off. "Did that bitch come see you last night? When I was out working, making money for *us*?"

"Baby, you've got to understand—"

Schneider's phone pinged with a message from Royce, his contact at Synth City Computers and Gaming. He straightened up and opened a file, which contained a full three weeks of video from the cat's POV. The footage was jarring. Quick pans showed the underside of the old lady's couch, a multi-tiered tower with carpeted flats, and closeups of other cats' faces. All of which is to say it was mostly garbage. Schneider closed the file and sent a message to Royce.

"My man, I need you to filter out everything except the street. I want to see people coming and going from the building, and every parked vehicle on the building side and across the street."

"On it." Royce's reply was almost instantaneous. He didn't exactly owe Schneider, but he hadn't forgotten either. Three years prior, at the tender age of 19, he'd gotten lit up for a work-for-hire hacking job. Unbeknownst to him, the hack was connected to a blackmail ring. Someone in the ring applied too much pressure and a dead body squeezed out.

Royce was pretty sure he'd have skated clear of it, eventually. But that would have taken months and the county holding center was not a good place for a bespectacled computer nerd prone to anxiety and digestive issues. Schneider had not only cut him loose but effectively scared him straight. "You're a lousy criminal, kid," he'd said. "Why don't you use those brains for something that won't get you stabbed in the shower by a man named Junior?"

"Like what?" he'd said. "I don't even have a GED?"

Schneider had shrugged. "You're good with computers. Start a computer business."

Which is exactly what he'd done. And it was why, on the rare occasion that Schneider asked for something, he delivered. Fast. In this case it took him five minutes to find and install the right editing software, and another five to make some adjustments and run it. Twenty seconds later, the file arrived on Schneider's holo.

"Thank you, Royce." Schneider scrolled. Nothing interesting. Mail and package deliveries. Residents carrying groceries and pushing baby strollers. A young woman delivering pizzas.

And then he saw it, time stamped at 12:46 p.m., Tuesday, the morning before they'd discovered Rachel Montgomery and Paul Chaffee's bodies: a man, pushing a hand cart loaded with a wooden shipping box.

"Bingo."

Schneider paused to enjoy this moment of discovery. It was always a thrill when the trail of dead ends opened up. He stopped the video and zoomed in. The man, who he immediately labeled the unsub, or unidentified suspect, wore gray coveralls and a ball cap with a hood pulled over it. Sunglasses, and a goatee shading the lower third of his face. Schneider put it through facial recognition, but there wasn't enough face to recognize. He let the video run again and observed that the cart had two sets of wheels that were motorized, the kind that could climb stairs. The box itself was constructed from high density fiberboard with pine framing, reinforced with steel straps. The whole thing secured to the cart's frame with 3" nylon webbing.

Schneider watched the video counter run while the guy was inside. Ten minutes. Fifteen. Twenty-seven. Enough time to gain entry, open the box, and unload its contents. Enough time to arrange two synth bodies without arms on a blanket on the floor. And smooth back Rachel's hair respectfully. Pack up the box and the cart, and head back down the stairs.

He kept watching. At the thirty-five-minute mark, the guy exited the building. Sure enough, he'd broken the box down into panels and stacked them flat on the cart. Yes, he was their guy. And it sure as hell wasn't Oscar Stanovich. Too tall and too fit. Stanovich was short and frail. This guy was about 5'11", broad shouldered, and fit. He moved like an athlete.

"Okay, Bambino, you beautiful bastard. Take me to the killer's car and please, oh please, look at the license plate."

The man wheeled the cart over the curb and into the street. He paused on the yellow centerline, waiting for traffic to pass, and then, predictably, the cat's attention shifted.

"No!"

The video panned down from the window and focused on the creature's extended hind leg, which he was grooming, and then his furry belly. It moved up and down over a two-inch section of belly fur for almost a full minute.

"Damnit."

Sudden movement across the carpet, weaving and slinking between the maze of other animals. Through a cracked door and up onto the rim of something. A piece of furniture, perhaps? Looking up at the far wall and a glinting mirror, then down into a shimmering silver pool. Head lowering, about to submerge itself.

Schneider sighed. He fast-forwarded over the whole toilet drinking sequence, until the cat made his way back to the window. Bambino jerked his head to track a fly and then, finally, returned his attention to the street. The parked cars on the building side were the same: a blue SUV, white sedan, red pickup, and a silver hatchback. But across the street, two spaces were empty.

Schneider scrolled back to an earlier sequence, just before the man's arrival at Rachel Montgomery's building. The first was a rusted white Econoline with a plumber's rack on the roof. The plates weren't visible, but there was a logo painted on the side: The Drain Doc. And ahead of the Econoline? A black RV. Mercedes Sprinter. Almost new by the looks of it. Set up like a camper with double air conditioning units on the top and the outline of what looked like a slide-out room on the side.

He'd start with the white van. With any luck, The Drain Doc would be a single operator business. That would save time. If not, he'd persuade the outfit's dispatcher to give him a name. And if the dispatcher refused? There was no way to get a warrant on a case that was officially sewn up. But there was nothing to prevent him from disconnecting his washing machine at home and calling in a repair. He could get a good look at the repairman. If it wasn't a match, he could ask him about any plumber colleagues that seemed odd or suspicious.

And if The Drain Brain proved to be a false lead? He'd pursue the Mercedes. It would be harder, with no plates or logo. If that dead ended he could always go back to visit Lawrence, the Xylene dealer, and push a little harder. Bring him to the station house and squeeze until something shook loose. If that failed too? He'd think of something else. He always did.

26

The Drain Doc office was a cinderblock square next to the railroad tracks half a mile from Stiehl's. The signage in the front window promised quality work at fair prices, and a one-hour guarantee for emergency calls. Schneider parked between two white Econoline vans but neither was a match. The first was too new, with shiny paint and no rust. Also, it was an extended model, a full 18" longer than the one in the video. The second, which was older and appropriately rusty, was lacking a roof rack. It was also missing half of the letter A in the logo.

He tripped the electric chime when he opened the front door. A small, middle-aged woman looked up from a crossword and tracked his progress across the checked linoleum. She was stationed behind a counter with organized stacks of manila folders, triplicate receipts, and parts manuals. There were computer monitors, too, but it was clear that, as an operation, The Drain Doc was old school.

"How can I help you, sir?" The woman looked up at him and, at the same time, looked down. Judgment. Disgust.

Schneider was used to it but he still noticed, which, he supposed, was the whole point.

He showed her his badge and tried to imagine the monotony of her life, grinding out a series of meaningless 9-5 days with retirement in a South Florida senior complex as the only salvation.

"I'm Detective Schneider, ma'am," he said. "I'm hoping you can tell me who would have been driving this van on June 7th at around 2:00 p.m." He laid down a still showing the van parked on the Dirty Boulevard. Just behind the black RV. "This is the 500 block of—"

She picked up a pair of red plastic reading glasses and installed them. "I know where it is. It's the part of town with all the drugs and sex shops. And synthetic prostitutes."

"I need to know who the driver is."

"I don't know what to tell you. We've got 12 plumbers, 8 plumber's assistants, and 4 subs. I don't even know how many vans. It could have been any of them."

Schneider pointed to a clipboard with dog-eared pages. "Look it up, please. You seem like a very organized person."

She huffed and flipped the pages, without reading, of course. "Guess I'm not as organized as you thought. But we've got full accident insurance, if someone wants to make a claim against one of our drivers. Fender benders do happen." She slid the glasses off and dropped them on the counter. Case closed.

"It's not a fender bender. I'm hoping the driver can help us solve a crime that occurred on this block." He tapped the part of the picture that showed Rachel Montgomery's building. "Some people were killed in this building, and your driver might have seen who did it." Especially if he looked in a mirror that day.

"Our men are busy from dusk till dawn fixing leaks and putting in toilets, not out in the street watching criminals. That's your job, right?"

Schneider registered the challenge with a raised eyebrow. In his periphery, he caught another white van pulling into the lot. Time to cut his losses with the small woman looking for a fight. He tipped his hat and said, "You could have helped, ma'am, but instead you've given me so much more."

She scowled and returned to her crossword.

The door chime rang on his way out, alerting the driver. The man was halfway out of the van when he noticed Schneider and froze. He was dressed in coveralls and a ball cap, just like the guy in the video.

"Afternoon, friend," Schneider said, approaching carefully. The guy looked twitchy.

A green Stanley thermos fell to the pavement and broke the standoff. In one fluid movement, the plumber slid back into the driver's seat, slammed the door shut, and cranked the engine to life. He pulled the column shifter into reverse. Skidded out of the lot and was gone.

Schneider hustled to the thermos and picked it up with a white handkerchief. He carried it to the Caddy and dropped it in the passenger's seat. Ten seconds later, he pointed the car in the direction of the escapee and punched it.

OPINIONS VARIED among cops about the best way to chase down a suspect. Many advocated a balls-to-the-wall approach, sticking as close as possible, pushing the driver to make a mistake or, in rare cases, give up. Sometimes it worked, but as often it produced spectacular wrecks. And a fair number of deaths. Some were bystanders or even cops themselves. Schneider owed his slight limp to one such disaster, in which his car had been t-boned going through an intersection. He'd been running the lights and siren, but the driver had been too drunk to notice. Schneider suffered a concussion, shattered front teeth, and a compound fracture of his right leg. It had taken him a full year to recover and was why now he slowed at every intersection, and checked the cross streets for the fleeing vehicle.

In this new way of moderate-speed-pursuit, he'd observed that suspects tended to flee in a relatively straight line. They didn't zig or zag much, presumably because turning corners required slowing down. It was human nature, he suspected, to want to gain distance from the pursuer. This was fine by him because it made his job easier. In this case, he cruised through two intersections and found the choke point he was looking for at the third intersection: a red light packed tight with commuters. And there, sandwiched between a black sedan and a red SUV, was his guy.

Schneider flickered his lights and pulsed the siren. As soon as the streetlight turned green, the SUV moved forward and then hesitated. Should the driver go through the intersection and pull over on the next block? Or stop and let the undercover police car go around? Schneider hit the siren again and, this time, left it on. The SUV jerked through the intersection and pulled over.

For the moment his guy was trapped behind the black sedan. The van laid on the horn, but the sedan continued at the same speed. When the sedan saw Schneider's lights two cars back and starting to slow, the van made a bold move and passed. There was a break in the oncoming traffic, but not enough. An approaching dump truck locked its brakes and swerved to the right, taking out two parked cars. The van blasted ahead, toward the promise of open road.

Schneider came up hard behind the black sedan with full lights and siren. The car pulled over, and he accelerated until he was one vehicle length length behind the white van.

"Take it easy now," Schneider coaxed. "Hold steady." The last thing he wanted was a wreck. Property damage and injuries would mean a ton of shit for him, and mountains of paperwork.

The driver of the van was getting twitchy. He jerked to the right of the lane and clipped the mirror of a parked car. Fragments of plastic flew into the air. The van overcorrected and fishtailed close to the centerline. An oncoming city bus hit its air horn and the van did something very surprising: it made a hard right turn when there wasn't an actual street. The front wheels hit the curb and the airbags went off. After that, the van climbed the sidewalk and magically careened between two oak trees without breaking off so much as a twig. Finally, it smashed into a set of cement steps in front of Jolene's Hair and Nail Salon, caving in the engine compartment and releasing a cloud compressed gas.

"Fuck." Schneider pulled into a nearby driveway and left the Caddy door open. He pulled the pin on his radio; it was linked to a GPS and automatically called for backup. Gun out, Schneider moved to the van from a line of sight behind the door pillar.

"Let me see your hands," he said.

The driver groaned. "I'm hurt. I'm bleeding."

"Are your hands broken?"

"No."

"Then put them out."

He did, but as soon as Schneider applied the cuffs, he started the fast-talking-I'm-innocent-I-swear-to-god routine. He promised on his mother's grave and his daughter's soul that he didn't do it, that he'd been working all day every day. He'd even paid his taxes on time.

None of this was good. The plumber's behavior was exactly what Schneider would expect from an addict or a low-level career criminal. Con men, hustlers, and small-timers, not the kind who could pull off a double murder and leave behind a spotless crime scene. The latter were almost always cool and composed. Or scornful.

Schneider pulled hard and dragged the guy out of the van and onto the ground. His nose was bleeding and he had a laceration over his left eye. Otherwise, he looked okay.

"You've got to believe me," the guy said. "I didn't do anything."

Schneider patted him down and found a wallet, a vape with three caramel-colored cartridges, and what looked like a grocery list: eggs, pepper jack cheese, chicken cutlets, and Bic razors—the pink ones. The guy was still talking a mile a minute. Scared.

Schneider dropped his stuff into an evidence bag and said, "Right now you have the right to shut the fuck up. Nod your head if you understand."

Jess stared hard at the bank check. She counted the zeros —seven—and counted them again. She held it up to her desk lamp to examine the watermark. Not that she'd know a fake watermark from a real one but, still, it seemed like the right thing to do. In the end, she called her team together for an emergency meeting and sketched out some quick notes.

"What's up, boss?" This from Kelly Alvarez, her always-smart, always-direct media specialist.

Jess smiled at Kelly and addressed the dozen or so souls gathered in the conference room, which was also their break room, lunch room, and main work space. "Hi, people. Thanks for coming." Polite laughter, since everyone had been there to begin with; the effort of attending one of Jess's all-hands-on-deck meetings involved swiveling their office chairs away from a computer monitor toward their boss. "I want to do a little thought experiment. Imagine an anonymous donor gave us $2,000,000 with the following rules: it can only be spent on advertising, and all the ads need to run before the SRA vote this Friday."

A hand shot up. Brendon Little, master of the bowtie and satin vest combo. "What if there's money left over? Do we get to keep it for other purposes?"

Jess shook her head in answer. "Spend it all. Every last cent." After she let that sink in, she said, "Let's take two hours, people, and give me your absolute best ideas. To fuel your brains, I've ordered lunch from Thai Express. It will be here at 12:30."

After a brief cheer from the staff—all except Brendon, who preferred The Kebob Connection—Jess retreated to her office to have another look at the mysterious check. She traced the signature at the bottom with her fingertip: Bharanda, the founder and chief stockholder of SynCorp, the world's largest producer of synthetics. Bharanda, author of such ground-breaking books as *The Machinery of the Soul, The God Circuit,* and *Handbook of Spiritual Computation.*

She understood why the genius who was credited with the invention of the Gen III synthetic brain and nervous system would want the SRA to pass. But why the check? And why ads? Two mil was probably a drop in the bucket for someone in Bharanda's income bracket but, still, it was a very significant contribution. She just wanted to make sure to spend it effectively.

"Knock, knock." Predictably, it was Kelly, the office den mother, coming on behalf of the others. To gain intel.

"Yes, Kelly."

"Is it real? The donation?"

"It's real." She held up the check, but not so close that Kelly could read the name at the bottom right corner.

"I know you said it's anonymous, but Jordan will find out when he does the paperwork and accounting. And he'll tell the rest of us. So, you may as well tell me now. It's more direct."

"You're a fierce negotiator, Ms. Alvarez. I'll give you one clue." She pulled a volume from her shelf, taking care to hide the title from Kelly's view. She opened to a dogeared page and read, "The central question of what it means to be human cannot be answered with os and is of code nor with the epigenetic flickering of DNA sequences, nor by clever Turing tests. It can only be answered by the heart, which is not to say the four chambered muscle that pumps blood throughout the body, but the simple measure of what moves one's soul."

"That's Bharanda, right?" Kelly covered her cheeks with her hands. "Really? Him?"

Jess smiled and closed the book. "Yes, him."

"Incredible. I thought he was a total recluse. No contact with the outside world and all that. No one even knows what he looks like. How is that even possible?"

"It's his name on the check."

Kelly looked away thoughtfully. "You know what the weirdest thing about this is?"

"What?"

"This could be the last piece, you know? The thing that finally moves the needle on the SRA vote."

"I hope so, but still, it's going to be really close. One of the Senators is going to have to change his mind."

"Or her's."

"You mean Bobbi Jo Talbot? Not a chance. She'll never change her mind. Or her vote." Jess slid the check back in its envelope. She kept a small fire safe next to her desk, for important documents. She pressed her thumb to the key pad and opened it. "I'm just grateful Bharanda trusted us." Outside of the office the food had arrived, giving the common area a party-vibe. Jess locked the safe and the two women joined the celebration.

28

Schneider sat on the concrete steps and contemplated the shitstorm he'd created. He was guilty of several different procedural violations from ignoring the chain of command to withholding evidence from the principal investigators, and pursuing a suspect without authorization or backup. Not to mention the property damage. It might be overlooked if the guy in the video turned out to be the unsub. If not? Shitstorm. Only one way to find out, though.

Schneider fished the wallet out of the evidence bag. It was a worn leather trifold containing a driver's license—Bill Spieler, age 37, not an organ donor—two credit cards, a coffee punch card, and a folded piece of paper with a phone number. He lit up a cigarette and held it out to the plumber, who lay prone on the walkway. The plumber nodded and Schneider placed the smoke between his lips.

"Thanks." He took a long drag and rolled it to the outside of his lips. A real pro.

"Here's what's going to happen." Schneider lit one for himself. "The uniforms are going to arrive soon. You'll get booked and assigned to some dumbass public defender with razor burns on his 27-year-old cheeks. He'll sit across from you and won't look you in the eye because he can barely comprehend his job and doesn't really give a shit anyway." He leaned forward and plucked the cigarette from Bill's lips. Bill watched intently as Schneider ground it under the heel of one of his wingtips.

"I told you, man. I didn't do anything. You've got to believe me."

Sirens screamed in the distance. "Do you hear that noise, Bill? They'll be here in two minutes, and then I can't help you. I'll walk away and forget all about you."

"What do you want me to say, man?"

"Tell me what you were doing outside of Rachel Montgomery's apartment last Tuesday."

Bill shook his head. "I don't know anyone by that name."

Schneider looked off in the direction of the sirens. "They're coming."

"I'll lose my job."

"Get another job. Plumbers are always in demand, and it beats prison."

"You don't understand. My wife will divorce me and get custody of the kids and move back to Arizona. I'll never see them again."

The first patrol car arrived. Two uniforms got out and eyeballed the situation. They didn't look happy. Schneider waved them over. "Time's up."

Bill the plumber tried to roll onto his side. "My chest hurts." But what he really meant was, *help me sit up and I'll talk.* Schneider pushed him over roughly and propped him up against the front driver's side wheel.

"I wasn't there for Rachel," he said. "I was there for Staci. I see her every week in between jobs. She's a synth." He looked at Schneider and then hung his head, ashamed. "She's really shook up about what happened to Rachel and that guy.

So when you showed up at work, I knew you'd seen my van—"

"She'll vouch for you?"

Bill nodded. "Totally. It's not what you think, me and her. We love each other. It started out with me being a regular customer, but—"

Schneider made a let's-move-it-along gesture with his hand to show that he didn't care. He didn't have time to listen to the synth version of *Pretty Woman*. "Staci knew Rachel and Chaffee?"

"I don't think so. It's not like they carpooled to work or anything."

"And you never saw either of them?"

Bill shook his head. "I'd text Staci whenever I got there and she'd let me in the back of the building. Where the trash cans and recycling are. Her apartment was the last one on the first floor, so I could get in and out without anyone seeing me. It wasn't top secret or anything, but people know people. My wife works with computers in Synth City. Just a couple blocks off the Boulevard, on Porter."

The uniforms were walking around the van inspecting the damage to the steps of the nail salon, shaking their heads about the stupidity of modern criminals.

Schneider hauled the plumber to standing. "Give me a timeline. On Tuesday. When exactly did you show up, and when did you leave?"

"12:30 to 1:55. I get half an hour for lunch, but I like to stretch it."

Schneider tucked one of his business cards in the pocket of the man's coveralls. "You'd better hope Staci will vouch for you. Call me if you remember anything else about that day. People you saw on your way in or out. An old woman, a kid selling candy bars for school, I don't care how insignificant you think it is. Understand?"

He nodded. Two new patrol cars arrived along with a tow truck. Schneider walked the plumber toward the flashing lights and the cluster of cops. Two he recognized from the 23rd, though he didn't remember their names.

One was short and stocky, with the standard cop-issue mustache. He nodded at Schneider and said, "Heard the news about Stanovich?"

"No." Schneider passed the plumber to Mustache's partner, a red-faced kid for whom it might have been his first day on the job. "Put him in your car and you can have the collar."

"Really?" the kid said.

Mustache narrowed his eyes. "But you're going to follow up with the paperwork, right?"

"Of course." Though he had no intention of following up or of setting foot in the Station House. As soon as the L.T. learned of this fiasco he'd be well within his rights to ground Schneider with a desk assignment, or maybe a suspension. Probably a suspension. Therefore, Schneider needed to lay low and avoid picking up the phone. And find the real unsub fast.

When the plumber was tucked in the backseat of the patrol car safely out of earshot, Mustache turned to Schneider and said, "Two of those stolen synth arms just turned up. Guess where?"

While Schneider waited, he moved them a few feet from the cruiser. Bill the plumber was watching them closely through his window. The fear of being arrested had the strange side effect of increasing one's hearing acuity.

"On the body of a senator's daughter."

"What do you mean *on the body of*?"

"Get this: someone abducted her, cut off her arms, and sewed on the synthetic ones."

"You're kidding?"

"No. How fucked up is that?"

"You know for a fact it's the synthetic arms from the Marquis-Chafee case?"

"That what they say."

"What about the vic? Where is she?"

"St. Joe's on life support. Rubin and Carter are waiting there with the mother. The Senator. In case the girl wakes up."

"And they still like Stanovich for it?"

Mustache shrugged. "Why wouldn't they?"

"Because how can he abduct someone and attach synth arms on them when he's in prison?"

"That's a good point." This from the kid.

Schneider thanked them, and pointed at the plumber. "Book him on vehicular assault and fleeing the scene."

"What about the report?" Mustache called after him.

Schneider kept walking.

29

Franco piled into the car with two shirt boxes and a vinyl dry cleaning bag containing his new suit. He looked pissed. "You and me need to talk. I've been waiting here for two and a half hours. I was one step away from—"

"Take it easy. I was running down a lead. It was time sensitive." Schneider started the engine and pulled out into traffic between a panel truck and a yellow convertible. Before Franco could explode, Schneider gave a bare bones account of his run-in with the plumber, talking as fast as he could to head off Franco's rage.

Halfway through the narrative Franco shifted from anger to curiosity. "You talked to his hooker girlfriend? Staci."

"By phone, on my way to get you. She cleared him. Says they're in love."

"You skipped over a few things. How'd you chase down a guy, take him in, do the paperwork and accident reports, and then square up with Carter and Rubin, and the DA?"

Schneider shook his head. "That's all on me. I know you're

on probation. That's why I went solo. I wasn't trying to ditch you."

"Yeah, right."

The woman driving the convertible honked at Schneider and gave him the finger. Schneider returned it with a wave.

"You know she wasn't being friendly?" Franco observed.

Schneider ignored him. "How'd it go with Murray?"

"About that. How come he won't take my money?"

"Ask Murray."

"I did. He said, 'don't worry about it.' He said you two had some kind of an arrangement."

"So?" Schneider skidded off the Boulevard and onto Porter, past rows of public housing—filled with synths and the most destitute humans—and the former city hall building, which had been abandoned three decades ago. Its four stories of concrete were slowly being reclaimed by nature, one crack at a time. A pair of stray dogs loped across the crumbling parking lot in search of ripe garbage.

"So I want to know: what kind of arrangement? Don't get me wrong, I appreciate you helping me out, you know, letting me crash at your place. And helping me get back together with Tina. But what's with the secret deal with Murray?"

"It's no secret. He's the best tailor in town and I give him a lot of business. I told him to put your bill on my account and you and I could settle up later."

"I can pay my own fucking way."

"That's what I said: you and I would settle later."

"You think, what, I'm a charity case? Some lost soul who needs to be taken in and fixed?"

Schneider looked at him and tilted his head, wondering where the emotion had come from. What story from the past did it connect to? He said, "What's this really about, Franco?"

"What do you mean?"

"What's the question behind the question?"

"Don't get all psychological on me." It looked like he might let it drop but then he pointed a finger and said, "I don't like you making decisions without asking me. That's what this is about."

"Okay, got it. Anything else?"

"Yeah, I'm getting the feeling that the L.T. told you to keep an eye on me. And you're doing his bidding, which I sure as hell don't appreciate."

"He told me you're a good detective with a hot head. That's it."

"Bullshit." And then, "He said I'm a good detective?"

Schneider slowed to watch a group of boys. They were attempting to rob an ATM machine. A skinny kid in an orange hoodie and oversized jeans stepped up with an aluminum baseball bat and whacked the hell out of the machine's casing. On the third swing the bat rebounded and hit him square in the face.

"Did you see that?" Schneider slowed to appreciate the spectacle. The boy, who had clearly knocked himself out, dropped to the sidewalk in a heap. His buddies tried to rouse him, but when Schneider flicked on his lights—hidden inside the Caddy's chrome grill—they fled in all directions. Schneider turned the lights off and kept going.

"What about that kid?" Franco said.

"Not our problem. We're headed to Maston Supermax. That's the next stop on the train to closing this case for real."

"The Supermax? Why?"

"Because that's where Oscar Stanovich is."

"So what?" Getting pissed all over again because of the way Schneider kept doling out the info. Bread crumbs for big, lumbering Franco. Worse, within the rigid world of police work, a trip to Maston was the same as going off the grid. Again. Not good for a person on such thin ice.

"We need to see for ourselves if he's our guy." He shared the news the cop from the 23rd had told him about the synth arms turning up, and the senator's daughter. Which meant one of two things. Either Stanovich was working with someone else, or he didn't do it.

Franco's eyes rose with surprise. "That's pretty fucked up, about the arms. What's it say about motive?"

"I don't know. It changes things, but I don't know how."

"Do Carter and Rubin know what we're up to? Or the L.T.?"

"What do you think?" He gunned it through a yellow light. The big car accelerated away from the Boulevard. They stopped before the green metal bridge that crossed the Chokee River, which today was running a darker brown than usual with a foamy scum riding the surface near the middle, which was supposed to be over eighty feet deep. The bridge was just starting to rise in anticipation of a rust-plated work barge passing through. The barge had a crane arm on the back end; the whole thing appeared to be moving at a slower-than-walking pace. It was going to be a while. "Listen, I know you're on the L.T.'s shit list. Say the word if you want to sit this part out."

He didn't hesitate. "No way."

Schneider put the car in park, shut off the engine, and returned to the subject of his new partner's paranoia. "So I've convinced you that I'm not on the take for free suits from Murray. Anything else you want to know about?"

Franco knitted his black caterpillar eyebrows. "Yeah. How come you got transferred from the 14th? You were there for a long time."

"I was in three different precincts before the 14th. My close rate was good, but—" He took a moment to consider the phrasing. "—I didn't play well with the others. Or they didn't play well with me."

"Because you're a Synth."

"Yeah. And my beautiful personality."

They stared out at the muddy river and the barge, which seemed to be standing still. A crumbling boat launch served as the main access point for the Boulevard. On the other side of the launch a scattering of fisherman sat in camp chairs smoking cigarettes and drinking beer. They used deep sea rods baited with corn, the tips rigged with small copper bells to alert them of any hits. An old man worked a Coleman stove, frying catfish filets in bacon grease with red onions. The smell wafted through the Caddy's open windows.

"You want to know about the kid I shot," Schneider said. "That's what this is really about."

"I think I deserve to know. We're going to be in situations where I'm going to have to trust you to have my back. And the other way, too."

Schneider nodded. "I'll tell you, but it's because I've got nothing to hide. Deserve has nothing to do with it." He dragged out the word *deserve,* a rare note of sarcasm from an otherwise straight shooter.

"The L.T. said it was a legit kill, that the kid was carrying. Two automatics."

Schneider laughed, but it wasn't the funny kind. "The kid was unarmed."

An old man in a Bronco backed a trailer down the ramp. It was loaded with a Grumman fishing boat with an antique two-stroke outboard.

"I don't get it," Franco said. "You admit you shot an unarmed kid? Why?"

"Because I wasn't aiming for him. It was an accident."

Franco scowled. Now he knew why he was so pissed at Schneider. It wasn't because he suspected him of being on the take—a guy like Schneider was too smart and too classy for that. It was because Schneider was always half a step ahead of him. Just like his wife, Tina. He watched the boat's propeller submerge and disappear into the brown water. "Alright," he said. "I'll play. Who were you aiming for?"

"My partner."

30

Elizabeth made a simple stew with cubes of nicely marbled beef, carrots, and shallots. She seasoned it lightly and served it over barley. A plate for her and a stainless bowl for the dog. The aroma filled the kitchen and drifted into the living room, where Louis lay on the carpet. He whimpered in his sleep and kicked his paws in a running motion.

"Aren't you coming?" she said. "I made your favorite."

Louis opened his eyes and sniffed the air. He thumped his tail three times. Three happy thumps.

"We're celebrating a big step forward. The girl survived the procedure." There was a lightness to Elizabeth's step as she set the bowl and plate down and glided across the wide plank floor. She knelt beside Louis and said, "I told you, old boy. No more deaths."

Louis licked her hand, but the smell of the beef was overwhelming. He twitched his nose and started to salivate.

"I know how you feel about my work, but I also know you're hungry." Elizabeth scratched the top of his head and behind his ears. "You are always hungry."

With the greatest of effort, Louis got to his feet and padded to his bowl.

Elizabeth returned to the kitchen and poured herself a glass of red wine. She sat at the small marble-topped table and ate her meal, scanning the pages Keven had prepared for her. At the front of the stack was a picture of their next subject, Steve Muncy, a twenty-six-year-old semi-professional triathlete. It was an action shot and the young man practically radiated health. A perfect physical specimen and a perfect choice. Of the dossiers she'd scanned on senator's children only Danielle Talbot, Steve Muncy, and two other women met their criteria for age, proximity, and health.

She smiled at her assistant's cleverness. The last subject, Danielle, had been especially difficult for him. He'd genuinely liked her, which had made the deception all the more unpleasant. But he would view a male athlete as a competitor. Someone as strong and fit as he. They could go toe-to-toe, best man wins and all that. Thus, no internal conflict. Such a clever Keven.

She sent him a text saying that she approved of his choice and that he should move ahead with the plan. After that, she put her dishes in the sink and grabbed her keys. "I'm going to the studio, Louis," she said. "I'll be back in a couple of hours." Altogether she was very pleased. It would be inconvenient without the RV, but she and Keven could handle inconvenient. The bigger problem was Schneider, whom she'd been working on for months. She was confident he didn't know anything. She needed to keep it that way.

31

When the Bronco's rear wheels kissed the water's edge the old man and a younger man, who looked like a synthetic, got out and released the winch. The handle spun freely as the thick yellow webbing paid out.

"You got it?" the old man said.

The younger man gave the thumbs up sign and the boat rolled smoothly off the trailer's rollers and into the water. He grabbed the boat's bowline and unclipped a carabiner attached to the business end of the webbing.

"More than half of the guys at the 14th were dirty." Schneider said it matter-of-factly. Not embarrassed at all. "You must have heard things."

"I heard things. Protection, drugs."

"Right. It was the culture there. From my very first day. I shouldn't have ignored it, but I did."

Franco nodded even though he had no idea. The 23rd was no model of ethics, but even assholes like Joe Dixon weren't dirty. As far as he knew, no one had crossed that line.

"The kid I shot was a synthetic. A nobody Xylene dealer

with just enough balls to kill the next guy up the food chain. Which got the next *next* guy concerned enough to reach out to his good friends at the 14th. My partner, Benny Dorsey, had orders to take the kid out. But before you make any judgments about Benny you should know this: he was a decent cop once. A good father and husband, too."

Franco waved his hand to get on with the story. "Spare me the good cop bullshit. What's the rest?"

The old man had parked the trailer at the edge of the silt beach and was now walking down a wooden dock where the younger man had tied up the boat. He straddled the gunwale, checked over the controls, and fired up the engine. It blew out a cloud of exhaust before settling into a modest rumble. The work barge had just passed under the bridge. Only a couple more minutes and they'd be on their way.

"Doesn't matter. Benny was in too deep and things were starting to unravel. He had a meet with the kid and Benny was going to shoot him. He was going to plant the two automatics, fire off a couple of rounds, and then call it in. The other guys were going to show up on cue and back his story. I got there first.

"I was twenty yards away, trying to talk sense to Benny. Reminding him about his wife and kids. All the years he'd done the job right. Benny said, 'Just turn around and go home, Schneider. It's none of your business. This has got nothing to do with you. You don't understand how this shit works and you should thank me for it because I kept you out of it. I let you stay clean.'"

"He *let you* stay clean?"

"Yeah, that's how he said it. Anyway, he had his piece out, pointed at the kid, but I could see he was nervous. His hand was shaking. He didn't want to do it.

"'Think about your family, Benny,' I kept saying. Then he waved his gun at me. He pointed it right at my face. I could say I just reacted, but I knew he wasn't going to shoot me. He was scared and confused."

"And?"

"And I shot him."

"Jesus," Franco said.

"Only at the last microsecond they both moved. Just a little, but enough so I missed Benny and got that damned kid. Twenty-six years old, technically. But a kid."

Franco rubbed his jaw. "The Department covered it all up?"

"Easier to explain than the truth. The truth would have put mud on everyone's face. So, instead, the public got to read in the paper about an early retirements and one transfer. The transfer was yours truly."

By now the old man was pushing the boat into the middle of the river, against the current. The younger man was getting their rods together. The old man opened the throttle. The bow rose up and over its own wake. A few seconds later they rounded a curve and disappeared.

"Where were you aiming when you tried to shoot Benny?"

"I told myself I was trying to hit him in his arm or shoulder. But I don't know, Franco. I don't know."

32

———————

Maston Supermax was unique in one respect: it had a separate wing for high profile prisoners. Mostly they were serial rapists, murderers, and those whose crimes had garnered media attention. As such, the Maston guards took their rules about visits very seriously, even when the request was coming from two detectives with their bonafides in order.

"You're not on the list." The guard working the front window couldn't stop gawking at Schneider. He was standard issue: six-foot-two and muscular, with a brush cut, goatee, and one cauliflower ear from an unsuccessful career in the WWE. He wore combat boots and at least fifteen pounds of gear on his black leather belt. A second guard stood behind him, nearly identical except he was a scaled down version, perhaps five-foot-ten.

"Since when do we need to be on the list?" Franco looked half a step away from challenging him to a bench press competition.

"Hipp-U rules." Hipp-U standing for High Profile Prisoner Unit, or H.P.P.U. The smaller guard looked at a computer screen and said, "I've got Detectives Carter and Rubin. Let me see. Nope, no Schneider or Lopinto. Sorry, guys."

"We're working with Carter and Rubin," Schneider said. "Task force out of the 23rd. The DA is feeling good about a conviction for this asshole, but Carter and Rubin needed us to get a couple of more details."

"Is that so?" Not buying it at all.

"It's time sensitive. We've got to be quick."

"Rules are rules," the first guard said. "Unless I hear otherwise from Detectives Carter, Rubin, or your Lieutenant, I've got to turn you away."

Schneider got out his holo. "I'll call the L.T. now if you send Detective Franco here down to the interview room. It'll save time." He felt the guard bristle, but didn't wait for an answer. He held the holo out so everyone could hear the dial tone. "Lieutenant? It's me, Schneider. Yes, we're at Maston right now. No, we haven't interviewed Stanovich yet." He looked at the guards and rolled his eyes. "Why not? I'm trying to explain, sir, if you'd stop yelling for a second."

Franco tapped the smaller of the guards and nodded in the direction of the door. "How about we let these two hash it out with Lieutenant Sinclair?"

The smaller guard looked at his partner, shrugged, and barked something into the intercom on the epaulette of his shirt. He turned to Franco. "Okay, let's go."

Schneider dragged out the fake call to the L.T. as long as he could. He hung up when Franco and the smaller guard passed through the electric security door. "He just chewed my ass out twice. Once for bothering him, the second time for taking so long to get to Stanovich."

"Bullshit," the big guard said. "You faked that whole conversation." He picked up his radio, presumably to put the kibosh on Franco's interview.

Schneider moved his thumbs lightening fast across his holo's screen until he pulled the L.T.'s direct number. He dialed. "Here." He passed the phone to the guard. "He's not going to want to hear my voice again. Maybe he'll talk to you."

The guard looked uneasy, but put the phone to his non-cauliflower ear. "Sir, this is Officer Dupre, at Maston. I'm here with one of your detectives who says—"

Schneider listened, genuinely curious about the outcome. He hardly knew the L.T., but based on his gut he guessed it could go either way.

"Who are you?" The guard shielded the holo and barked at Schneider.

"Nick Schneider."

More listening. After a few more seconds, the guard hung up and returned the phone. "Your partner can finish his interview, but you stay here. And he wants you to come to the Station House as soon as you're done."

"The L.T. said I need to stay here, or is that your ruling?"

"It doesn't matter, does it?" He pointed at a chair. "Sit your ass down."

33

———

Danielle awakened to harsh light and the oversized, frosted hair of Bobbie Jo. Her mother.

"Oh, honey. You're awake. Thank God." Bobbie Jo wiped at her eyes and dragged a streak of mascara across her cheek. She wasn't used to crying and had little awareness of what it might do to a makeup job as heavy as hers.

Danielle rolled her eyes to the left and right. Nothing but IV lines and machines. She tried to speak, but her mouth felt pasted shut.

"It's going to be okay, baby," Bobbi Jo said, but her eyes didn't believe it. "You've been through a lot, and you're going to be okay."

Danielle tried again to speak. This time she managed a feeble, "what?"

Bobbi Jo smoothed her daughter's hair back. Danielle didn't feel it, though, because her arms were on fire with little needle pricks. Like when you sit in one position too long and your foot falls asleep. They ran up and down both of her arms, yet when she tried to move them nothing happened. Even her fingers felt dead and unresponsive.

"Mom," she said, more clearly this time. Throat as dry and painful as sandpaper, but at least it worked. She could speak. "What. Happened."

"Oh, honey." But Bobbi Jo did not answer.

"What. Happened?"

A doctor hovered into her view and said, "Good. She's alert. Blood pressure is not what I want it to be, but the instructions say not to worry. It will come up on its own."

Instructions? What instructions? Shouldn't a doctor *know* what to do? She didn't understand why he wasn't speaking directly to her. She was awake. She could see him and he could see her. But it was like she was in a T.V. drama. Everyone in the room was an actor with a script. Except her.

"Okay, Danielle." Finally, the doctor turned to her. "We're giving you a mild sedative, and then we can talk. I will explain everything that's happening as soon as you wake up. But now it's time to rest."

She tried to nod, but a warm liquid feeling was flowing into her body.

"That's it," the doctor said. "Just relax now. There's plenty of time for explaining—"

The needle pricks went away and, along with it, her fear. She closed her eyes but did not sleep right away. The words around her seemed distant, but she did her best to listen. They washed over her in waves of semi-understanding; it was all she could do to keep track of who was speaking.

"Can't you take them off and give her human arms?" Her mother's voice. Bobbi Jo.

"No." Doctor's voice. "The nerve connections are too delicate. It's impossible."

"But you said yourself what he did to her was impossible."

"It is. I can't even guess how it was done. We don't have the technology. No one does. Even if the problem of nerve attachments were solved, there's still the issue of compatibility."

"I'm not a doctor. I don't understand."

"Human blood, nerves, and fascia cannot connect directly to a synthetic limb. Which means there has to be some kind of interface at the amputation site. Not only has that never been done, I'm not aware of any work even at the conceptual level."

There was more, something about a pair of detectives waiting to talk to her, but of course that wasn't possible. And then semi-understanding slipped into non-understanding, and the beautiful nothingness of sleep.

34

If the god of intelligence and the god of sleaziness met at a bar and had sloppy, drunken, and moderately angry sex, Oscar Stanovich would have been the illegitimate love child. Gifted with a genius IQ and a mean spirited, hopelessly corrupt soul, Oscar struggled through his first forty years to find his place in life. It was only after a series of dead-end jobs, three failed attempts at college, and an unremitting porn addiction that he discovered his true calling: founder and president of S.E.S.H., or the Society for the Eradication of Synthetic Humans.

S.E.S.H. was unique among America's hate groups in that it welcomed everyone, provided that *everyone* meant those who hated synthetics. Once that criterion was met, S.E.S.H. was wholly democratic and open to all regardless of race, creed, color, sexual orientation, gender expression, age, height, weight, physical or mental ability, veteran status, and marital status. Oscar was proud of this openness.

Oscar was also proud of the S.E.S.H. website, which he'd designed himself. It included an exam for membership with just two questions:

1. *Are you a biological human? If you have to ask what this means the answer is no, and you will be PURGED. Enjoy what little time you have left!*
2. *Do you believe synthetics represent a threat to the human race? If no, you are a sympathizer. You will be PURGED too.*

Basically, Oscar was big on purging. Needless to say, with the upcoming SRA vote, membership in Oscar's organization was growing at an alarming rate. And Oscar himself had become something of a hero among the far right. Prior to his arrest he'd been making rounds on the talk show circuit, galvanizing the hate vote. And after his arrest? Surprisingly, his popularity increased. His ranting bearded image started showing up in cartoons and memes like, "Want to know how to create jobs? Easy. Kill more synthetics!"

Franco hadn't given much thought to synthetic rights. He'd skimmed a few articles in his news feed over the past years, never taking any of it too seriously. He knew synths in the Department—patrol, not detectives—but he'd never been friends with any of them. They'd kept to themselves, possibly in an unspoken attempt not to stand out. Same with the synth couple that had moved into his neighborhood last year. Quiet and private, but a frequent topic of conversation among Franco's neighbors. Time to move they were saying.

Now, as he approached the interrogation room, the whole thing seemed much more relevant. Schneider was still an asshole, a little too arrogant for his liking and not nearly as forthcoming as a partner should be. But he'd been there for Franco when he needed a place to stay. Then again, Franco didn't owe him anything. He needed to be careful because he was on probation, and they were way off the map. One more screwup and he'd be suspended. How would Tina respond to that?

He stopped and scratched his chin. The smart thing would be to call off the interview. Go back to the Station House and get started on the next case. Except recognizing the smart thing and actually doing it were light years apart.

"Hey." Franco got the guard's attention. "Does Pete Stovall still work here?" Franco knew for a fact that he did, but it would work better to play it casual.

The guard nodded. "How do you know him?"

"We played football together in college."

The guard eyed him more closely. "At American?"

"Yeah."

"He's here. He just got promoted to Assistant Warden."

"The lucky bastard. What pay grade is that, 23?"

"Twenty-seven."

"Franco whistled in appreciation."

THE MASTON INTERVIEW room was square and bare except for a stainless table and two chairs. Oscar sat at the far end stroking his graying beard, squinting at Franco through thick round lenses. He looked like a bored professor, although one that's mildly psychopathic and wearing an orange supermax jumpsuit.

Oscar leaned forward and greeted Franco with a friendly, "I can smell him on you."

"Who?" Franco said, already weary of the I'm-cleverer-than-you convict game. He'd played it more times than he cared to count. It always ended in him being disgusted.

"That skinless abomination you call a partner."

"Abomination," Franco repeated. "That's a big word. How do you spell it?"

"You look like someone who would have difficulty spelling. It's correlated with mouth breathing, you know, which is, in turn, correlated with low IQ, something that afflicts many of your police brethren."

Franco smiled. He'd expected Stanovich to try and rattle him. He was surprised, though, that Oscar was so well informed. As far as the newsfeeds were concerned Carter and Rubin were assigned to his case, not Schneider and him. And yet Oscar had known his last name. Since their visit hadn't been arranged ahead of time that meant one of the guards had tipped him off through the prison communication network, which everyone knew worked faster than the internet.

"Orange looks good on you," Franco said. "It brings out the crazy in your eyes."

Stanovich looked down at his fingernails and resumed picking. "How can you stand it? That smell. It's so unnatural. So foul. I would transfer to a different precinct. Or maybe I'd just cut off his arms and let him bleed out all that weird synth blood."

"To be honest, Oscar, I can't smell so great. On account of being a mouth breather. It screws up the sinuses." Franco took his seat opposite him. Slowly, he rolled his sleeves up and placed his beefy tattooed forearms on the metal table, next to the convict's pale thin ones. "So, why'd you do it?"

"Do what, rid the world of two synthetic prostitutes? I hardly think they'll be missed. No one has even come forward to identify the leftover pieces."

"Why'd you cop to a double murder you couldn't possibly have committed?"

Oscar scoffed. Kept picking. "You want me to prove to your satisfaction that I committed a crime? Your colleagues didn't have any trouble believing me. The police commissioner and the courts don't seem to have a problem with it, either."

"Yeah, I'm not surprised, but you don't look so torn up about it. Most guys I talk to in these places are bitching and moaning about injustice. *Help me, I'm innocent. I didn't do it. You've got to believe me!*"

Oscar looked up. "To answer your question, I kept the arms as trophies, but they started to smell. So I threw them in a dumpster behind a souvlaki place on the Boulevard and then got something to eat. The lid on the dumpster was secured with a chain, but I broke it using bolt cutters. Shall I go on?" He waited a breath. "I keep the cutters in my shed They've got red handles. There."

"Which souvlaki shop? There are two on the Boulevard, and one on Porter."

"The one that's in between the needle exchange and the Social Services building."

"Pita Garden?"

"Maybe. That sounds right."

"What'd you order?"

"Souvlaki. Chicken, with extra tzatziki. And a plate of stuffed grape leaves."

Franco slid his arms back off the table and crossed them over his chest. "Dolmas they're called. I like those. I can eat a dozen and still be hungry."

Oscar studied his fingernails.

"You're full of shit," Franco said. "Nobody found any arms in a dumpster, and every criminal in the free world owns a pair of bolt cutters, so that proves nothing. Finally, there's no Pita Garden on the Boulevard. The place near the needle exchange is The Caribbean Cabana."

"So my culinary memory is a little off. And maybe I didn't throw the arms in a dumpster. Maybe I saved them for another purpose. A more important purpose."

"Like what?"

"I don't feel like explaining."

"If you cooperate, maybe—"

"I don't need to cooperate. I'm at peace with what I've done, because the reason behind it is a righteous one."

"How'd you cut the arms off so cleanly?"

Oscar sighed. "I'm good with sharp tools, if you must know. I built a lot of models when I was a kid. You remember those little X-Acto knife kits? The parts on the balsa wood blanks were supposed to be precut, but they never came off cleanly. You'd have to trace the lines with that #1 knife. It was tedious."

"Just like this conversation."

"What kind of models did you build when you were a boy, Detective? I'll bet you were into tanks and muscle cars. I was partial to German airplanes, and ships from WWII. Talk about a purge! The German's knew how to do it. Fully committed, if you know what I mean. Willing to go all the way."

Franco struggled mightily to keep the violence inside of him, instead of letting it free where it might bounce Oscar's sanctimonious head off the table. "That layer of titanium under a synthetic's skin is thin but it's super hard. Do you even know what *would* cut it? I'll bet you don't, because you didn't do it. You're not the type who gets his hands dirty. You're more the ranting, raving, and writing type."

Oscar smiled. "I like the alliteration, Detective. Do you need me to spell any of those words for you, too? Cretin. Mouth-breather." He yawned and stretched. "As much as I'm enjoying this, you are hopelessly ignorant and poorly informed, Detective. Tell the guard I'm ready to go back to my cell. It's time for my nap."

"Okay, we're done here anyway." Franco pushed back his chair and motioned for the guard. As soon as Oscar went back to his nails Franco whispered something to the guard.

"Really? You're serious?" the guard smiled wickedly.

"Do I look like I'm joking?"

"Sure," the guard said. "I'll ask him."

35

Charlie Armstrong had a superpower that had made him the top Mercedes salesman in his region for three years running: he could see inside a person and know what made them tick. And he could do it in less than sixty seconds. It didn't matter if the person was a 70-year-old grandmother looking for a safe sedan or a thirty-something venture capitalist wanting to show off with a six-hundred horsepower coupe. He'd take one look at him or her, and he'd know.

When Franco and Schneider pulled into the lot after their less than enlightening interview with Oscar Stanovich, Charlie met them with a smile and handshakes. He looked admiringly at Schneider's ride and said, "63 Coupe De Ville? Am I right?"

Schneider nodded.

Charlie whistled, and touched the hood lightly, lovingly. "If memory serves she's got a 390ci 8 cylinder with a 3-speed automatic. Tell me you're here to trade in that piece of rolling art and I'll be a very happy man."

"Not here to buy," Franco said gruffly.

"That's a shame," Charlie said. "Because I've got a sweet G

Wagon that just came in on trade. Twenty-thousand miles. Not even broken in."

Franco shook his head.

"You could pile the kids in it on Saturday, and then haul your buddies and their bags for 18 holes on Sunday. Big discount for members of the police force, too."

"How'd you know we're cops?" Schneider said.

"Forget about that," Franco said. "How'd you know I golf?"

Charlie walked slowly toward the part of the lot where the G Wagons were parked. They were big and muscular, but the chrome trim lent a touch of class that hit Franco in a place he didn't even know existed. "Come on, guys. It's my job to read people. We're not so different, you and me."

Schneider produced a still of the RV. "Charlie, do you recognize this vehicle?"

He touched the edges delicately and studied it a long time before speaking. "I remember this sale. Very unusual, and it's been heavily modified since it left us. That's why it took me so long to recognize it."

"What can you tell us?"

They arrived at the G Wagons, the first six of which had sticker prices exceeding three hundred. Charlie kept going until they reached the last one, which had no sticker. "That RV was the weirdest sale of my career. By far."

"How so?" Franco couldn't help but admire the boxy muscular vehicle before him. It was gunmetal with wire wheels and running boards.

"To begin with, it was a special order." Charlie opened the driver's door and pushed the hood release button. "Heavy suspension, extra soundproofing, and an open layout with no seating and just the rear bunk. Can you believe that? Who buys an almost-empty RV?" He walked around to the other side of the engine compartment, so Franco had to look past the gleaming coils and induction ports to continue the conversation.

"What else?"

"Rubber floor." Charlie slid into the passenger's seat and gestured for Franco to join him. Reluctantly he did. "Can you believe this dash? It's real walnut burl. That came from a goddamned tree!"

Franco touched it, mesmerized.

"What kind of a floor was standard?" Schneider could see he'd just lost his partner to the hand-stitched burgundy leather upholstery. He came around to Charlie's side.

"There are many options, but diamond plate rubber with a central drain isn't one of them."

This broke the spell for Franco. "Tell us about the buyer."

"It was a corporate purchase. A nonprofit with deep pockets. I dealt with an assistant."

"Name?"

He put up his palms and said, "Fellas, this is as far as I can go. I can't disclose the details of our customers. Unless—"

"Yes?" Schneider couldn't help wishing his partner was half as sharp as this salesman.

Charlie's eyes twinkled. "Unless we take this baby for a little test drive." He pushed the starter button. The engine purred, smooth as silk but with a throaty undertone that only hinted at its real power.

Schneider looked at Franco. Franco pulled his door closed and wrapped his hand around the leather shift knob.

"I look at it this way." Charlie closed his door and fastened his seatbelt. He was in his stride, ready to drive home a sale. "Going on a test drive is like flying a plane over international water. The regular rules don't apply."

As soon as they cleared the city limits Franco opened it up, pushing past one hundred. The tachometer wasn't even close to red.

"She's beautiful," Charlie said, "but she's also a beast."

Schneider brought them back to the investigation. "International waters, Charlie. What's the assistant's name?"

"Bruce Morgan. You won't find anything on him, though. It's a fake."

"How do you know?"

"I checked. The corporation is real, though. It's called New Hope, LLC. Their website says they raise money to buy medical equipment for 3rd world countries. Haiti, Sierra Leone, Liberia."

"Uh-huh." Franco opened the roof and stuck his hand into the current.

"Which is fine, because it's really none of our business so long as the credit is good and the check clears. But I was curious so I looked. There's no address or phone numbers listed for New Hope. And get this: the sale and delivery was totally anonymous."

"What do you mean? Tell me you got a look at this Bruce character when he picked up the RV."

Charlie shook his head. "Per instructions, which were conveyed via email, we dropped the RV off on the Boulevard, outside of a smoke shop."

"I'm surprised no one stole it."

"Keys were locked inside. A second set was mailed in advance to a P.O. Box."

Franco groaned. "There's no CCTV on that part of the street."

"We're going to need that P.O. Box number," Schneider said. "I'm sure the account's closed out by now, but it's all we've got."

BACK AT THE DEALERSHIP, Franco parked the G Wagon in its slot. He lingered a moment too long behind the wheel.

"So," Charlie said. "What do you think?"

Franco grunted. "I think you're a good salesman, but you

have no clue what cops earn or how much it costs to raise kids in this city."

Charlie fished the key fob out of his pocket and dropped it in a cup holder. "Tell you what, Detective. Why don't you keep her for a few days?" Franco stiffened, but before he could say no, Charlie pulled the clincher. "If I can dig up any more details about this Bruce Morgan character or New Hope, LLC, I'll let you know when you drop it off."

36

Franco and Schneider waited in the L.T.'s office like a pair of 6th graders about to get bitched out by an Associate Principal for setting off smoke bombs in the girls' bathroom. Which was, in effect, the tenth-grade equivalent of what they'd done by conducting an unapproved interview in a supermax prison.

Franco elbowed Schneider and said, "I can't believe we went through all that and got nothing."

"The absence of something isn't nothing," Schneider said. When Franco's face twisted with disdain, he added, "look. We've ruled out Stanovich, and soon we'll have a P.O. Box."

"Like I said, nothing."

Schneider waited a moment and said, "I want to go back to Rachel's building. Something's not right with the drug dealer's apartment. I think he's hiding something."

"Imagine that. A drug dealer who lies."

The L.T. came in and slammed the door so hard it shook the frame and bounced open again. Schneider moved to close it.

"Leave it," the L.T. said. "Maybe your colleagues can learn

something from your screwups and this day won't be a total loss."

"Yes, sir," Schneider said.

L.T. glared long and hard at Franco. At last he said, "What do you think I'm about to say to you? I want to know what's rattling around in that thick skull."

Franco cleared his throat. "I think you're going to say that you're proud of us for working together and showing so much initiative. That you wish you had sons just like us. Well, maybe not the metal part of the pair, but you get the idea."

Outside of the office several of the guys laughed.

The L.T. pinched the bridge of his nose and made a sound halfway between a cough and a honk. "Just when I think you couldn't be more of an asshole you take it up another level. How many more levels are there, Franco?"

"Sir," Schneider interrupted. "If I may—"

"Shut up, Schneider! I expected more from you. You were supposed to keep this jackass in line, not become his collaborator."

"Yes, sir."

"Do you have any idea what your little stunt today cost the investigation in terms of forward progress? Do you know what it's going to cost the department in terms of credibility with the public?"

"With all due respect, sir," Franco offered, "all I did was ask Stanovich a few questions. No one outside of the three of us even knows about it."

"Wrong. Stanovich told his lawyer. Who told reporters. And then a judge reviewed the lawyer's emergency order to vacate the charges. So that's where we're at now. Because of you." He waited for it to sink in.

"I don't understand." Franco looked at his partner.

Schneider shrugged to say, *it's news to me.*

"No shit you don't understand. While you two were out

breaking your arms patting each other's backs, Stanovich walked."

"On what grounds?" Schneider said.

"He's claiming coercion of the initial confession." The L.T. rolled his eyes to the stained ceiling tiles and back. "Which is a whole other matter involving the officers who took the confession. But the important part is we're back at square one."

Outside the office, all ears were trained. Most of the other detectives had been on the receiving end of the L.T.'s unique mix of anger and disappointment, but it was a special treat to hear Franco and the new guy getting it.

The L.T. said, "You can close the door now." As soon as the brass bolt hit the strike plate, he lowered his voice. "Now which one of you geniuses had a synth gang leader moved into Stanovich's cell?"

Franco raised his hand, expecting more wrath.

The L.T. bared his teeth. They were not pretty, but the effect was almost like a smile. "That was smart, Franco. Just enough push to get that smug bastard to drop his story. We should have done that from the get go. Honestly, I don't know why we didn't. Actually, I do. The powers that be were pushing for a quick conviction."

Schneider looked at Franco, then at the L.T. "Why'd you go along with it if you didn't buy it?"

"Schneider, if you think the world is supposed to be just and fair you're in the wrong business." The L.T. pulled out a bottle of cheap whiskey and a stack of Dixie cups. He poured and passed them around. They drank and enjoyed five full seconds of silence.

"Let me get this straight," Franco said. "Even the wrong story is better than no story?"

"Now you're learning. And if you want to make sure it's the right story, you got to work even harder to find it. Now get out of my office and do your jobs."

37

In the kitchen, Schneider got out plates and silverware while Franco chopped garlic and onions and started a pot of water for the pasta. He dumped two tablespoons of Kosher salt in the water and said, "Most people fuck up their pasta because they don't put enough salt in."

"Really." Schneider uncorked a bottle of red and poured it in a decanter. To breathe.

"Or even what kind. Table salt gives the food a tinny, bitter taste." He sautéed the garlic for thirty seconds before adding in the onions and spreading them in a thin layer.

"I don't cook. I'm the king of takeout and the prince of the late-night diner."

"At least you keep good olive oil in your kitchen. They cut the cheap stuff with canola oil. Can you believe that?" He held up the bottle and swirled it around. "The good stuff—like this —is green. It has a peppery aftertaste on the back of your tongue."

"You're full of surprises." Schneider drifted to the dining room. He cued up John Coltrane on the sound system and switched on the fireplace. When the food was ready, Franco called him over.

"This is Pappardelle ai Funghi, Tina's favorite."

"Smells fantastic."

"Here, try some."

Schneider loaded a fork while Franco waited impatiently. "That's incredible."

Franco beamed. "The salad's got shaved parmesan, red onion, and fresh cherry tomatoes. And for dessert I made zabaglione with glazed strawberries. Only a few ingredients, but it's surprisingly easy to fuck it up."

Schneider lit some candles and carried them to the dining room table. He appraised Franco's new suit and said, "Looking good, man. Are you ready?"

Franco bobbed his head. "Yeah. Nervous, if you can believe it."

"I can." He resisted the urge to straighten his partner's tie. Then did it anyway. "It's a good sign, being nervous."

Franco looked out the window, watched the headlights of his wife's minivan. She pulled into the driveway and parked beside the Mercedes. "Me and Tina, we've known each other forever. But this feels like a first date. I hope I don't mess it up."

"Don't be yourself and you'll be fine."

"Fuck you."

Schneider grabbed his hat and cane and headed for the door. "You two kids have fun. I'll be home late."

TINA STOOD in the floodlit driveway wrestling with her emotions. On one hand she was still hurt and angry, and doubtful that Franco would ever change. She knew the kind of guy he was when she married him: a musclehead cop with absolutely zero subtlety or sensitivity. He was just living up to the stereotype.

On the other hand, he'd been calling every night to talk. And during these talks he'd actually asked her about herself and listened to her answers. But the real surprise had come when he'd showed up to the kids' parent-teacher conferences. Tina wasn't sure who'd been more shocked: herself or the teacher.

Schneider stopped at a distance and cleared his throat. He was acutely aware of the effect his appearance had on people, especially during first meetings. "Hi, Tina. I'm Schneider, your husband's new partner."

She clicked towards him on delicate heels. No visible shock or surprise at the metal face. Or if there was she made sure not to let it show. "It's nice to meet you, Schneider." She transferred her purse to her other hand and shook. "I like your house. It's really nice."

"Thank you. You look lovely, by the way."

She seemed uncomfortable but pleased. "I like this big Mercedes, too. You've got good taste."

Schneider laughed. "It's not mine."

"Who's is it?"

"I'm going to plead the fifth." Schneider jingled his keys and examined his motives for helping. He discovered it was a mix of selfish and altruistic. He wanted Franco out of his house as soon as possible. But he genuinely wanted this couple to work their shit out. To save their family where he hadn't been able to save his. "It was nice to meet you, Tina," he said. "I hope you have a nice evening. Franco's been looking forward to it."

38

Derrick Carter's linen jacket was ruined and he hated it. Worse, he was pissed at himself for being such a prissy bastard about a stain on his clothes when the real problem was the girl, Danielle. She was dying. And he was out in the hallway with Javier bitching about his favorite suit. It was petty. But hell, clothes that fit his tall lanky frame didn't just grow on trees.

"You put two packets each of ketchup and mustard on your cheeseburger," Javier Rubin said. "That's part of the problem. Two packets is too much. One packet of each is the way to go."

"Uh-huh."

"The rest of the problem is you wearing a white suit. A linen suit. Who wears linen? Look at those fucking wrinkles!"

"I should wear maroon and brown polyester like you?"

"Polyester my ass. It's a blend. You don't have the depth of character to pull off maroon and brown, not to mention my beautiful and exotic complexion. Your pasty self should go with navy. Spill as much condiment or whatever on a navy jacket and no one's going to notice."

They carried on for a while longer but neither was taking

any pleasure in the banter. Normally they could keep it going for hours. As long as they needed to pass the time and entertain themselves. But now, not ten feet away on the other side of the wall Danielle Talbot was coding. First the machines went off, then the docs and nurses came running. Soon enough the girl's mother, Bobbi Jo Talbot—the big shot Senator—was going to want to talk to them and ask questions like, "who did this?" and "what are you doing to catch him?"

Carter knew how to answer those questions. He'd done it enough times. Not pleasant, but it was a big part of the job and he was decent enough at it. Mix 20 percent official cop demeanor with 60 percent compassion. The final part? Personal. *Senator Talbot, I give you my word of honor that we will not stop or rest until we get this guy.* Something like that.

What really worried him was the question of why? Twenty years on the force and he'd seen all manner of horror. But this? Cutting off human arms and attaching synthetic ones? Never. Never in his wildest imagination. If the girl's mother, the senator, asked him why someone would do that, or if it was connected to her anti-synth politics, he'd have no answer. He was both expecting and dreading that moment.

"Hey." Rubin read a text on his holo and said, "L.T. wants us to go. He wants us to give a statement to the press outside."

"And say what?"

"The usual. Ongoing investigation. Pursuing all leads. Etc." He continued to scroll. "And then there's a whole bunch of stuff about what not to say."

"Let me guess. We have *not* yet established any connection between this crime and the Marquis-Chafee case."

"And," Rubin continued, "no connection between either of those cases and the SRA vote. Or with Senator Talbot's role as chair of the Committee on Synthetic Rights."

"Got it. No connection to anything." Reluctantly, Carter took off his jacket. On their way out, he tossed it in the nearest bin and straightened his tie. "You know what bugs me most about this, Javier?"

"Tell me."

"Schneider."

"I know what you mean. The way he looks without his skin. It's beyond weird. I keep trying to accept it but I can't. What do they call that, the uncanny valley?"

"Not that. I mean, yes, his appearance is weird as hell, but that's not what's bugging me. He knows something. Back at the crime scene and at the diner. He just sat there watching us, not saying a damn word."

"So he's quiet."

"He's holding out."

"On what?"

"I don't know. That's the problem. He's got some kind of synth insight about this case and he's not sharing."

"We can make him share." Rubin pushed the double doors leading to the parking lot outside the ICU. "We've done it before."

"You think we need to play that card?"

"I don't know yet, but let's keep it in our back pocket."

The detectives faced the crowd of reporters and camera crews and waited for the noise to die down.

Carter took in a breath and said, "Okay, people, I'm going to tell you everything we know, and everything we don't know."

39

———————

It was their first real date but they'd corresponded for over nine months. Schneider wasn't sure he wanted to take the risk, but he knew it was time. Every relationship had its own ticking clock; he couldn't expect a woman to wait forever just because he was afraid to let his heart out of its cage. He'd done it once with Jess's mother, Lauren, and it had nearly destroyed him. He wasn't sure he was ready to take the plunge again, but it was time to find out.

"It's a little studio behind Kobo Coffee, on Prospect," Beth's text said. "Green steel door at the end of the alley. Give the secret knock and I'll let you in."

He found it easily enough and stood outside the door. The secret knock comment was surely a joke, but he gave a four-tap rhythm nonetheless and waited.

"Come in. It's unlocked."

He liked her voice. Crazy he'd never heard it before. But that's what had drawn him in: her request to get to know each other through letters. Real letters. Old-fashioned letters with paper and stamps and hand printed words. It had seemed safe enough, at first. Schneider had never written one before and was surprised to discover how much he liked it. How danger-ously exciting and intimate to see what spilled out onto the pages, almost like he'd tapped a line through his mind and personality into his soul.

It felt wild and dangerous.

And even more wonderful to receive a letter from Beth. To discover its narrow spine hiding among the bills and circulars with the promise of that most unattainable commodity: connection. He'd hold it in his open hands, feeling the weight of the pages within. Was it just one page or more? He'd become greedy not just for the volume of paper but what those pages might contain. Greedy for the words and thoughts of a woman he'd never seen nor spoken to.

And now they were going to meet. It was both terrifying and exhilarating.

Schneider opened the door a crack and took in the warm earthy smell of clay and kiln. He looked at the far wall lined with wire racks containing molds and vessels. Opening the door fully, he saw Beth. She sat in front of an industrial sink at an electric wheel, letting her fingers run over the rim of a bowl. When she finished rounding it she looked about for a rag. Finding none, she wiped the residue of wet clay on the shoulder of her blouse.

"It's me," Schneider said.

"Come in, please." Beth turned off her wheel and stood up. She waved her hands around her studio. "I was so nervous I had to do something. Working always does the trick."

Schneider leaned on his cane, keeping his distance. He'd first started using it while rehabbing from his accident. Techni-cally he no longer needed it, but it helped with his very slight limp. Moreover, he'd come to like it. Leaving home without now felt like forgetting his badge or gun. "I'm nervous, too, though I'm not sure why I should be. I feel like we already know each other."

"Yes." She moved toward him until they were just inches apart. "I'd like to think I know you. And you me."

When he leaned forward she met him in space. It was a simple kiss. After, they held hands and walked slowly around the studio. Schneider pointed at bowls and sculptural pieces. Beth told him a little about how each was made or the idea behind the work. He was surprised by how matter of fact she was. She talked simply, without pretense or lofty ideas.

"This one was a mood." She pointed to a raku piece with a dark glaze over a lightly burnished green. I remember when I made it I was very restless. Unsettled. It was when we first started writing. "And this..." She pulled a thin wooden board toward the edge of the shelf. It was a small sculpture, incredibly detailed with vines and chunks of wood growing out of and around a man's face. "I don't know what or who it is. It's a mystery." She leaned up and kissed him again. "I'm so happy you're here. Are you hungry?"

"I'm happy, too." He took a moment longer to linger over her work. "Yes, I'm hungry. Should we go? My car's in the alley."

40

K even hated Steve Muncy the moment he saw him gearing up beside his Range Rover Defender. It was good, the hate—or contempt, if he wanted to be more precise about his feelings—because it would make his job easier. So much easier to befriend and abduct an elitist prick whose idea of a *job* was traveling to exotic locations to participate in races with other elitist pricks. His enmity would give him the emotional distance required to do his best work. And given the fact that the first test subject, Danielle Talbot, had just died, Elizabeth had made it very clear: she was going to need his absolute best on this job.

The reason for Keven's hatred of Steve—aside from the fact that he secretly envied his lifestyle and dreamed of the freedom that came with being paid to train and compete—had to do with the difference between specialists and generalists. He'd thought a lot about this topic and wasn't surprised to discover which side of the line he fell on. Jack of all trades, master of none was he. Factotum. Man of all work. Believer in the Pareto Principle, or at least his own version which amounted to this: he could achieve 80% of the desired effects with just 20% of the inputs provided, of course, that he knew which of those inputs were the most important. Therein lay the art.

Steve Muncy, on the other hand, was without a doubt a specialist of the highest order. Keven could tell just by looking at his musculature, which was far too quad and calf-centric for a triathlon competition. It was standard for serious roadies, sure, the result of thousands of miles of training in the saddle, pushing ever-larger gears and punishing hills. All great for stimulating the adaptation needed to sustain such a level of high power output during a season of extended road races. But it was lousy for the health of the neck, back, and shoulders. And the hip flexors, which had a tendency to shorten and stiffen.

Not that Keven was overly concerned with Steve's health and wellbeing. He wasn't. But he was conscious of what this meant in terms of race strategy: Steve was dominant in the cycling portion of the triathlon and would expect to make most of his time in the saddle. Which meant that Keven didn't have to beat him on the bike. He just had to lose less badly than Steve would lose to him in the running and swimming portions.

Truth be told, Keven wasn't convinced he *would* lose on the bike. In a bike-only event a specialist like Steve would beat him by a landslide. But in a multi-sport event like triathlon a strong generalist might have the advantage, especially if one factored intangibles like confidence and strength of will. And as Keven pulled his Ram pickup alongside the Range Rover, he felt very confident. His will was strong.

"Nice rig," Steve said, referring to the Specialized bike and carbon disc wheels Keven was pulling down from the rack.

"Thanks." Keven made sure to take notice of Steve's lavish spread of high-end gear. And his clipboard-carrying assistant, who was busy working through a checklist. This was a vital part of competitive race culture: the sizing up of an opponent. Not so different from medieval knights judging each other by the quality of armor and the strength of one's horse. Only now it was about weight and the aerodynamics of their bikes. And the level of support they could afford to have in place during changeovers, between events. "I'll trade for your matched set of Pinarellos. That's a sweet setup."

Steve flashed a self-deprecating smile. "It's a sponsorship thing. If I had to pay the bill I'd be riding an old Schwinn. With a steel frame."

Bullshit, Keven thought. The sons of senators don't ride old steel bikes. He dropped the Ram's tailgate and started fishing out his gear. Wetsuit and goggles, swim cap, and waterproof lube to keep the suit from chafing at the arm and leg cuffs and the back of the neck. Helmet and cleated shoes. Hydration belt and energy gel. Tossed it all in a pile on the pavement, next to a folding camp chair and a Yeti cooler.

After he slotted the carbon disc wheels into their dropouts and loaded water bottles into their cages, he sat down dramatically in the camp chair. "Ready," he said to no one and plucked a cold IPA from the cooler. Beads of icy water ran down the sides of the bottle and onto the hot pavement.

"Really?" Steve looked on from an oversized yoga mat. His assistant had spread it out and Steve was busy limbering his muscles on a vibrating foam roller. "Before a race? You're kidding."

Keven flashed his own self-deprecating smile and said, "Just 5% alcohol. Want one?"

Steve shook his head. "Good luck out there, buddy."

"You, too." *You're going to need it,* Keven thought, *because I'm going to tear you up.*

41

After dinner, Schneider took the long way to Beth's apartment. The Boulevard was slowly releasing its heat from the last day of a week-long hot streak. They kept the windows down, talking about everything and nothing while the lights cast shadows across the white leather bench.

"Do you mind?" Beth unbuckled and slid from the far side of the seat to the middle. Their shoulders touched. "I'd like to be closer."

Schneider put his arm around her. "It's like we're in an old movie."

"Which one?"

"Casablanca."

"You've got all the right answers, don't you?"

He smiled and gave her shoulder a playful squeeze. "It does hold together nicely for a first date. But beyond that?"

She put her head on his shoulder. Warmth flowed through him and around the places that had been iced over by hardship and loss. He tried to enjoy the moment, but he didn't know how to turn off his cop brain. To stop mulling over details and complications, trying to see the old stuff in a new way. He knew he was missing something, but what? The sickly jade plant in Rachel's kitchen. The crooked paint-by-numbers on Lawrence the drug dealer's wall. Bodies without arms.

It had been the same with Jess's mother, Lauren. When they'd settled in for the night and opened a nice bottle of wine. She'd curl up next to him on the couch and, if the phone didn't ring, his mind would latch onto a problem with his current case and run wild with it.

In this moment he moved quickly from the oddball details to Oscar Stanovich. Stanovich had been a wrong lead, sure, but it still didn't make sense. The publicity served Stanovich's cause, but weren't there easier ways to get attention? Then why confess to something he didn't do?

Schneider and Franco needed to find out.

"I'll give you a dollar-thirty-seven for your thoughts," Beth said.

Shit, he'd heard that before, or something like it. "Didn't it used to be a penny?"

"Inflation."

"I'm thinking about how nice this is." True, it was nice, but that was not what he'd been thinking. "The cynical part of me is wondering how I'm going to screw it up."

She laughed and sat up straight. "Don't be cynical then." When he didn't respond, Beth said, "Do you remember that story you wrote me about the Portuguese man who worked in a 3D print shop?"

Schneider searched his memory. Too many letters back and forth, but he remembered the guy who'd done some printing for him years back. Desouza.

"You said he saved for years to buy a printer so he could be his own boss. And when he finally did it, and the money started coming in, you asked him—"

"When he was going to buy a second machine and expand."

She nodded, smiling. "He said, 'Why would I need another machine? With this one I make enough to eat, pay my rent, and go to the bar on Fridays and watch a Benfica game. I don't need anything else.'"

"I can't believe you remembered all that." Schneider entered a residential neighborhood with painted brick row houses. Expensive looking, with the understated elegance of a Manhattan millionaire's home. He found a parking space on the street and angled in. "You're saying I shouldn't overthink things."

"I'm saying you should be the Portuguese 3D printer guy of dating."

~

BETH'S WAS the last row house on her side of the street. It was set up like a townhouse with four levels of living space. She waved her hands to encompass the twenty-foot ceilings and a curving staircase in the main entrance. "If you're wondering, *how can I afford this…?*"

"It never crossed my mind." Schneider grinned for sarcastic effect.

"My father left me some money when he died. I invested in some tech stocks. Most of them failed but one did *really* well. I bought the whole building, which was undervalued because it had been condemned. I fixed it up and now rent the floors I don't use."

"Nice." Schneider ran his palm along the smooth walnut bannister leading to the second floor. As an afterthought he said, "What was the stock?"

She hesitated. It was the first time and Schneider noted it. "SynCorp."

"Hmm." Schneider couldn't even begin to wrap his mind around this little nugget. SynCorp was synonymous with

Bharanda, who was essentially the Supreme Creator of synthetics. His God, he supposed. Which made Beth as a stockholder what, a disciple? Or a prophet? It was crazy.

"Is that uncomfortable for you? I imagine it would be, but I don't want to lie, Schneider. Not to you."

"It is uncomfortable, but I don't know what to do about it." He stopped near the top of the stairs, holding the bannister for support. "There's no way around the fact that SynCorp made me." He touched his chest and stomach while trying to explain. "They grew my bones and organs in a vat, wrapped me in foil, and covered it all up with skin. I'm a creation experiment. A science project."

She stopped and turned around. "I'm sorry, Schneider. I didn't mean to open up any—"

"It's okay." But was it? These days he rarely dwelled on his synth existential dilemma, but it was always present in the back of his mind. So why was it coming to the forefront now? The truth was he'd been enjoying the evening and he didn't want it to end. Not on this note. "The truth is I've been working on a case that's pushed me to think more about this stuff."

"Do you want to talk about it?"

"No, but thanks. And I know that owning SynCorp stock isn't the same as working there as an engineer. I don't even have bad feelings about SynCorp. It's just complicated."

She held up her hands and pointed at a spot of dried clay on her wrist. "Well, I'm definitely not an engineer."

Schneider finished climbing and checked out the second floor, which housed a dine-in kitchen, living room, and master bedroom. He pointed at a pair of ceramic bowls on the floor. They were white with brown milk bones painted on the sides. "Your dog, Louis. Right?"

She smiled. "Now who has the good memory? He's probably sleeping in the back room. He's very old. I don't like to think about it, but he doesn't have much longer to live."

Schneider drifted to a bookshelf and checked out the titles. He touched the spines of *Moby Dick*, *I Know Why the Caged Bird Sings*, *Dalva*, and *Heart of Darkness*. A couple of *Moosewood* cookbooks. There were a few volumes of poetry and many on art, mostly focused on ceramics and sculpture.

"Would you start a fire for us?" Beth was busy uncorking a bottle of red. "I thought we might get cozy. We could stay up late talking."

"Only if you insist."

"I do." She bustled about the kitchen before disappearing into her bedroom, presumably to change out of her dress and heels.

AFTER HE BUILT THE FIRE, Schneider spread a blanket on the floor and made room for Beth. They watched the flames and kissed.

"That was nice," she said. "I wondered what it would be like."

"Kissing someone with a metal and silicone face—"

"Yes, that, but mostly just kissing you."

When they finished the bottle, Schneider said, "I know it's impolite to ask, but if I didn't know any better, I'd think you like me."

She laughed. "I do like you, Schneider."

"How much?"

"This much." She kissed him again.

He felt heat from the fire and the light touch of her lips. It had been so long since he'd felt close to someone. Too long. Why had he waited? He didn't know but, hopeless bastard that he was, a few seconds later his mind circled back to the problem of Oscar Stanovich. And he got it, the new way of looking at the old thing. Stanovich's arrest was bullshit. Had been from the very start. He'd learned that early in his career.

Any solution that looked too easy or too convenient probably was. Just like it was too convenient with the Brooke Marquise case Carter and Rubin had mentioned, the one from six months back. What was it they'd said? Full confession from a pervert named Pelletier, who shortly after was killed in prison. Too convenient.

No way to prove it, unless he could raise Pelletier from the dead and question him. He'd mention it to Franco, though. At least they could read the file, check it against the Montgomery case for the quality of cuts in the amputation and whether or not the victim was placed on a blanket.

"Hey, Schneider." Beth grabbed his face gently and pulled it to hers. "Focus."

"I'm here." He did his best to stay in the moment, but his brain was edging close to something important. A question. What if Stanovich was not just a publicity whore? What if his confession was a predesigned strategic decision? Which led to further questions. Who could have devised such a strategy? Stanovich, or someone else? And why?

"Is something wrong?" she said.

He pulled away and registered the hurt in her eyes. "I'm sorry," he said. "Even in the presence of an amazing and beautiful woman, I can't turn my brain off."

"It's okay. My mind races, too." She lay down and patted the blanket. "Lucky for you, I know how we can fix it."

42

―――――

Near the end of the swim, Keven strengthened his kicks to ready his legs for the awkward transition onto sand and the short sprint to his bike. He emerged from the water second in the pack and immediately peeled off his cap and goggles and unzipped and shrugged off his wetsuit. He wore his cycling clothes underneath, black Lycra shorts and a light blue top. Next, he fastened his helmet, which he'd left upside down on his handlebars. Like the other racers he'd draped the straps over the sides to save time.

Last, he stepped on the towel he'd set up by his bike, weighted down at the corners with rocks. He allowed himself three scuffs with each foot to dry them. Then into the shoes and *click*, locking the right cleat into its matching clipless pedal. He pushed the bike with his left leg over the remaining feet of sand and then *click*, locked into the left pedal.

Ahead, he caught a glimpse of the race leader, an Australian who was likely to win the whole thing. Keven didn't care. He had a different goal, the first part of which involved preserving his lead over Steve as long as possible. If he could hold out until the eighty-mile point, that would be ideal.

"Eighty miles," he said to himself and put the power into his pedal strokes. He shifted to his big chainring up front, 54 teeth, and dropped his arms into position on his aero bars. Ready for the long haul.

THE FIRST RIDER TO pass him was Topher Comey, who he recognized as one of the top pros. He wasn't surprised to see someone of Comey's caliber participating in a non-sanctioned event; it was considered good off-season training. Also, the sponsors loved it. Comey blew by Keven like he was standing still. Before he was too far away, he called back over his shoulder, "Hey, who are you?"

Keven almost slipped and gave his real name. "Ah, Aaron Banks. From Boston." The repetition of the B in the last name and city was good. It helped people remember, if ever questions were asked.

"Pretty good for an unknown, Aaron from Boston." Comey shifted to a lower gear and climbed out of the saddle, pumping like mad. Three seconds later and he was gone.

Keven maintained his pace. Two dozen other riders passed him, but that was fine. He kept track of his miles and it wasn't until the 75th that he recognized Steve, who ghosted by on his red Pinarello. He took no notice of Keven; he was completely in the zone.

"Alright," Keven said to himself. He picked up his pace until he was drafting, his front tire just inches behind Steve's rear. Steve seemed to feel the intrusion and shifted up. Keven did the same but dropped back a couple of feet. He'd keep up the game of cat and mouse as long as he could, just a little extra tension to rattle Steve and pull him out of his rhythm.

"You?" Steve said at last. It was a slight descent and he was able to turn around and look at his pursuer. "Mr. Beer Guy."

Keven panted and said, "Yeah, that's me."

"Doing pretty good."

"Thanks," Keven managed. "You too."

They might have been evenly matched in terms of raw strength and ability. But Steve's training was showing. Each mile he pulled farther ahead and Keven had to all-out sprint to catch up, at which point he'd be too gassed to keep up and then he'd fall back and the cycle would repeat. At the 95th mile, he was sure he was going to lose him for the last time. "Make a bet?" he huffed.

Steve wasn't even breathing hard. "What kind of bet?"

"Loser buys drinks after the race."

Steve looked back one last time. "Okay, but I like my beer ice cold. Don't forget that."

43

———

The computer work was Franco's least favorite part of the job. Not only was he inept at it, he had no patience for the guys who were the undisputed masters of that world. To Franco, the staff at the Forensic Tech Unit were a different species. More like naked mole rats than men, sitting behind their screen arrays watching fields of data through filtered glasses. Fighting crime like it was a video game, hiding behind tinted lenses and dorky t-shirts with prints from old sci-fi movies that no one cared about.

"You don't have to hang out and become friends with them," Schneider said.

"Don't worry about that." Franco grabbed his holster and jacket, and the file he and Schneider had put together on New Hope, LLC. It was practically empty. "I'll be in and out of there in ten minutes."

An hour later, Franco was deep in the bowels of the tech department talking excitedly with James who, he was pretty sure, had just become his new bestie. Not only did James not wear glasses or nerdy graphic tees, he was a champion body-builder and former Olympic weightlifter.

"This is you?" Franco couldn't get over the first picture on the wall, which was next to one showing the rest of the tech team at Comic Con. Collectively, they posed as the main cast of Altered Carbon. James, of course, was Takeshi Kovacs. But the photo that interested Franco showed a slightly younger James on the Olympic podium looking spectacularly jacked. He was receiving a bronze medal for his performance in the clean and jerk event.

"That was a long time ago. I managed 200kg."

"Jesus," Franco said. "That's incredible. I'm going for 800 in the squat. That's my next goal."

James tilted his head to study Franco. "That's doable." He led Franco past the main work area, which was lit up like the control deck of a spaceship. The other members of the tech team toiled in the blue-green half-light of their monitors. They didn't even look up when the two big men walked by. "I want to show you something I've been working on. These guys..." James gestured at his colleagues. "They think the human body is just a meat sack whose only purpose is to support the brain."

"That's because it is," said the nearest meat sack, still not taking his eyes from his screen.

"Totally," another added.

"This is it," James said. "The future of muscle."

Franco stood before a wall-mounted exercise machine with elastic bands and hoses. It looked like a kid's toy. "Where are the weights?"

"Don't need them." James adjusted two pairs of pneumatic cuffs on Franco's upper biceps and thighs. He tapped a button on a screen and the cuffs inflated, much like on a blood pressure machine.

"Whoa." Franco extended and contracted his arms, feeling the pressure. He looked doubtful. "No offense, James, but this thing isn't going to do shit. I push a lot of iron when I train. Like, a lot."

"With this you'll only need to do 20% of your one rep max, because the pressure from the cuffs limits venous return from the working muscle. Which traps metabolic waste inside the tissue, which signals adaptation in the form of hypertrophy, or muscle growth. That's fairly old tech in and of itself, but the algorithms and interface are transformative. They do all the thinking and coaching for you."

"Thanks, but I'll stick with the old way. If it was good enough for Arnold and Frank Zane and Dorian Yates it's good enough for me."

James was clearly loving the conversation, and the opportunity to talk shop. "Yes, but what do we know about those guys? They had open minds and they were fully committed to doing whatever necessary to win. If they had this technology, they'd have used it. For sure." He opened a fridge in the nearby kitchenette and handed Franco a small aluminum cylinder. "Drink this quick. It's tastes like shit but it's loaded with creatine, collagen, and BCAAs. Your muscles are going to love it."

Franco swallowed it down and grimaced.

James adjusted the cuffs on Franco's arms and secured them with velcro. "I designed an AI coach, but we don't have time to set that up. I'll walk you through it. Go ahead and try some bicep curls. I want to see thirty reps."

Franco started. There was a slight whir as the magnets engaged, providing the correct amount of resistance. At the same time, the cuffs on his arms inflated, adding more pressure. "I feel it, sure." He kept going. "I still prefer iron. No computers. No magnets. No screens. It's simple. It works."

James grabbed a stack of manila folders off a nearby desk. *New Hope, LLC* was written on the tab of the one on top in black Sharpie. He returned his focus to Franco. "This is going to give you the same amount of hypertrophy as conventional training, but with reduced load stress on joints and ligaments and tendons. It cuts recovery in half, and stimulates VEGF."

Franco was starting to grunt and strain, especially at the upper part of the concentric phase. "Veg what?"

"Vascular Endothelial Growth Factor. Makes new blood vessels." James looked at the readouts on his screen then back at the detective. "Come on, man. I want to see thirty. Really squeeze it at the top."

"Hurts." Franco couldn't believe it, but he was already sweating. There was no way he'd make it through the set. And even more of a surprise, he had twice the burn compared to a monster session with heavy weights.

"Don't be a pussy, Franco. Come on. It's only twenty-percent. I thought you said you were used to moving a lot of iron?"

Franco growled through three more. But at the bottom of the twenty-sixth rep, he gave up. The cuffs deflated for thirty seconds of rest. "Jesus, that's crazy."

The cuffs inflated again. "Second set," James said. "Same number. Go."

This time he only managed sixteen reps.

"What? You don't want to keep going?"

"I'm done. I give."

James grinned while disconnecting the machine. He tapped the manila folder on top of the pile. "Okay. Ready to talk business?"

Franco nodded, but he was breathing too hard to speak.

"New Hope looks legal, but it's clearly a ghost company. Here. These pages are shipping manifests." He flipped through. "Next are tax records. What's surprising is 100% correspondence between the two. That almost never happens."

Franco grabbed a towel and mopped his forehead and the back of his neck. "You're saying they're not laundering money."

James handed the pages to Franco and tapped in the middle. Highlighted in yellow was a list of medical equipment. It was seven pages long. "These are all the items that were ordered but not shipped."

"So they're cleaning medical equipment not money? I never heard of that one before."

"And the RV, which was supposed to go to Sierra Leone. Put it all together and you get a person—or more likely persons—who went to all this trouble to build a mobile surgical suite with state-of-the-art equipment."

"And none of it can be traced."

James smiled and held up the last folder. "Not necessarily."

"Tell me you figured out who's behind this bullshit."

James put out his palms to slow Franco down. "New Hope has a board of directors, but they're squeaky clean. A couple of philanthropists. Several MDs from universities and research hospitals."

"How do you know they're clean?" Franco was getting impatient now. "That just means we have to dig more. Everyone's got dirt."

"My guys are thorough, Franco. Trust me on that. The board members' financials are spotless, and we've looked at three points of data—interviews, meeting notes, and correspondence between members. It all matches."

Franco continued scanning the pages, but he knew what James was telling him. "So what you're saying is it's hopeless."

James shook his head. "Not hopeless." He handed over the last folder. "There's one name that came up in several key places. Well, not a name, per se. More like a digital signal that we were able to trace back to a name. Very hard to do because this guy is so well protected."

"Okay." Franco reached for the folder. "Who is it?"

"See for yourself."

Franco opened the folder and scanned the top page slowly making sense of the data table and the name that it eventually pointed to. "You've got to be shitting me. I don't believe it."

44

In the morning, Schneider found a French press and a bag of Columbian in Beth's kitchen and made two cups. He wasn't sure how she took it so he put half and half in one, and left the other black. The dog, Louis, was awake, watching him from a distance.

"Good morning, fella." Schneider held out his hand but the animal did not move. His eyes had cataracts, and his fur was patchy.

"Don't worry, old boy," Schneider said. "I'll be out of your space in a few minutes. You're still the king of the palace."

He carried the coffee and a newspaper into the bedroom.

"I love coffee in bed." Beth rolled over and stretched. She sat up and took the steaming mug. "You have impeccable manners."

"And you're a luddite." He sat on the edge of the bed and shook the newspaper. The front page had stories on Danielle Talbot's death, and the SRA vote.

"Actually, my first career was in tech and I'm not against it at all. It's just that at home I like my life to be as simple as possible. It helps keep my mind clear. And my work benefits from a clear mind." Beth leaned over and wrapped her arm around Schneider's waist. "Besides, I like a lot of the old things, like records, paper books, a good coffee press. They're perfect objects."

"Perfect objects, huh?" He held up the paper and started to read.

"A perfect object is something that can't be improved."

"How about people?"

"You mean human beings?" She scrunched her eyes, thinking. "We're very far from perfection. We're really quite fragile. People get sick and die all the time."

Schneider skimmed the Talbot story, which quoted Derrick Carter. "Oscar Stanovich remains a person of interest," it said, "but we are also pursuing other leads." He folded the paper closed and tossed it on the bed.

Beth picked up the paper and looked at the front page. "What do you think about the SRA vote?"

"As a cop, I think the increased penalty for hate crimes and homicide are long overdue."

Beth folded up the paper and set it aside. "And as a synthetic?"

"I'm not sure. Marriage, health insurance, and other benefits, absolutely. But it's hard for me to believe that people's attitudes will change."

"I think people can change."

He smiled. "Maybe, but then there's the one in a million chance that the amendment will pass through the senate. There's so much opposition."

"What if you could change that and influence the decision? Would you?"

Schneider tilted his head, trying to understand the question, which was a new one for him. If he had to parse out his identity, he was equal parts synth and homicide detective. If he had any power to change the world, it would come from solving cases. Specifically, solving synth murder cases that the rest of the world cared little about. "Influence it how?" he said.

"Magic button kind of thing. Push it and the world changes."

"Do you have a magic button?"

"Maybe." Beth climbed back under the covers and made room for him. "But let's finish this conversation another time. Come back to bed."

SCHNEIDER DIDN'T STOP at home. He drove straight to the 23rd, but this time parked a block away from the precinct, in front of a 24-hour laundromat. He almost made it to the front door before spotting trouble in the form of Joe Dixon. Put simply, the newest member of the Sewage and Disposal Unit did not look right. His face had the sallow bloat of a person making the shift from solid food to an all-liquid diet. In Joe's case, his liquid of choice was Canadian Club. It had the perfect price point. It was cheap enough to buy in bulk but no so cheap that the clerk at the liquor store would give him that pitying look that said, "are you sure you really need this? How about a smaller bottle, buddy?"

Joe Dixon's gait was unsteady, too. Shambling, with half his shirt untucked, on his face an iron shadow of stubble.

"Hey," Dixon called out. "I want to talk to you."

Schneider looked at the double doors and sighed. He didn't have time for this. There was too much work to do.

Dixon didn't waste a second. He got right up in Schneider's face, so close that Schneider could see the roadmap of exploded capillaries in Dixon's nose. "I want to hear it from you."

"Hear what?" Schneider took half a step back, out of the high-octane draft of Joe Dixon's breath. He noticed a small crowd of uniforms gathering to watch. Half were ending their shifts and turned their attention from cleaning the fast-food bags and coffee cups from the cars, ready to go inside and write up their reports. The others were just getting started. None were averse to a little entertainment.

Dixon closed the distance. "I want to hear you say it, and I'm not leaving until."

Schneider looked to the now-sizable crowd to the exhausted faces of the end-of-shifters, and those of the equally tired beginners. He weighed the options. One, he could summon all the horseshit pop psychology he'd learned at the academy and try and talk Dixon down. Remind him he was close to retirement and his pension. Or two, he could tell him to fuck off. But there was a third option: he could take the Franco route and be a wise ass. He surprised himself by choosing door number three.

Schneider sighed, for dramatic effect. "I love you, Joe. I've always loved you, and I always will. There, I said it."

Dixon's eyes dilated dangerously. While the cluster of cops howled with laughter, he drew his sidearm and leveled the muzzle six inches from Schneider's nose. "I know it was you. You set me up, you dirty synthetic fuck."

"Easy, Joe," Schneider said.

"Don't *easy* me. Do you know what you did?"

"Maybe you should tell me." Buying time. He didn't think Dixon was unhinged enough to shoot a detective in front of the precinct. With half a dozen cops watching. But then again, he'd have lost the bet on whether Dixon would pull his piece in the first place.

He panned his gun from Schneider to the other cops. "You all think I'm a fucking joke, don't you! You think this is funny?"

In unison the watchers shrank back.

Schneider sidestepped into the line of fire. "I'm right here, Joe. I'm the one you're pissed at."

Dixon returned his attention. "Maybe it is funny, I don't know. You tell me. Is it funny when a guy's wife leaves him because he likes to have some drinks after work?"

"No, Joe. I don't think that's funny."

"Shut up, Schneider! Twenty-six years we've been married. Twenty-six fucking years." He swiped at his eyes before picking up the original thread. "Do you think it's funny when a guy has to swallow his pride and go to work on the goddamned sewer beat because he's less than a year out from retirement and then he gets sent home because the supervisor, who isn't even a real cop, sends him home?"

"No."

"And do you know why he gets sent home?"

Schneider could make a guess but didn't. "Why, Joe?"

"Fuck you, Schneider. Let me tell you something. Ever since you showed up here my life has gone to shit. That's the effect you have on people, did you know that? You shot your own partner! People hate you and no one will ride with you except Franco, and he's an even bigger fuckup."

Out of the corner of his eye, Schneider could see the L.T. coming out of the double doors of the precinct. He needed to stall for thirty more seconds. "I've heard that before, Joe."

The watchers noticed the L.T., but Dixon stayed focus on the object of his hate.

"Dixon!" The L.T.'s voice boomed from twenty feet away. "Why in the hell is your weapon drawn on another officer?"

Dixon looked at the L.T. Bewildered. Caught between two conflicting desires.

"It's okay, L.T." Schneider stepped up to the gun, close enough for the tip of the muzzle to make a soft tap against his chin. He reached up, covered Dixon's hands with his own and brought the gun down. "This is not what it looks like."

"I sure as hell hope not, because what I'm seeing is Dixon going straight to the disciplinary review board."

Dixon seemed to come out of his trance. He started to stammer something but Schneider took over. "I was busting his balls, L.T.," Schneider began. "I told him he was too fat, cross-eyed, and hung over to aim a gun straight. He said he'd prove me wrong."

Dixon looked down at a crack in the pavement.

The L.T. eyed Dixon and then Schneider. He knew an off-the-rails cop when he saw one. What he didn't know was why Schneider would cover for him. It was common knowledge that Dixon had trashed his beautiful Caddy.

"It's unloaded," Schneider said, "and the safety's on. Right Dixon?"

Dixon nodded unconvincingly.

One of the onlookers coughed. The L.T.'s eye twitched. "I don't know what's going on here, but—"

"Nothing's going on," Schneider said quickly. "Like I said, we were just messing around."

The L.T. stared hard. "I'll be watching you two."

45

———

Schneider found Franco hunched at his desk behind a tower of file boxes. He had a pile of colored Sharpies and was busy writing on index cards.

"Are these from the synth prostitute case Carter mentioned? What was the name?" Schneider snapped his fingers, trying to remember.

Franco ignored the question. "You didn't come home last night."

"No." Schneider offered no explanation. Privately, he was surprised his partner noticed or cared. They were getting along better, true, but still a far stretch from friends. "How was your date with your wife?"

"About that. I need to run something by you."

Schneider pulled up a chair. "Okay. Let's talk."

Franco looked around, decided the buzz of action around them provided enough cover. "She wants us to go to marriage counseling."

"That's good, right?"

"No, it's not." Franco soured his face. "I don't want to sit in front of a stranger and air our dirty business. My dirty business, I mean. But I guess I've got no choice."

"You have a choice."

"You know what I mean." He pulled the top box down and pushed it toward Schneider. It was full and heavy. The notecard on top gave the date followed by, "Brooke Marquise, 137 Doherty Boulevard, Apt. 18, Cause of death: blood loss subsequent to bilateral limb amputations, Estimated Time of Death: 3:00 a.m., Principal Investigator: Derrick Carter."

"It's basically counseling or a divorce," Franco said. "And I don't want to get divorced, so..."

"I get it." Schneider lifted the top off the box and looked inside. It was filled with manilla folders. The first two held pictures. The second and third held case notes. The rest were filled with forensics reports and miscellaneous notes. "What are you afraid is going to happen if you go to counseling, Franco?"

"The therapist is a woman, which means she's going to side with Tina. That's a fact."

Schneider shook his head. "Women cheat, too. If this therapist has been working longer than two-weeks she'll have seen dozens of people in your exact situation. You think you're the only married person who's had an affair?"

"No, but I'm going to sit there in front of Tina and spill my guts. Any therapist in the world is going to back Tina because she followed the rules. She was loyal. And I'm going to end up living in a crappy apartment paying child support. I'll only get to see my kids every other weekend."

"Franco."

"I'm not done. After that, after I move out of my house and say goodbye to my daughters, Tina's going to meet some skinny vegetarian guy who watches foreign movies and... drinks English tea."

"English tea? What the fuck are you talking about, Franco?"

Franco stood up, getting agitated. His voice climbed. "This vegan guy, he's going to move into my house and sleep in my bed!"

"Easy, man." Schneider held out his hands in a calm down gesture.

Franco unclenched his fists and dropped back into his chair. All at once the anger went out of him. "And they'll all live happy ever after. Without me."

Schneider tried hard not to laugh. He could see the fantasy of doom taking shape and growing. Inside of Franco's thick skull it was as real as the box of files in front of him. "First," Schneider said, "the therapist's job is to help you and Tina stay together. Not take sides and wreck your life. Second, you didn't answer my original question. How was your date with your wife?"

"Good." Franco said it grudgingly, finding it hard to shift from the blackness of his fears to the mixed light of reality.

"Just good?"

"What do you want me to say? My life sucks right now."

"How was the dinner? You could try being half as descriptive as you were with that epic of despair you just painted."

"She liked the pasta and the music. And the dessert. She stayed late."

"Nice."

"She said if the first therapy session goes well, we can talk about me coming home."

"There you go." Schneider waited a beat in case there was more. When Franco kept his mouth shut, he pointed at the boxes. "All this from the Brooke Marquis case?"

"This one's Marquis. These two are related cases."

"Separate from the ones Carter and Rubin mentioned? I didn't think there were any more."

"I did some digging. All synthetics who lived or worked on the Boulevard."

Schneider said nothing but inside he seethed. Murdered synths didn't rate high enough to get real attention.

"The investigations went nowhere," Franco said. "The cases were closed. Also, different detectives on each case, so they all got treated separately." Franco stood up and hefted two of the boxes.

"That would never happen with humans," Schneider said.

"Nope."

"Did you see the press conference with Carter and Rubin? They said no connection between the cases, and the reporters didn't even question it. They totally let it go."

"Guess there's not as much heat when the vics are synthetics."

"That's just how it is," Schneider said. "How it's always been."

They carried the boxes downstairs and loaded them into Tina's minivan, which was parked closest to the precinct. Schneider closed the cargo door and gave it a thump with his fist. "What happened to the Mercedes?"

"Don't ask."

Schneider grinned. "I'm asking."

Franco's face turned pale. "She thought it was a makeup present."

"And you went along with it?"

Franco pursed his lips together and nodded. "Yes, I did."

THEY DROVE to Schneider's and got to work. After carrying the boxes inside, they established a sorting system. The Brooke Marquise folders went on the dining room table. The second box, which was for Dante Deveroux, a forklift operator in a shipping facility, went on the kitchen counters. And the third,

Lisa Jankowski, a hairdresser, they spread out on the living room floor.

Franco, who now knew the layout and contents of the kitchen better than the house's owner, set about brewing coffee and slicing some cheese and pepperoni he'd bought the day before. He arranged the slices on a plate with crackers and garlic-stuffed olives.

Schneider was at the dining room table flipping through the pages quickly, pausing only to study the pictures and handwritten detective's notes. The last were from Carter and Rubin.

Franco poured two steaming cups of coffee and went back to his own files. "Forensics got nothing, except for some dirt on the carpet at Jankowski's apartment, which could have been there before the body was dropped off."

"But the body was definitely dropped off."

"That's what I said."

"What about a blanket?" Schneider picked up a pack of cigarettes and lit one. "Look at the pictures and check the crime scene notes."

"No, I looked. The bodies in both sets of pics are right on the carpet." He brought one of the Deveraux pictures into the kitchen to show Schneider. "The cuts look the same, though. Clean. No blood or torn tissue, no crimps on the edges of the metal."

"Let me take a look." Schneider held the cigarette between his lips and flipped through the stack of photos. He went through them again, turning each one around carefully. He put them in a line on the counter. To the right of it he put the Deveroux pictures. And to the right of that, the Marquise pics. "These are in chronological order, oldest to newest. What stands out?"

"None of them have any fucking arms."

"What do you see in these pics that isn't here in the Marquise set?"

Franco waved the cigarette smoke away and leaned in close. "No blanket."

"Which means what? What does the blanket mean to this guy? What's it represent?"

"Comfort or warmth."

Schneider dropped his cigarette into the dregs of his coffee and watched the smoke drift and swirl as it went out. "No. For warmth he'd have covered them with it. Or if he wanted to give them the respect of being covered like we do in morgues. So it's got to be something else."

"You think he feels bad about killing them?"

Schneider shrugged. "No, I think he needs them."

"For what?"

"No clue, but I think he's got his own code, and part of that code is to return them home when he's done with them. He spreads a blanket and then lays them down gently."

"So if it's not warmth or respect, what then?"

"An apology maybe."

Franco grabbed Schneider's mug. "No offense, but this shit stinks." He dumped the butt in the sink and rinsed the mug. "You ever been hunting, Schneider?"

"Do I look a hunter?" He lit another cigarette, ignoring his partner's dirty look when the smoke issued forth.

"I've got this cousin. Through marriage. He took me hunting once. We froze our asses off and I didn't even fire my gun, but he got one. A doe."

Schneider grabbed a chair and settled in for what sounded like the beginning of a lengthy story. He hoped it would tie in.

"This deer is lying dead in the snow, right? Clumps of bloody fur everywhere, only my cousin says it's hair not fur. Anyway, he spreads out this green canvas tarp over the snow and rolls the deer onto it. He field dresses it with his knife, and we take turns hauling it out of the woods."

"So the tarp is like the blankets?"

"Yeah, but also the whole time we're hiking out he's telling me how you have to respect the kill. I said, 'Martin, you work in a paint shop. What are you talking about *respect the kill*?' And he said, 'You can kill something and respect it at the same time.'"

"Uh-huh."

"He said he hated the guys who killed the big bucks just for the rack."

"What's a rack?"

"The horns. Antlers. They get them mounted to hang on the wall. Trophies."

Schneider nodded. "Okay, so he's not a trophy hunter. And he returns the bodies to their homes, lays them out on a blanket to show respect."

"It's not much to go on," Franco said.

But Schneider wasn't so sure. He was starting to put together a picture. "Look. We've got an expensive RV purchased anonymously through an untraceable shell corporation. Which speaks of money and resources. And the killer is using the bodies in a very unusual way: attaching them to human victims."

"But why? We still don't know shit about his motivation."

"Right." Schneider started to gather up the files and put them back in his box. "We're not going to learn that from these files."

Franco gathered up his boxes and followed Schneider to the front door. "Where to?"

"Where else? We're going to the Boulevard. I've got an idea about Lawrence, the drug dealer. I think I know what he's hiding."

46

———

Carter handed his holo to Rubin. "Here. You've got to see this."

Rubin started the six-minute and forty-second video of two men beating the shit out of each other in a steel cage. "Is this who I think it is?"

"Yes."

Rubin turned the holo sideways to enlarge the picture. "How'd you get it?"

"My youngest, Josh, was watching it. Him and his friends send each other videos all the time. It's what they do these days instead of playing sports or riding bikes."

"You sound like an old man." Rubin watched as Schneider staggered to the center of the cage. His opponent, who might have been the largest man—or synthetic man—he'd ever seen, came up behind him and prepared to pummel him. Schneider seemed to feel the blow coming but he didn't duck or jump back. Instead, he leaned and turned toward his opponent. The movements were subtle, a matter of fractions of an inch, which was just enough to push him out of the line of strike and into position for a counterattack.

Rubin, a serious boxing fan and former welterweight himself, watched with growing interest. Schneider responded with a lightning-fast combination that frustrated his opponent more than it caused any real harm. His opponent lunged forward with a right hook which Schneider evaded easily. "Jesus," Rubin said. "He's fast. And look at how attuned he is to the other guy's movement. It's like he can feel it before it happens."

"Yes, he can fight. Seen enough?"

"No." In the video, Schneider rolled away from another potentially killer blow and found the soft opening he'd been waiting for. The big synthetic's miss and follow-through left his side and back exposed; Schneider peppered him with punches, two good ones to the kidney and ribs. When the video sequence ended, Rubin paused it and said, "I don't think you understand what we're looking at. Do you know who he's fighting?"

"Some genetic monstrosity. Who cares? You're missing the big picture here, Javier. What this video means in terms of our investigation."

Rubin was undeterred. "That *genetic monstrosity* is Crusher Carlson. He was thrown out of the WBA and the IBF after he killed a guy in a title fight."

"I know. You're a fan. Tommy Hearns and Sugar Ray Robinson. Right?"

Rubin finally looked up from the holo. "So tell me. What's this video mean to you?"

"Now we've got leverage. Picture the headline: public law enforcement officer in a cage fight." Carter poked the air with a slender finger. "And I'm no fight expert, Javier, but I'd say he's tripping his balls off in there. Did you see near the end how he was wandering around, looking up at the ceiling?"

"What are you proposing, that we blackmail him?"

Carter looked indignant. "Who do you think I am?"

"What then?"

"I'm going to let him know *we know*. And then we're going to find out what he's holding back in the case."

Rubin scowled.

"Hey, if it makes you feel any better, we can share the credit with him and his moron partner when we close the case. I think that's generous."

But Rubin was only half-listening. He'd restarted the video. The phone's tinny speaker broadcast the crowd's boos, which changed to gasps, followed by raucous cheering. Rubin tapped his partner on the shoulder and said, "Hey, Carter."

"What?"

"Schneider's one hell of a fighter. Really impressive."

"Great. You can start a fan club."

"Hey, I'm just saying. He destroyed Crusher Carlson in a cage fight and he works with us. You have to admit: that's something."

47

Steve Muncy was triumphant at the end of the race. He hadn't placed as highly as he'd have liked—5th out of a field of 324. But the competition with Keven had been intense and, surprisingly, fun. From the point he'd first passed him in the cycling event at the 75th mile, they'd played an elaborate game of cat and mouse. It felt more like the drag races he and his friends used to have on their BMX bikes. Back when they were kids and there were no prizes, rankings, or sponsorship deals. Just the wind in your face and, later, bragging rights.

After he chatted with some of the other athletes and posed for a few pictures with his sponsors, Steve wheeled his bike back to the parking lot. He'd expected Keven to be waiting with a cooler of beer, but it looked like he'd set up a full-scale tailgate party. Even Steve's trainer, Rory, was involved.

"Nice race," Rory said from his station behind a portable grill. He had a beer in one hand, a spatula in the other.

"Thanks," Steve said. "What's all this?"

Keven greeted him with a beer and pointed to the row of camp chairs. "Have a seat. Rory's taking care of the bison burgers and corn. I'm going to fetch us some ice packs."

"This is awesome." Steve eased into the chair and kicked off his running shoes. He rested his swollen feet on the indoor-outdoor rug Keven had rolled out and sighed. "Thank you. It's Aaron, right?"

Keven almost forgot his pseudonym. Aaron Banks. He held his beer up to clink against Steve's. "You beat me fair and square. A bet's a bet."

"Yeah, but our wager was for cold beer. Not all of this."

"Hey, I just do this for fun. There's no way I'm grueling through an Ironman without a little R&R at the end."

"I hear that."

Rory served the bison burgers on paper plates. They ate the corn straight out of tinfoil wrappers and watched the majority of the racers and fans exit the parking lots in their vans, pick-ups, and SUVs. Probably going to the race-sponsored after-event dinner, which was almost always a shitty keto-friendly buffet with gluten-free suds.

Steve was into his fourth beer when his speech started to slur. "I'm sure you know this, Aaron, but you could train professionally. If you wanted to."

"I thought about it," Keven said. "But my job is too demanding."

"What job?" Steve gave his assistant a kick with his bare foot. Rory had fallen asleep in his camp chair and was snoring loudly.

Keven took a bite of his bison burger. It was delicious. "I work for Bharanda."

The surprise cut through the effects of the alcohol and scopolamine. "You work for Bharanda? The Bharanda?"

Keven nodded and wiped a smear of ketchup from his chin.

"Bullshit. The man's a myth. A ghost." Steve waved his beer and dropped his ear of corn onto the rug. He almost fell out of his chair trying to retrieve it. "No one even knows what he looks like. What makes you think he's still alive?"

"Would you like to meet Bharanda?"

Steve laughed. He kicked Rory harder. "Rory! Did you hear this guy thinks—" He lost focus mid-sentence and turned back to Keven. "What were we talking about?"

Keven smiled benevolently. "It's time to get in the car, Steve."

"Okay."

"Do you need a little help?"

Steve shook his head. "I can do it." He stood up and winced as his massive quad muscles tightened. He tried to step into his running shoes and stumbled. His coordination was shot.

Keven took him by the upper arm and led him to the passenger's seat of the Range Rover. Steve tried to ask about Rory, but he was slurring very badly now.

"Rory can come, too," Keven said. "I'll drive and he'll ride in the back."

"K." Steve smiled and closed his eyes.

48

———————

Schneider knocked at the door and gave Franco the cue. They'd returned to Rachel Montgomery's building to shake down Lawrence, Rachel's drug dealing neighbor in 2D. They had a plan.

"You think he's in there?" Franco cranked up the volume for Lawrence's benefit. "I can bust it down. It's a cheap lock."

Schneider cupped a hand around his mouth. "Yeah, might as well. I don't want to bother with a warrant. Do you?"

"Shit no." Franco backed up and made a show of scuffing his boots for traction. "Here goes." He took in three loud breaths and—

"Whoa. Hey!" Lawrence opened the door as far as the chain would allow. "What the fuck are you guys doing?"

Schneider flicked the chain with his index finger. "Open up, Lawrence. We need to talk to you."

"I don't have any more Xylene, man. Go somewhere else."

Franco raised an eyebrow at Schneider, who shrugged. "Open the door, Lawrence."

"Why should I? I told you. I don't know anything about anything."

"That's a very true statement," Schneider said.

Franco was growing impatient. He took a step back and threw his beefy shoulder into the door just below the chain's attachment point. The chain held, but the screws securing the brass plate tore through the wood veneer into which it had been attached. Lawrence jumped back but not fast enough. The door caught him in his chest and the side of his face. He reeled back into the dirty kitchenette, whining. "You can't do this, man. This is illegal."

"You should call the cops," Franco said, inspecting his work. The damage to the door was minor, and the frame relatively untouched. Not bad.

Schneider went straight for the fridge. He opened the left freezer door and found what he was looking for: a bag of peas. "Here. Hold this on your cheek. It looks like it might bruise."

Lawrence took the bag. "You guys are real assholes, you know that?"

"Are you ready to talk business, Lawrence? The quicker we get to it, the quicker you can go back to your fulfilling and productive day."

"What kind of business? I told you I'm not holding."

"The movie business, Lawrence."

His eyes narrowed. He dabbed his face with the bag of frozen peas.

Schneider crossed the living room and pointed at the paint-by-numbers. "This is a nice horse, Lawrence."

"It came with the apartment." Lawrence took a step toward Schneider. Franco blocked his way.

"Back to the movie business, Lawrence." Schneider pulled the paint-by-numbers off its nail. Taped to the back was a small device, about the size of a quarter. It had a tiny fiberoptic stalk, long enough to be threaded through a pinhole in the wall. Nearly invisible. "If your work is up to par, if it's helpful to us, your lucrative payment package will include the option of not going to prison."

"That isn't mine." Lawrence pointed at Schneider and the miniature camera with the bag of peas. "I've never seen it before."

Franco came in for a look.

"You planted it," Lawrence said. "This is entrapment."

Franco touched it with his thick forefinger. "It's too small to store anything. He must be uploading to a computer. You want me to toss the place? Might be quicker than bracing this schmuck."

Schneider turned to Lawrence. "What do you think? We're only interested in your computer, but if my partner happens to find anything else, we'll be obligated to—"

Lawrence took a look at Franco. He dropped the peas on the counter and turned to go. "I'll get it."

As soon as he was out of the room, Schneider tapped the painting and said, "I can't believe I missed this. Rachel's bedroom is on the other side of the wall."

"Don't be like that. We got it now." When Lawrence returned, Franco snatched the laptop out of his hands. "Now go get a piece of paper and write down your username and password, and the file names and locations."

"You can't take that with you." Lawrence looked hopefully at Schneider. "That's how I earn my living."

Schneider produced a pen and notebook. Handed them to Lawrence. "Time to find a new vocation, my friend."

49

─────────

Carter kept the message short. In his vast experience, the less one said the better. "Let's meet. You pick the place."

The response came in a few seconds. "Antonio's in thirty."

Carter cursed under his breath. He should have known: Antonio's was on the Boulevard, which meant it was suitably dark and dirty. Not the kind of place he preferred for this kind of talk. They made good Brazilian rice, though.

"I don't like this." Rubin took his frustration out on the steering wheel and squealed their undercover cruiser through a U-turn. "It doesn't feel right."

"I'll tell you what doesn't feel right: a couple of hacks fucking with our case."

"I get that," Rubin said, "and Franco is definitely unfit for service. You'll get no argument from me there. But—"

Carter was busy cueing up the video on his holo. He stopped and said, "But what? Just how badly do you want to make Sergeant, Javier?"

"You know what my goals are."

"Good, because we're out of leads. And Franco and

Schneider are working behind our backs. We need to take control and get back in the game."

They drove the rest of the way in silence. Rubin parked outside of Antonio's but made no move to get out.

"What. You're staying?"

"This is all you, partner. My way? We'd chase down our own leads instead of worrying about what Schneider's doing. But hey, I'm not going to stand in your way."

Carter got out and slammed the door. He straightened his suit, passed through two windowless doors, and entered the semi-darkness of Antonio's. He spotted Schneider right away. Hard not to; he was the only skinless man in the place. Or anywhere. He was at end of the bar next to an old-timer in a green-visored fishing hat. They each had a plate of grilled skewered shrimp and a frosted mug of dark beer.

Schneider gestured to an empty stool.

"How about some privacy?" Carter stood stiffly, watching the old man eating his shrimp. He didn't bother removing the shells.

"Mickey is deaf and mute." Schneider snapped his fingers in front of the old man's face. "Your secrets are safe with him."

"More like your secrets." Carter pulled up a stool and raised a finger to the bartender.

The bartender looked hard at Carter and his tan cotton suit.

"I'll have a Stella and a small bowl of yellow rice."

"What do you want in the rice?" The bartender took a green bottle from a mini fridge and set it on a coaster.

"Get it with shrimp and chorizo," Schneider suggested.

Carter nodded his approval and said, "I need an update on the case, Schneider."

"Sure," Schneider said. "When do you want it?"

"Now."

"Okay, here's the full unedited version. First thing I did was take Franco shopping for new clothes. As a man of style, I'm sure you can appreciate—"

Carter rolled his eyes. "Don't play games, Schneider."

"Fine. I ran down a solid lead on an alternative suspect."

"Why?"

"Because you and I both know Stanovich isn't our guy."

"My guy."

"Whatever. The new lead was a plumber. He was putting it to a hooker in Rachel Montgomery's building near the time of her death. He's clean, though. I was wrong about him."

"What else?"

"Old lady with a cat in the downstairs apartment."

"Yeah, we talked to her. Mrs. Donato."

No need to include the part about Bambino the synthetic cat. "And, last, we went back to the drug addict neighbor, but that guy couldn't tie his own shoes and doesn't know what day it is. That's pretty much the whole story."

"Pretty much."

"That's right."

The bartender dropped a large bowl in front of Carter. Yellow rice with onions and carrots, spicy shrimp, and slices of chorizo. He picked up a fork and took a bite. Nodded appreciatively. "Where'd you take your knuckle dragging partner for clothes?"

It was an unwritten rule among detectives: when food was present, you ate. And when you ate, it was considered bad form to talk shop. Most likely it had to do with the unpredictable nature of police work; a cop could go five or six hours without food or even a bathroom break.

"Murray's." Schneider plucked three shrimp off his skewer and handed the rest to Mickey.

Carter took another bite and realized he was starving. He scarfed the rest of the small bowl and asked for another. "Murray is a good tailor." While he waited for the food, he returned to business. "Here's the thing, Schneider. That stunt you and Franco pulled at the prison with Stanovich fucked up our case."

"*Your* case."

"Don't act surprised. I know you've heard that directly from L.T. Me and Rubin are the lead investigators, which means it's *our* case. And you're obligated to share everything you know about it. So, tell me about the RV—"

"What RV?"

"Don't play dumb. It's embarrassing."

Schneider thought he'd borrow one from Franco's playbook. "Oh, *that* RV. I thought you meant a different one."

Carter rolled his eyes.

"Tell you what. Since I'm running low on trust these days, and since it's *your case*, how about you tell me what a couple of A-Team investigators like you and Rubin have come up with. Go on. Dazzle me."

Carter checked his watch, which was German, and expensive. "We looked into Paul Chafee, the male victim. He had two priors for prostitution. We talked to his boyfriend, who didn't know Rachel Montgomery, but he knew of her. He said if ever Rachel got a client who wanted a three-way she'd call him. And vice-versa. They looked out for each other that way."

"Was Chafee's boyfriend a sex worker?"

"No. He drives a delivery truck. Produce route. Regular kind of guy."

"Human?"

"Yeah. Said they were waiting for the vote to pass so they could get married. Is this weird for you? It feels strange talking about it with you."

"It's fine. Go on."

"He said Paul's work was temporary. They were trying to bank enough money to move away from the Boulevard and buy a fixer-upper in the Heights." Carter turned his bottle of Stella around in his hand, picked at the label. "Anyway, Chaffee got a call from Rachel Montgomery on Tuesday at 3:00 p.m. for a job at 4:00. He was going to meet his boyfriend after for drinks, at a place nearby."

"But he never made it."

"The boyfriend waited for two hours then went home. He started to get worried, but he didn't know Rachel's number. Or where she lived. He called the 23rd at 9:00 p.m. and tried to file a missing person, but they told him—"

"Right. I know the drill: can't file a missing person on a nonperson. What else?"

Carter spread out his hands. "He kept calling. After the 24-hour mark, well that's when you and Franco came into the picture."

"Okay, but aside from talking to Chafee's boyfriend, what have you and Rubin actually done?"

"We put a lot of work into Stanovich. And you should know, at the time—"

Schneider hung his head and shook it.

"And we talked to Rachel's neighbors. That brings us up to the present. I came clean with you, now tell me about the RV."

Schneider took a sip of beer and said, "It was an almost-new Mercedes Sprinter. Expensive. Someone saw it parked outside of Rachel's building."

"Who? You have a new witness we don't know about?"

"The old lady's cat."

"Very funny."

"Fine. The old lady saw it."

"She didn't tell us that."

"Maybe you didn't ask the right way. Franco used his staggering charisma to jog her memory. She didn't see much, though. Just the color and some of the vehicle's features."

"There's a lot of those on the street these days. How did an old lady who doesn't even drive know the difference between a Sprinter and a Freightliner?"

"Good question." He didn't bother with the explanation, though, which would have involved backtracking to Bambino and Royce, his computer guy. "Franco and I talked to a salesman at the Mercedes dealer who remembered making the sale." He paused for another drink and then gave a compressed version. He described the weird vehicle specs, as well as the anonymous drop off on the part of the Boulevard that had no CCTV.

"That's a 9 out of 10 on the suspicious scale."

"Right. So we're looking at a ghost vehicle that's some kind of a mobile surgery theater."

"Didn't you trace the registration?"

"Franco's buddy in Tech tried. It's registered to a company called New Hope, LLC. Lot of money flowing through it, but no actual office or headquarters. The board of directors is loaded with doctors and professors, but they don't actually do anything outside of attending closed meetings."

"Budget? Accounting?"

"Kind of. They take donations, but most of their endowment comes from a single anonymous donor, and no one takes a salary. They spend everything they get on hard goods and medical supplies, which they donate to third world countries and NGOs."

"What about the DMV? Start locally and get a list of Sprinters that are registered as RVs. Expand the circle until we get a hit."

Schneider nodded at the logic of it. He was also pleased to hear Carter's use of the plural *we*, but it was easy to be inclusive when the flow of information was one-way. "Over the last ten years, New Hope LLC has purchased two dozen Sprinter RVs, so they use fleet plates, and they're privately insured, too. It's a group rider that covers the whole fleet. It's kind of brilliant, actually. Like the car share programs most cities have."

"It's unlikely someone created all of this just to experiment on a couple of synthetics."

"That's a good point, and I'm still short on motive. It's possible New Hope is for real but they've got a rogue lunatic in their midst."

"With unheard of scientific and medical abilities."

"I know. It's too far-fetched. Another possibility is that Danielle Talbot wasn't a random victim."

"Does anyone think she is?"

"Again, it's too much work to go through to try and sway a senator's vote. Too many moving pieces."

"Right. Much smarter to kidnap and blackmail. But he didn't do that, so that blows that motive."

"I'll give you the file," Schneider said. "Maybe you and Rubin can see something new in it."

From his stool, Mickey appeared to be following the conversation with interest. Carter noticed him noticing, and Mickey flashed an enormous, toothless grin.

"What else?" Carter pushed. "This is not the time to hold back on me."

"That's all I've got."

The bartender brought another bowl of rice. Carter thanked him and took out his holo. He swiped it on and slid it toward Schneider.

"What's this?"

"See for yourself."

Schneider recognized the scene. It was him, at Stiehl's. "I was going through a rough time." What he hadn't realized was how, in the middle of the fight, the crowd had gone silent. He was in the zone, taking his giant opponent apart one quick punch at a time. The spectators looked stricken. Horrified. Was it because he was on X? Or was it because he was so much smaller and had a shiny metal shell? "Listen, Carter. Why are you showing me this? What are you getting at?"

"It's time for you to walk away from my case. Leave it to the professionals, like the L.T. already told you to do."

"You're going to strong arm me? With this?"

"That's up to you." Carter picked up his fork, then thought otherwise and put it down. "We both know it would be bad for the Department if word got out that a drug using, cage fighting synthetic was working on something as high-profile as this."

Schneider nodded. He got it loud and clear. He drained his beer and stood up, clapped Mickey on the back in lieu of a goodbye.

"You ready to cash out, chief?" the bartender said.

Schneider gestured toward Carter. "He's paying for the three of us."

A moment later Mickey turned to Carter said, "Are you going to eat the rest of your rice?" His voice was as clear as a bell.

50

Elizabeth wasn't used to prepping the surgical suite in the country house. That was Keven's job, but he was busy bringing in Senator Muncy's son. Which he'd insisted could only be accomplished by participating in a ten-hour race.

"If you want to compete," she'd argued, "why not wait until our work is finished? Take a few months off and do it properly. Rent a place in California, or Maui, or wherever those people gather. Hire a professional trainer and coach. I'll bet you would enjoy that."

But Keven had been resolute. "Would I tell you to use a different peptide bridge in the microsurgery gaps?"

"No," she'd conceded.

"Then trust I know how to do my job."

"Of course." And he was right. In their many years together, Keven might have asked why she'd chosen a specific compound, or why it was better than another. But his questions were pure questions. Aimed at clarifying or gathering informa-tion, not doubting or criticizing.

Which is why in the end she'd agreed with his plan to

abduct the senator's son at the ironman event. And it was also why now she was up to her elbows in heavy rubber gloves, spraying surfaces with disinfectant. Surprised at how much she enjoyed the lemony bleach smell and the slight metallic tang of stainless steel.

Predictably, Keven's text came through just as she was finishing. Even with the dozens of contingencies he'd been faced with he was still punctual. "Be there in fifteen minutes," he said.

She put the cleaning supplies in a metal cabinet and met him by the carriage house. He pulled into the first bay and cut the engine. It was a vehicle she'd never seen before, a dark green Range Rover loaded with bicycles.

"Any trouble?" The windows were heavily tinted, but she could see a second person in the car. Slumped in the backseat.

"No trouble." Keven followed her focus and said, "that's Rory. The trainer."

She nodded, understanding at once the steps Keven had taken to cover his tracks. Obviously, he'd scrubbed the pickup truck and left it at the race parking lot. And terminated the trainer, who could have easily identified him. She also understood the future steps he might take, like driving the Range Rover to the shredder place he'd told her about. And, later, traveling across state lines with Steve and Rory's holos. He would send clever texts to the people on their contact lists. Perhaps post some pictures of odd landmarks. He'd become good at that sort of thing.

"How was the race? Did you enjoy it?"

He tried unsuccessfully to suppress a smile. "I did, thank you. Have you enjoyed your time with the detective?"

She made no attempt to hide her smile. "He's a very interesting man. It makes me wonder about the different directions our lives might have taken. I could see myself being happy with him. Living a small, quiet life. Is that surprising?"

"No. You've made many sacrifices over the years. It's natural to think about different paths we might have taken."

"Have you wondered about another life for yourself?" But before he could answer she shook her head and said, "Never mind. I know you're a private man."

"It's okay," Keven said. "I've wondered. I've thought about it."

"Jess?"

He didn't answer, which was itself an answer. "I'd like to be loved, but I'm not sure that means the same for me as it does for you or other people. Will you be able to do what is needed with Schneider? When the time comes?"

"Of course."

"But you said you could see yourself having a different life. With him."

"It's true. But our work is bigger than any of us individually. Will you be able to do what's necessary with Jess?"

"I don't have to like it, but I will do it. When the time comes."

"Then let us begin."

Together, they transferred Steve from the passenger's seat to a wheeled gurney. She closed up the carriage house while Keven pushed the gurney. They'd commissioned the construction of the house with automatic double doors in the back leading to an elevator. Keven keyed the elevator open and waited for Elizabeth. She joined him shortly and said, "I'm worried about that man in the back seat of the Range Rover. Won't he smell?"

By appearances, the elevator ran one floor down to the basement. It housed the furnace, water treatment equipment, backup generators, and storage. Beneath the basement—accessible by code only—was a subbasement that contained the surgical suite. Keven typed in the numbers and said, "After the procedure I will take care of it. The vehicle and the body."

"How? I don't want him disposed of on this property."

"I said I'd take care of it."

She accepted this and waited for the soft bell to chime, announcing their arrival. The anteroom was for washing, and Keven took fifteen minutes to clean himself thoroughly and dress in scrubs. He assisted Elizabeth in cutting away Steve's triathlon clothes, and they transferred him again to the surgical table. Keven started IV lines and hung bags on racks.

"I can take it from here," Elizabeth said.

"You don't need me to help?"

She hummed pleasantly, completely absorbed in her work. At first Keven thought she hadn't heard him. But then she stopped humming and said, "No, thank you. I would prefer you work on getting rid of the car and that man. Otherwise it will be an unnecessary distraction."

51

The detectives were on their way in to the 23rd, Lawrence's laptop in tow. They had the username and password, and James was on standby for tech support. Just in case.

"What are you so excited about?" Schneider said. They hadn't worked together long enough to be overly familiar with each other's moods, but Franco didn't strike him as the happy or enthusiastic type.

"You know how it is when you're working a case and it's going nowhere and then all of a sudden you get something, A little piece of evidence that ends up breaking things wide open?"

"Yeah, sure. Not as often as I wish, but—"

"I think that's what we've got. Inside this laptop. If we get a clear picture of this sonofabitch—"

Schneider's phone announced a call from the L.T.

"This is Schneider," he said. "Go ahead."

"Put me on speaker. I want both of you to hear this so I don't have to explain it again." The L.T.'s voice sounded angry, which is to say he sounded like he always did. "Schneider, you're suspended. Without pay. Starting now."

Franco looked at his partner, mouthed *what the fuck?* He didn't know about Carter's shakedown at Antonio's.

"I can see Carter didn't waste any time," Schneider said dryly.

"Don't make this about him. It's not. It's about you."

"It is about Carter, though. Doesn't it concern you that he seems more focused on a pissing match with me than solving the case?"

The L.T.'s voice deepened with anger. "Did Carter force you to go to a fight club and get in a cage?"

"No."

"Was he responsible for you trying to bite the ear off someone named Crusher?"

"No."

"That's right, so you can drop whatever it is you're doing and turn in your badge and gun at the station. Jesus, Schneider. A fucking cage fight? Really?"

"I was working off some steam, sir."

"You'll have plenty of time to work off steam now. Franco, you paying attention?"

"Yes."

"I want you to stop with the Montgomery case. Come in later and we'll talk about your new assignment."

"But sir, we've got a new lead—" Franco was still trying to reconcile the image of Schneider in a cage fight. Biting off someone's ear, or at least trying to. It sounded crazy but, still, he felt some obligation to note his opposition.

The L.T. ignored him. "One last thing, Schneider. Do you know what I'm most disappointed about?"

"What's that, sir?"

"I had my money riding on you two. Everyone thought I was nuts. *Schneider's too much of a loner,* they said. *Franco's impulsive and doesn't listen.* But I went out on a limb. I told them you were going to surprise us all. Well color me surprised." He hung up.

FRANCO PICKED THE BAR—CAPPY'S Lounge—and paid for the first three rounds, all of which were doubles.

"That's enough for me," Schneider said.

"One more." Franco gave the sign to the bartender. By all accounts he appeared to be taking the news harder than Schneider. He wasn't the kind of guy to whom friendships came easy. But despite a rough start with his new partner, the relationship was starting to grow on him. Now it was over. "You're going to fight this, right? Talk to the union rep at least."

"What's the point?" Schneider tipped back what would be his *last* last drink. "If Carter hadn't thrown it in his face someone else would have. Just a matter of time. I've got no one else to blame but myself."

"Yeah, sure. I get it. But you know what's really messed up about this?"

Schneider shook his head. His speech was slurry around the edges. "That I made it this far in life and haven't learned a goddamned thing?"

"No. It's Carter. Why does he have such a hard on for keeping us off the case? I know he's ambitious, and an asshole. But it's more than that."

"What do you mean?"

"What do you think of him as a detective? Unbiased opinion. Purely based on skills and abilities."

"He's good. Not the best, but better than most."

"That's right. Everyone who knows him says he's smart and thorough. So why did he get fooled so easily by Stanovich? He didn't even check out the guy's story. It's sloppy work. Too sloppy."

"Stanovich is a persuasive psychopath. He persuaded Carter. Simple as that."

Franco thumped a meaty fist on the bar top, an indication that the whiskey was doing its job. "I hate to admit it, but I think you were right about him."

"How?"

"Carter steered the whole case in the wrong direction. On purpose."

"I didn't say that. I just put it out that there was a possibility. A suspicion."

"As soon as you—we—started to get the case back on track, and found a new lead—"

"He got me suspended."

"Yeah."

"You think this is a conspiracy as opposed to one guy having it out for another? Maybe he just hates synths. It could be as simple as that."

"Hey, I'm just repeating what you said, buddy. 'Among real detectives, there's no such thing as coincidence.'"

Franco and Schneider looked at Lawrence's laptop before returning their attention to their drinks. It represented the unknown. The great mystery of what comes next.

"Aren't you curious?" Franco said. "Where all this goes?"

"Sure." Schneider picked it up and turned it over in his hands, as though he might be able to see through the plastic case to the data files inside. "Tell you what. My career is already in the toilet. I'll take this home and have a look. If anything useful comes up, I'll let you know."

"No way. That's stupid."

"So is losing your job. The smart thing is to keep your distance from me and this case."

Franco scratched his head. "I don't know, Schneider."

"Seriously. You should treat me like I'm poison."

52

———————

Keven made a decision. He would dispose of Rory's body and the Range Rover in one fell swoop using the shredder. He was sure Wade would play along, though probably with a demand for more money, which was fine. What he wasn't fine with was the volume of blood and fluid. One to two gallons worth. Would it drip out or spray? He didn't think so, but it wasn't worth the risk.

Exsanguination was called for. But he lacked the proper equipment which meant, once again, he'd have to improvise. He dug through the minimal rigging gear on hand and found several locking carabiners. They were stainless steel and of good quality; they would substitute nicely for pulleys. He also found a coil of 11mm static line from his rock climbing days, and a bag of small diameter parachute cord for binding.

First step. He dragged Rory's feet out of the back seat and lashed them together with the parachute cord. Clipped two carabiners over the lashing and ran the working end of the static line through one of them.

Second step. He secured two more carabiners to the center

rafter, the one that lined up over the drain. These would serve as the upper pulley points. He tied off the working end of the static line on the rafter itself and ran the other end through one of the leg carabiners. After that, it was a matter of threading the rope through the remaining pulley points and working the slack out of the system.

When he had enough tension, he pulled and moved backward, hauling Rory out of the Range Rover and across the floor. He continued hauling and watched the body swing and climb until the head came to rest six inches above the drain. He ran the rope around one of the Range Rover's wheels using the gap between the tire and the concrete as an improvised cleat.

"Not bad." He wished Elizabeth could see his fine work. It was true that she cared little for rough, physical tasks like this, but he still craved her attention. Her compliments were rare things that he valued above all else. He unfolded the serrated blade of his knife and cut a little too hard.

"Damnit!" He stepped back, but it was too late. Stupidly, he'd sliced through Rory's trachea. Blood sprayed in a fine mist. Worse, he'd apparently under-dosed the phenobarbital and Rory appeared to be working his way back across the mysterious threshold of consciousness. His eyes were open. He started to make gurgling sounds and thrash about.

"Fuck." Keven rarely used this word, but his fine work was turning to shit. He paced around the swinging, flailing body. It took thirty-two seconds before Rory stopped moving, and a full four minutes before the last of the blood ran down his forehead and dripped from his matted hair into the drain. Keven hosed the splattered blood from the floor and positioned a PVC body bag under the corpse.

Keven grunted as he tried to tug the rope loose. It had become wedged under the tire. It only came unstuck after he changed position and jerked it free. He lowered Rory's body into the bag, zipped it, and dragged it into the Rover's hatch.

Then he stripped naked and burned his clothes in a bin behind the carriage house.

Start to finish it had taken forty-five minutes. Another fifteen and he was showered and dressed in clean clothes. The last step—which proved the hardest for him—was to disassemble Steve's bikes and toss the wheels and frames into the back, on top of the body bag.

AT THE SCRAPYARD, Wade put up little resistance and settled for three grand in cash. But when Rory's liquified remains came through the shredder he negotiated for four. Apparently, exsanguination hadn't been enough.

"IRS my ass," was Wade's parting comment.

Keven left the yard feeling unburdened. Back on track. He walked 1.2 miles to Cup of Joe, a five-table café in a random strip mall. He ordered a decaf latte, took a seat by the window, and dialed Jess.

"Hi," she said, maybe a little coolly because of how they'd ended the last call.

"Please tell me I can take you for dinner," Keven said by way of a greeting. "Now. Or soon. As soon as you can get ready."

"What?"

"It's a spontaneous gesture of how much I miss you, Jess, and how much of an ass I've been to focus on my dumb job when you needed me. I'm sorry. I will not make that mistake again." He knew as he spoke them that the words were true. At least the part about his feelings toward her. Did this matter? He thought so. He would still do what was needed vis a vis his and Elizabeth's plans. But this did not obviate his love.

She paused, trying to wrap her mind around Keven's fast and honest invitation-apology. "Okay."

"Okay? Really?" Trying to nail the excitement level at an 8.7 out of 10.

"Really. Just give me half an hour to get ready."

53

Franco was the first to sober up, thus they took his wife's minivan. "I fucking hate this thing," he said, beckoning toward the rows of child seats in the back, which were littered with stuffed animals and little-kid snack wrappers.

"It's a suburban abomination on wheels," Schneider agreed. "But think of it this way: every time you get behind the wheel, your risk of having an affair drops to zero."

"Yeah, it's kryptonite for hot women alright."

"Exactly."

"Listen, we're going to have to do this at my house. Tina wants me to watch the kids." He looked out the side window, rubbing his jaw. "The marriage counselor says it's a critical moment in our relationship and I need to show Tina I can be different. You believe that?"

Schneider looked skeptical. "What about going in to the station house today? You're supposed to get your new assignment from the L.T."

"I called in a personal day. He didn't question it."

"You're sure?" When no answer came, he said, "Okay,

Franco, but if we're going to your house you're going to want to keep those girls far away from what's on this laptop."

"The garage is private and soundproofed. I work out and watch football in there."

Tina met the two of them at the front door. She was dressed to the nines in a tight skirt and heels with a low-cut red blouse.

"Where are you going?" Franco's eyes drew together with menace.

"I told you. I'm going out with Lauren and Jacqui. Happy hour."

Schneider gave him a nudge. When he didn't respond, he gave him another one. Sharper.

"You look beautiful," Franco said.

Tina beamed and gave him a kiss. "The girls need a snack, and don't let them watch T.V. the whole time. You need to engage with them, you know?" She touched Schneider's arm and said, "Hi, Schneider. It's nice to see you."

"Good to see you, Tina. Love that Mercedes. It looks great on you."

They watched her depart in the G Wagon. Franco gritted his teeth and was immediately assaulted by his girls. Clad in matching princess pajamas, they jumped into his arms and shouted, "Daddy's home! Daddy's home!" He kissed them both and then let them slide down to the floor. "Girls, I want you to meet my new partner, Schneider."

The girls faced Schneider with big eyes.

Schneider smiled and tipped his hat.

The older of the two, who was missing a front tooth, said, "I'm Chloe and I'm eight. I'm in the third grade. I go to P.S. 31 and I'm in Ms. Shank's class."

"Hi, Chloe, I'm Schneider."

"He looks funny." The younger girl clung to her sister's arm. Half of her face was covered by her long dark hair.

"It's true," Schneider said. "I do look funny because I'm

partly made out of metal. Thank you for noticing. What's your name?"

Chloe spoke for her younger sister. "Her name's Molly. She's shy and doesn't like to talk to adults." She pointed at Schneider's cane. "What's that? Why are you carrying a stick?"

"I just like it." Schneider held it in front for the girls to see.

"What's that, on top?"

"It's amber. Do you know what amber is?"

The girls shook their heads in unison.

"When the resin from a tree gets to be millions of years old, this is what it becomes."

"What's resin?" Chloe said.

Molly pushed the hair out of her face and said, "Did you hurt your leg? Is that why you need a stick to walk? I hurt my leg once. I had to get stitches."

Franco took the moment to slip away to the kitchen and started gathering snacks.

"My leg is fine." Schneider knelt down and handed his cane to Chloe. "It just suits me to use a stick when I walk."

Chloe examined the amber knob. She covered it with her palm, tapped it with a fingernail, and then handed the cane to her sister, who followed the same protocol.

Franco reappeared with a bowl of popcorn and a bag of candy. "Alright." He herded them into the kitchen and said, "Twenty questions is over. Daddy and Schneider have some work to do, so you two are going to watch a Disney movie and have a snack."

The girls went along, but looked back over their shoulders at their father's strange new partner. "Mom said we're not supposed to watch—"

"Mom's not here," Franco said. "I'm in charge, and I'm ordering you to eat this gigantic bowl of popcorn and the entire bag of candy. The fate of the world depends on it. Understood?"

The girls laughed, and soon Schneider heard the sound of

dramatic intro music from the T.V., and the crunching of popcorn.

54

____

"You need to go home." At 7:40 p.m. Brendan Little, one of Jess's staff, hovered in the doorway of her office. He looked concerned. "When's the last time you slept?"

Jess picked her head off her desk and focused. Brendan was wearing a pink satin bowtie and an olive quilted vest despite the summer New DC heat, which was oppressive. "Is that a Barbour?"

His face lit up. "Why, yes, it is. Thank you for noticing."

She rubbed her eyes and stretched. "Brendan, where do things stand with the ads for the SRA vote?" They'd settled on two but hadn't closed deals with the networks. One of the ads was a common ground scene with the tagline, "Synthetics are people, too." The longer one was a montage showing synthetics as first responders: firemen, paramedics, nurses, and cops helping humans.

"Give me a second and I'll check." Brendan pulled out a chair and turned on his tablet, then took an extra few-seconds to adjust his vest. "It looks like we're all set, Jess. The shorts are already running on Netflix, CBS, and NBC. And the longer ones run tonight on ESPN at halftime." He turned his tablet around for her to see the schedule. "You said not to bother with Fox."

"That's right."

"And here's the really cool part: if the ads run up until the SRA vote like we've arranged, the bill will come in just five cents under the total amount of the Bharanda check."

"You spent it all. Excellent work, Brendan."

He clutched his tablet tightly against his chest and said, "Can you believe she flipped?"

"Who?" Brendan had a habit of switching abruptly into gossip mode. Usually, Jess could follow the thread and keep up, but not today. Not after three straight all-nighters, working like mad to meet the advertising deadlines. She'd spent most of that time with the video crew and had been surprised to learn that they no longer used real actors. From start to finish the ads had been computer generated, which seemed ironic given the context.

"Bobbi Jo. Senator Talbot. She's changing her vote."

Jess looked at her watch. It was 4:30. She'd been asleep for over an hour. "How do you know this?"

"It's all over the news. She had a press conference and everything."

"No kidding? That's amazing." Jess needed a moment to process this, but she was sure she was late for something. Another interview maybe? She took out her phone and looked at her schedule. Nothing.

"It's because of her daughter."

"I'm sure, but it's a horrible reason. I still can't believe that happened." Then she remembered. Keven. Dinner. She grabbed her purse and ran out of the office, trusting that Brendan could lock up after her.

JESS DICTATED AS SHE DROVE. "Sorry, Keven. I'm running late, but I'm on my way. Are you still able to meet me? I hope so."

"No problem." The reply came almost instantly. "I'm on a bench out in front of the restaurant and I've got a book. So don't rush."

She relaxed a little and checked her hair in the rear view. A mess. She dug out a brush from the center console and did her best while driving. The Thai restaurant, Spicy Basil, was across town but she knew a shortcut. She got lucky and managed to blast through a yellow light, which put her on track to hit the next three, which were synchronized, on the green.

When she pulled into the parking lot she caught the smell coming from the restaurant. She realized not only hadn't she slept in days, but she hadn't eaten either.

Keven was exactly where he said he'd be, but he was empty handed. He wore black jeans and a white cotton button down.

"Where's your book?" Jess said.

"I lied. I didn't want you to feel bad for being late."

She frowned. "I do feel bad."

He grabbed her gently and pulled her in for a kiss. "You're here, and I'm happy to see you. So let's take this inside and get a table. Are you hungry?"

"Starving."

55

Franco's garage had been converted into a Franco-specific paradise. It was split into two sections, one with an enormous T.V. and matching leather recliners, the other with a row of kettlebells, a hex bar with iron plates, and a gym-quality squat rack.

"It's surprisingly masculine, Franco," Schneider said. "I was expecting something a little more... androgynous and artistic."

"Shut up."

Schneider carried the laptop to the T.V. He entered Lawrence's username and password and spent a few minutes connecting the laptop to the big screen. Franco turned on all the lights and retreated to a fridge in the corner.

"I'm guessing you don't want any more alcohol," he said.

Schneider shook his head no. Franco returned with two Cokes. He arranged the laptop on a small table between the recliners, and they settled in.

"I never thought I'd be using this space for something like this," Franco said.

"You're sure the door's locked?" Schneider said. "We'll do the first run-through with the volume way down." He began slowly, scrolling through Lawrence's files, the state of which was nothing short of catastrophic. There were at least two thousand pictures and videos all mixed together. Unlabeled, of course.

"Dates and times," Franco said.

Schneider narrowed the pool, creating a new folder and dumping the potential hits in it. Gratefully, the first videos were short and they were able to disqualify Rachel's customers quickly. One was obese, another too short. The third was a woman.

"Stop," Franco said.

Schneider froze the third video. "Yeah, that's our guy."

"You're sure?"

"It's him. He's dressed a little different, but it's him. Look." He unfroze and they watched Rachel in her bedroom with two men, both mid-thirties, handsome, and well-built. Paul Chafee, the one whose limbless body would soon end up next to Rachel's, was dressed in skinny jeans and a tight black t-shirt. He was slim but muscular and stood close to their unsub, who wore the same ball cap as in the video feed from Mrs. Donato's apartment. No coveralls, though. Instead he had on a pair of khakis and a navy hoodie.

Schneider stopped it and took a screenshot. "I'm sending this to Royce."

"Why not James?"

"Because I'm suspended and you're off the case, remember?"

Franco nodded. "Let's see the rest. Call Royce after."

"This is enough for him to run facial recognition."

"It's not that. My kids are going to be banging on that door any minute. We need to confirm he's the killer."

"He is." But Schneider unfroze it and they watched. Rachel sat on the edge of the bed looking provocatively at the unsub. She swept her long chestnut hair over one shoulder. The audio was poor and they had it set low, but she distinctly said, "Money first, sweetie."

The unsub reached into the pocket of his khakis. He brought forth a stack of bills, which he handed to Paul Chafee. While Chafee counted the money, Rachel wriggled out of her skintight dress and crossed one long shapely leg over the other. The unsub ignored her in favor of Chafee. He went in his pocket again and came out with was a yellow and orange plastic cylinder. "You both deserve better," he said.

Chafee stopped his counting long enough to look up. Curious.

"I promise that it will be meaningful."

"What will?"

"Your sacrifice." He raised the cylinder, which looked much like an epi-pen and unceremoniously plunged it into Chafee's chest.

Franco leaned over and hit the space bar to pause it. "What is that? What is that thing?"

"Just watch." Schneider hit the space bar again and the film advanced.

"No!" Chafee cried out and grabbed at his chest. The money fluttered in the air. Before the last of it settled to the carpet, he collapsed in a heap.

"It's like an EpiPen," Schneider said. "One that's able to punch through titanium."

"Yeah, but what's in it? Poison? Sedative?"

"No, please." Rachel, now naked, backed to the center of the bed and then up against the headboard. She covered her breasts with her left forearm, then looked around for something to throw or defend herself with. She grabbed a table lamp, but the cord was tangled. She shielded her face with her right arm. "Don't! Please."

The unsub advanced and struck her in her forearm with the EpiPen. Rachel shrieked and, seconds later, slumped onto one of the pillows. Whether she was dead or knocked out, they couldn't tell.

"I DON'T GET IT," Franco tracked the unsub's retreat from the room. "Where's he going?"

"He'll be back."

"Maybe there's two of them working together. It's not a complicated disguise."

"It's just him," Schneider said. "He's going to get the hand truck with the box."

They were interrupted by the sound of tiny fists pounding on the door. "Daddy, Chloe ate all the—"

"Tattletale!" Chloe said. "You're such a little tattletale."

There was a thump against the wall, and then one of the girls began to cry. A second thump followed by both girls crying.

"Jesus." Franco cursed and righted his recliner. "Give me a few minutes."

When he returned, Schneider backed the video up for Franco to see what he'd missed. The unsub had returned. This time he was dressed in coveralls with a dark hood and sunglasses. He dragged Paul Chafee to the corner. He laid the hand cart down with the box on top of it. From a pocket of his coveralls, he took out a small cordless driver and removed the box's lid.

Carefully, he arranged the two bodies in the box and stuffed the money and Rachel's dress between their legs. Then he secured the lid with screws. He reinforced this with steel bands at the top and bottom.

Lastly, in a display of tremendous strength, he bent his knees, hinged at his hips, and lifted the cart.

"Jesus," Franco said, impressed. "That's a four-hundred-pound dead lift if you count the weight of the box and everything else. I mean, I can hit five on a good day, but that's still impressive."

"You can challenge him to a bench press contest when we catch him."

"Fuck you."

But they were both happy. Not because of the violence they'd just watched on the big screen, which they knew was a prelude to something far worse. But because finally they had a face. And with that face, Royce would be able to get a name and an address. And with those two pieces they would find him.

56

"Where are we going?" Chloe climbed into her seat and expertly worked the buckle.

Franco helped the younger of the two, Molly, into her seat while Schneider distributed a trio of stuffed animals. He gave Chloe her much loved and badly patched rabbit, and Molly her panda and a sad-eyed sloth.

"We're going on an adventure." Franco chucked each girl under the chin, and jumped into the driver's seat. "Extra fun dad stuff."

"What kind of dad stuff?" Molly said.

"We're going to pretend we're detectives hunting down some bad guys."

"That doesn't sound fun at all. That sounds like your job."

"This is a bad idea," Schneider said.

"You have anything better? I know this is a do or die moment in the case, but it's the same for me at home, you know?"

"Drop me off at my car and I'll take care of the next couple of steps. It's just grunt work anyway."

"No way."

"Be smart, Franco. We'll reconnect as soon as Tina's home. We'll bring him in together."

Franco shook his head. He was in stubborn mode. "Where are we going anyway? What's taking Royce so long?"

"I don't know. He said it would take a while to hack and run the program."

"Yeah, well, we don't have *a while*."

The argument was interrupted by the holo. "Yes, go ahead, Royce." Schneider gave Franco the evil eye. Punishment for his impatience. "Uh-huh. Yes."

In the back, Molly leaned over and whispered something to her sister, who giggled.

"What are you two doing back there?" Franco had one eye on Schneider's holo and the other on the girls. There were no eyes left for driving.

"Watch the road." Schneider pointed at the car ahead that was braking. Franco locked the wheels and skidded to a near miss.

"Daddy!" Molly shouted from the backseat.

"What?" Franco took his foot off the brake and got them moving again. "Don't yell, honey. Schneider's making an important holo call."

"With who?" Molly said.

"We want to make a deal," Chloe said through more giggles.

"Yeah? What kind of deal?" Franco's attention was on Schneider's conversation. How long did it take to give him a name and address?

Chloe cleared her throat and straightened up in her chair, a rather nice impersonation of an uptight, self-important type. Molly laughed hysterically.

"You take us for magic frosty sparkles," Chloe said, "or—"

"Or what?"

"We'll tell mom you took us on a stakeout."

"What?" Franco turned to glare at Chloe, then back at the road. "How do you even know that word?"

"It's on T.V. When the police are trying to catch the bad guys they do a stakeout, which is like a sleepover in a car but they don't watch movies and there's no pillows and blankets. They do eat popcorn, though, and talk a lot."

Schneider turned back to the girls and said, "You're very smart. That's exactly what a stakeout is."

"Don't encourage her," Franco said. "She's leveraging both of us and the case for ice cream."

"Royce, hold on." Schneider shielded his non-holo ear. "I didn't hear that. Can you repeat?" He listened for a few seconds and said, "Kevin Danvers."

Franco mouthed the words, trying them out. "Kevin Danvers."

"Got it. Text me the address?" Another few seconds of listening, then, "Hey, Royce? Thanks. You did good. Now I owe you."

57

———————

Elizabeth wanted to look after Steve Muncy for a couple of extra days but it wasn't possible. There was a schedule to keep, after all. And one more piece of the puzzle that was hers and Keven's work to assemble. She did what she could to stabilize him for transport, and tried one last time to reach Keven. For the first time in their many years working together, pursuing their greater cause together, her call went straight to voice mail.

She tried not to dwell on it. Keven clearly had feelings for Jess. She wanted to remind him he was entitled to those feelings just as she was entitled to her own feelings toward Schneider. Strong feelings, she had to admit. Powerful enough to let her cognitive flywheel spin out an alternate future, one in which she and Keven did not change the world. Instead, she lived as an ordinary woman named Beth. She made pottery and sculpture in her studio and, after, went for late night drives with Schneider in his old car.

But she'd stopped being Beth long ago. She knew what was real and she knew what was important for humanity. Neither she nor Keven could afford to let something as trivial and fleeting as feelings—mere energy patterns moving through the body—interfere with their work. She just hoped he would remember this.

The printer spit out the same hospital instructions as before but with an added personal touch at the top of the page.

"You may ask yourselves if the changes to this young man were intended as enhancement or debasement. They are neither. What you are looking at is adaptation. Evolution. The next step."

That done, she loaded her patient and the supporting equipment into the cargo area of a black Honda Odyssey. It fit nicely with the back seats folded down. The low tailgate height made it easy enough for her to collapse the front legs of the gurney and slide it in. She dressed in black clothes and grabbed a black knit cap and sunglasses. She was ready.

On route to the hospital she called Carter, whom she found unpleasant but useful. He was one of those ambitious but predictable types. He liked to talk about the moral high road but, in the end, he would always put himself first.

"I can't talk," he said. "It's not a good time."

"Then hold the phone to your head and listen." She was able to navigate to the hospital without thinking, but there was something Keven had told her about the camera situation. Yes, she remembered now: they were placed in the parking lots and entry points. She'd have to drive to the back lot by the loading docks.

"My partner," Carter said. "He's watching me closely on this. He doesn't know anything, but I don't have a lot of room to move."

"You'll manage," she said. "About Schneider. He's getting close. Do you know what to do?"

Silence.

"You are not instilling me with confidence, Derrick."

"Listen, Elizabeth—"

"It's past the time to change your mind," she said. "The money is already in your account. You are connected to me and we are connected to what is about to happen."

"I know what to do."

"Good."

She ended the call and steered through the maze of one-ways, patient parking lots, and service roads. When she reached the back of the hospital, she pulled up to the first loading dock and popped the automatic hatch. She checked Steve's sutures and made sure the lines and bags were running clearly. She took her time unloading the gurney, even when she heard a vehicle in the distance. There was no cause for worry, though. She was beyond the cameras' reach, working within the shadows of the building. She felt practically invisible in her dark clothes, cap, and sunglasses. In less than sixty seconds she'd be in the van, calling the hospital's emergency line.

"Listen carefully," she would say. "There is a man in need of medical attention. Send an emergency team with the following equipment to the back of the main building. By the first loading bay. Are you writing this down?"

58

Schneider waited in line at the ice cream stand while Franco and the girls reserved a picnic table. The line was long and he was packed in, front and back, with almost a dozen stressed-out parents and hyperactive children. A boy of four or five stared at him, his mouth hanging slightly open at the sight of a metal-faced man in a hat and sunglasses. Schneider couldn't tell if he was scared, fascinated, or mentally disabled.

"Stop staring, Silas," the boy's mother said. "It's not polite."

The kid stared even harder and Schneider made a little show of tapping his forehead with his knuckles. It made a faint tinny sound. He flashed a smile he hoped would come off as goofy.

The boy screamed. Schneider stepped back, alarmed. The boy's mother took in the situation and made a fast decision. She scooped him up and walked briskly away, giving Schneider a parting dirty look.

"Next," the kid at the ice cream counter said.

Schneider could feel eyes on him from the rest of the line. He stepped to the counter and ordered two magic sparkle frosties and a large chocolate-vanilla twist for Franco. He brought the treats to the picnic table and pulled Franco to the side. "What's the plan?" he said. "We've got a name and an address. I want to move."

"I'm in a jam here." Franco took a bite of his chocolate vanilla swirl. "I told you. I've got to watch the girls."

Schneider tapped his cane nervously. "We need to go, Franco. As in now."

"What do you want me to do?"

"Call Tina. She'll understand."

"You don't know my wife. Here, hold this." Franco gave Schneider his ice cream and took out his holo. "Look, I'm calling the babysitter. She lives nearby. We'll swing over and drop the girls off."

Schneider looked at the ice cream. Drips of chocolate and vanilla were running down the sides of the cone, ready to coat his fingers and the toes of shoes. He left Franco on the holo with the babysitter, nodding and saying, "yeah, I understand." At the picnic table, he set Franco's cone on a napkin. "How are the frosties?" he said to the girls. Chloe and Molly nodded slowly, their faces blank with the kind of concentration and deep relaxation that children only know when they're eating ice cream or dreaming. "I have to go for a little bit. Tell your Daddy I'll be back later."

The girls nodded again. He doubted they'd remember, but it was time to go. Schneider grabbed his cane and walked around the corner of the ice cream shop out of Franco's line of sight. Around the back he passed through a small municipal parking lot and onto a residential street. He scanned the line of parked cars on his side and made sure no one was watching. The first car was an Impala, but the driver's door was locked. So were the next three. He got lucky with the fourth; it was an electric blue Mustang with red leather seats.

"Sorry, Franco," he said out loud. Twenty seconds later he

used a small—and highly illegal—device to connect to the car's electronic control unit. The instrument panel came to life with a soft blue glow. He opened the navigation program and said, "249 West Euclid Avenue." He followed the directions, ignoring the stream of texts pinging his holo. He was sure they were from Franco, and not of the friendly variety.

59

K even insisted on sitting next to Jess instead of in the customary across-the-table chair. Which was unusual because, up to that point, she'd thought of him as a little standoffish. Not cold or aloof. Just a touch distant. Which had been fine with her, really, because she hated guys who were clingy and needy. Keven had been just right: kind and thoughtful, just not in an overly demonstrative way. And independent. He had his own life and didn't seem to want to intrude on or control hers. But now he was sitting next to her, holding her hand, talking excitedly about the future. Their future.

"I've got an idea," he said. "When the vote is finished and your work settles down, let's take a vacation. Is it too soon to talk that way?"

"No," she said, amused at the change that had come over him. "Where would you like us to go?"

"I don't care, so long as we're together."

She contemplated asking if he was high or had been replaced by a fictitious soap opera boyfriend. Instead, she gave his hand a squeeze and said, "that's sweet."

"Seriously. Where do you want to go, Europe? The Caribbean? Iceland?"

"Where's this coming from, Keven?"

"What do you mean?" He let go of her hand and tensed his posture.

"I mean, can you even take off from work? I'm not one to talk, but when's the last time you took a vacation? Or a sick day?"

Keven relaxed his shoulders. "That's what I'm saying, Jess. We both work too hard. For good causes, sure, but what about us? When do we get to have time for ourselves? For each other."

"Wow." Jess couldn't help enjoying his display of emotion. "This is a different side of you. I like it, don't get me wrong—it's just very honest."

He waved at the waiter. "More wine, please?" He turned back to Jess, his eyes blazing with intensity. "I've realized what's important, Jess, and I don't want to waste time. I hope that doesn't scare you off, but I don't want to hold back or pretend to be less interested in you than I really am."

The waiter brought new glasses and poured. They waited politely for him to leave.

"I've had too much." Jess pushed the glass a few inches away. "I'm going to have to drive home."

Keven waved his hands. "I'll drive you home."

"I don't want to leave my car."

"You won't have to. I walked here."

Jess shrugged and retrieved her glass. "Virginia Beach." She swirled the wine, which was a deep ruby color, and took a sip. "That's where I'd like to go on vacation."

"Really?" It was Keven's turn to be surprised. "Why Virginia Beach? I'd love to go to the ocean with you, it's just not somewhere I'd think of."

Jess looked at the table to their right, which was occupied by two middle aged couples who appeared to be on a double date. She hardly noticed them; her vision was focused inward, toward her past. "I went there once. With my family. Before my parents split up. I have very good memories from that trip."

Keven waited to make sure she had nothing more to add. She liked this about him. Most of the men she'd dated couldn't stop interrupting or talking over her. Like she was a sounding board for them to share their boring stories and brag about themselves. "We haven't talked much about our families."

"No, we haven't."

"Is it a painful subject for you?"

Jess shrugged. "I was about to lie and say no. But yeah, it still hurts. Probably always will."

Again, Keven listened, giving her space to continue.

"The man who raised me was a synthetic, which made things difficult for my mom. Well, it wasn't difficult for her. He was the love of her life. It was a problem for everyone else. I was too young to understand. I just loved him. He was my dad."

Keven nodded.

"When he left, it felt like I was being abandoned. He stayed in touch and I know he still loves me but I can't get rid of that feeling, you know? It's like I want to be close and have a relationship, but every time I talk to him all this anger comes to the surface."

"Did your mom remarry?"

Jess nodded. "Dwight. He's a conservative asshole who hates synthetics. Can you believe it?"

"Based on what I know about people, yeah, I can. Besides, his name is Dwight. Who names their kid Dwight? It's a setup."

Jess laughed and took a long sip of wine. "I don't talk about Schneider to many people. Thanks for listening."

"Schneider's a good name," Keven said. "Much better than Dwight. It sounds cool. Like a tough guy. Schneider."

She nodded. "He is cool. And tough. What about you? What kind of people do you come from?"

Keven took a while to respond. He wanted to tell her the truth, especially after what she'd said about Schneider. After all, who better to understand him than Jess, who was raised in part by a synthetic? Who loved a synthetic. But no, it was too risky. Or maybe he'd worked too hard to pass for human. He didn't have the strength to go against all of the conditioning.

"Keven?"

He drank his wine and let her initial question hang a little longer. When he spoke, his voice was constricted. His posture changed, almost like he got smaller, less upright. "I didn't grow up with a father. I have a mother, though. She's not my biological mother, but that's never mattered to me."

"It didn't matter to me, either, with Schneider. What's she like?"

He smiled and straightened back to his full height. "In two words, brilliant and elegant. She trained as a doctor but now she's more of a researcher. And in her spare time she's an artist. Pottery and mixed media sculpture."

"She sounds amazing."

"She is. I'd like you to meet her sometime. I think you'd really hit it off."

Jess excused herself to the ladies' room. While she was gone, Keven ordered coffee and mango sticky rice. He turned his holo on, sent a text to Elizabeth, then shut it off again. He paid the bill in advance and held Jess's chair when she returned.

"I can't eat this," she said. "I'm stuffed."

"It's really good. You should try a bite."

They ended up finishing all of it. And despite a second cup of coffee, which was stronger than she was used to, Jess could hardly keep her eyes open. She yawned and leaned against Keven, letting her head rest on his shoulder.

"That's it?" Keven said. "Shrimp Pad Thai and a couple glasses of wine and you're done for the night?"

"Guess so. I had a great time, though." She started to slump in her chair. Her eyes closed and she said in a sleepy drawl, "When are you going to take me to Virginia Beach?"

"When you stop falling asleep on dates."

"I'm awake." She opened her eyes wide to prove it.

"Come on then." Keven helped her out of her chair. By the time they made it her car, she was leaning fully on him.

"So tired."

He helped her into the passenger's seat and buckled her in. "Keys?"

Jess's head lolled but she felt around in her purse, which was on her lap. She found the keys and tried to smile, but her lips felt thick and immobile. Her hand still worked, though, and she gave the keys a little jingle.

"Are you sure you're okay?" Keven leaned in and touched his lips to her forehead. "You feel a little warm."

"Just tired. So tired."

Keven lifted her head and placed it back against the headrest. "Let's get you home."

"Keven?" With great effort she managed to turn her head and focus her eyes on him.

"Yes?"

"I don't feel right. I think something's wrong."

He started the car and reached out for her hand. "It's going to be okay. I promise."

As they drove she watched the lights streak by in the darkness and began to cry. She'd made a terrible mistake, even if she didn't know how. The hamster wheel of rationalization was spinning madly, telling her she'd had too much to drink or she'd eaten something that had spoiled. Or perhaps it was exhaustion from the succession of late nights preparing for the

SRA vote. But deep down she knew it wasn't any of those things. It was far worse.

"The next few hours are going to be very confusing, Jess." Keven steered with his left hand so he could stroke hers with his right thumb. It was meant to be a comforting gesture but had the opposite effect. She tried to pull away, but her limbs no longer responded.

"It's going to be okay," he reassured, though he was beginning to have doubts. On a purely technical level, Elizabeth had been so confident about the last test subject, Danielle. And she was dead. But on an emotional level things with Jess weren't going the way he wanted. She looked upset. And afraid—of him. He talked faster, eager to reassure. "After the procedure, we can go far away from everyone."

She began to cry.

"We can be happy together. Trust me. You'll see. When you meet Elizabeth it will all come clear. She'll explain everything."

60

Javier Rubin maintained a perfect tail on the stolen Mustang. Far enough not to lose sight of it, but not so far that he risked getting shaken loose with a sudden turn. It helped that the car was a screaming electric blue, but it hurt that it was low slung, especially since the vehicles in between were massive SUVs. The one in front, a big Infiniti, was like a moving building and he had to weave back and forth to see around it.

"I don't get it," Rubin said. "Why can't I hit the lights and pull him over? He's officially suspended, and driving a stolen car."

"Discovery," Carter said. "We want to find out where he's going. What he knows. Then we can arrest him."

"And you're sure the L.T. has our back?"

Carter tilted his head. If he held the right angle, he was able to track Schneider through the Infiniti's windows. "He's turning right onto Euclid."

"Why? There's nothing on Euclid but rich people. Our case is on the Boulevard, not out in the burbs."

Carter knew why but he wasn't going to say. The less his

partner knew the better. Better for Rubin and his family. They slowed and watched Schneider cruise the blocks of restored Victorians with a few upscale new builds mixed in. They sat on half-acre lots, each one with a manicured lawn, the kind that's only possible through chemistry and hired crews. Indeed, two houses down, a zero-turn mower zig zagged across a front yard while a kid patrolled the perimeter with a battery-powered vacuum, sucking up every errant leaf, pine needle, and blade of cut grass.

"What the hell is he doing?" Rubin pulled over and parked a couple hundred yards back from the Mustang.

"Just wait," Carter said.

They watched Schneider get out and approach the house, which was an impeccable atomic ranch of brick and glass with an overhanging roof. The plating on his face gleamed white in the sun. Schneider rang the bell and stood off to the side, his gun drawn but held low.

Rubin wondered where Franco was but didn't ask. Carter had no answers for him today. Maybe that meant something, maybe it didn't. He'd have to wait and see.

"What?" Carter said.

"Nothing," Rubin said. "You want me to roll with this cloak and dagger shit and trust you and not ask any questions? Fine. This is me not asking questions."

Carter nodded as if to say *good*.

"But you can bet your ass when this day's done, we're getting a table at the Golden Horseshoe and you're going to tell me everything."

"Yes. I promise."

"And another thing."

"What?"

"You're buying."

61

The unsub's house on 249 Euclid was filthy with cameras. In Schneider's experience this was emblematic of being an AI paranoid motherfucker. He'd come across some normal types who were extremely security conscious, armed to the teeth with motion detectors, police scanners, and all manner of tech surveillance gear. Usually worried about break-ins and theft, though there was often something darker under the surface. He remembered one guy, a banking exec, who had caught a burglar in his kitchen and had dumped half a clip of .45 ACP rounds into the poor bastard's back. Later he'd given Schneider a rather unusual explanation: "I'd been waiting for years for this to happen. Fantasizing about how I'd respond. You know, would I choke or be a hero?"

And when Schneider had asked him a few more questions, like, "what did you think he was doing in your kitchen?" he'd gotten the surprising answer of, "I just put myself in his shoes and pictured what I'd be doing in someone else's house at 2:00 a.m."

"Which is what?" Schneider had said. "What would you be doing?"

"I don't know. Choking someone out in their sleep. Or raping someone. Something bad like that."

It was weird the shit you remembered in the middle of working a case. Things reminded you of other things and right now he was staring up at three high-end security camera lenses, absolutely certain their unsub, Keven Danvers, was watching him. He took off his sunglasses and gave him a good look before walking around to the back of the house.

On the way, he slipped off his jacket and wrapped it around his gun. His holo had been buzzing nonstop for the last five minutes. He knew it was Franco, but he couldn't answer it. Not now. He was too close.

The back door was solid oak, but a long thin window ran along one side of it. Schneider looked around to make sure the coast was clear. The adjoining yards were empty so he banged out the window with his cloth-covered gun and cleared the jagged pieces from the sides. Reached in and unlocked the back door.

His holo continued to buzz the whole way up the stairs and into the kitchen. It was all hard lines and gleaming surfaces, nothing out of place. Expensive, too. Quartz countertops and one of those massive restaurant-level stoves you find in the homes of people who don't actually cook. Same for the range hood, which might have belonged in a modern art collection.

Through the kitchen and into an open living room. The furniture and furnishings looked unused, and he got the distinct feeling the house was not so much of a front as a standby. Like a west coast businessman who buys an apartment in Manhattan and only uses it for two weekends out of the year. Schneider moved quickly, opening doors. He didn't expect to find anything and wasn't surprised. A closet by the front entry held a broom and vacuum and a few men's jackets, size large. A pair of leather boots, size 10. Italian, very pricy. Several pairs of running shoes and an umbrella.

Back through the living room and into a study with an antique desk and a single bookshelf. The shelf was all nonfiction, mostly medical texts, heavy on Bharanda titles.

Schneider rifled through the desk but found nothing of interest, just a few legal pads, a stapler, and two boxes of Pilot pens. Upstairs it was much the same. The bathroom contained ibuprofen, cream, floss, and Band Aids.

He moved quickly through the bedroom and stopped cold at a bedside table.

"No."

Schneider picked up a photo and held it close. It was Jess, posing by a lake next to Keven Danvers, the man who had abducted Rachel Montgomery and Paul Chafee. Jess had her arm around him. She was leaning in, giving him a kiss on his cheek.

"Fuck."

Schneider thought back to his last conversation with Jess. She'd mentioned something about a guy she was dating, but no details. She certainly hadn't given him a name, which wasn't unusual for Jess; with few exceptions, since he and her mom had split up, she'd kept her private life to herself. But how was she connected to Danvers? Their unsub? It could not be a coincidence.

Two things: first, Jess did not know who this guy really was. Schneider wasn't going to try and fool himself into believing he knew anything substantive about her life, but she was a good person. He had no doubt about that. She would never be with a murderer unless she were completely in the dark. Second, Danvers's connection to him through Jess was purposeful. It was a classic sociopath move except, for the life of him, he couldn't imagine what Danvers would gain from it. Unless—

He realized his holo was still buzzing. He ignored it and it stopped, then started again. He took it out and saw a mess of calls and texts, all from Franco. The last one said, "Get out. Now!"

62

———————

Carter had never lied to his partner but what could he say, that he'd been paid an ungodly sum of money to keep Schneider off the trail? That Bharanda had reached out with a very long arm and chosen him? Bharanda, founder of SynCorp and the wealthiest person in the world? It wasn't believable. Carter knew he was a better-than-average detective and he was smart enough. But he wasn't stellar. He wasn't world class. Someone of Bharanda's status would never choose someone like him. Unless there was a very good reason for it.

There were other questions he didn't want to answer. Like, why had he agreed so readily—when he'd made it through his entire career without so much as being tempted by corruption? And why did Bharanda have such a thing for Schneider?

No, he wasn't going to touch those questions until it was over. Until he'd done his part and the second half of the money was transferred into the secure, untraceable account Bharanda had set up for him. Five million plus five million meant he and his wife could disappear. Buy oceanfront in cash and measure out the next twenty or thirty years in micheladas and fish tacos.

All of which justified his lie to Rubin. "L.T. asked me to minimize the blowback," he said. "Because of the promotion."

"What are you talking about?"

"Everyone knows you're a shoe-in for the Sergeant opening, right? And this thing with Schneider is going to get messy. So the L.T. wants to keep you out of the mud. That's it."

Carter thought about it for a moment. "He said that? I'm a shoe-in?"

"Yeah."

"Because he hasn't said shit to me."

"He wasn't going to talk about it but I pressed him. At the coffee machine yesterday." Carter watched his partner's skepticism turn to pride. And gratitude. "Seriously."

Rubin thought about it for a moment and said, "Thanks, Derrick. Thanks for looking out for me. I appreciate it."

Carter waved it off. He felt a pang of regret about the lie and vowed he'd make it right by taking care of his friend. When all was said and done he'd make sure the promotion happened. Hell, with ten million dollars he could grease the wheels. Offer a ridiculous donation to the Police Benevolent Association with a strong suggestion that Rubin get his due. The guy was heading for the promotion anyway. A donation would make it happen a little quicker.

"I'll give you ten minutes," Rubin said. "After that I'm coming in."

"Good." Carter skirted the side of the house. Once he was out of sight, he drew his sidearm and traversed the back patio, closing in on the door. There was a line of shattered glass and the door was cracked open. He almost took the edge of it in his face as Schneider came flying out.

"Fuck!" Carter said, jumping back. He lowered his piece but did not put it back in his holster.

"What are you doing here?" Schneider said.

"I'll ask you the same thing." Carter felt the urge to hide his piece but kept it out, flat against his thigh. Schneider didn't seem to notice or care.

"I'm looking into something," Schneider said. "Not that it's your business."

"You're off the case. Suspended."

"Did the L.T. put you up to this?"

Carter liked this. In fact, he wished he'd come up with it himself. "Yeah. He said, and I quote, 'You're not to do shit except sit at home and wait for your review.'"

Schneider closed the door and started to leave. "Goodbye, Carter."

Carter stepped in front of him and put a hand on his shoulder. He'd never touched Schneider before and was surprised at the warmth of the metal.

Schneider looked down at Carter's hand, which was pale and slender. Graceful for a man. When he looked up, the barrel of Carter's gun was eye level. "What are you doing?"

Carter jangled a pair of cuffs and tossed them. "Put these on."

Schneider caught the cuffs. He considered disarming him, but Carter said, "don't," and backed up to a safe distance by the edge of the patio stones.

"You're mixed up in this, Carter," Schneider said. "I don't know how, but I'll find out."

"You're barking up the wrong tree."

Schneider held his gaze.

"Listen. Whatever you might think, no one's going to listen. You just stole a car and broke into someone's house. You're officially suspended. You and Franco are fuckups. You're not believable."

"Who turned you, Carter?" Schneider fastened one of the cuffs. Metal touching metal. "You're a good detective. A bit of an asshole, sure, but still a good detective. Why throw that away?"

He gestured with his gun for Schneider to hurry up. "You

don't know shit, Schneider, and we're going to keep it that way. It's better for everyone, including you."

Schneider opened the other cuff and caught movement around the corner of the house. A large shape edging into his line of sight. Slowly, carefully. At first he thought it might be Keven Danvers, returning home. Or Rubin, arriving for backup. But it was neither. This person was too broad. Too massively built.

"Hey, dickface," Franco shouted.

Carter turned his head.

Franco delivered a straight punch that would have earned him cheers back at Stiehl's. The slim man dropped straight and fast.

"Dickface?" Schneider bent down and rummaged Carter's pockets until he found the keys to the cuffs.

"I didn't have time to think of anything better. You could just say thank you."

"Thank you." Schneider attached one of the cuffs to Carter, and the other to the barbecue grill. He fished in Carter's pockets for his holo, and then tossed it into some shrubs in the backyard. "Let's get out of here."

Franco led the way through the neighbor's yard. They came out on the street a hundred yards behind Rubin, who was just getting out of his car.

63

They managed to sneak around the back of the G Wagon without tipping Rubin off. Schneider had his holo out, dialing Jess. It went straight to voice mail. He climbed in the passenger's seat and relaxed a bit behind the safety of the blacked-out windows. "Where's the minivan? And the girls?"

"Yeah, about that." Franco was getting settled behind the wheel. He turned and punched Schneider in the arm. The titanium alloy hurt his knuckles, but he didn't let on. "Why'd you fucking leave me?"

"I'm sorry, Franco. It had to be done."

"At an ice cream stand? Really? I had to call my wife to come tap me out. Do you have any idea how embarrassing that is?"

"I'll bet she understood."

"Lucky for you."

"Tina's a good woman."

"She is, but I don't need you to tell me that." He started the car and said, "You mind filling me in on what just happened?"

Schneider took a long breath. "It's Danvers. He's got Jess."

He explained about the picture in Keven Danvers's bedroom. Franco said nothing as he pulled in the driveway of a massive Victorian while an elderly couple in matching glaucoma sunglasses watched from the porch. He backed out and headed the other way down Euclid, past Rubin's now-empty car.

"You didn't read any of my texts, did you?" Franco white knuckled the steering wheel.

"I was busy."

"Yeah, while you were searching the house and ignoring me, I had James check Danvers's phone and financial records. You said not to, I did it anyway. In a second you're going to thank me."

Schneider was only half-listening. He texted Jess, telling her she was in danger and needed to call right away. "Please," he muttered. "Let her be okay." He paid no attention to the speed they were going, nor the direction.

Franco kept talking. "So this guy Danvers is a ghost. Extremely well protected. Very careful. Did you know he's synthetic?"

"A synthetic who kills synthetics. It's rare, but not unheard of."

"So, like I said, he's careful but he slipped. Just once, and it was recent. A few days ago." Franco cranked the wheel and took them onto the highway. Soon they were crossing the muddy river where they'd watched the old man launch his fishing boat. "He ordered some weird-ass carbon fiber bicycle parts. Can you believe that? Had them shipped to a private address in the Heights."

Schneider looked at him, his face a question mark. "The Heights?"

"That's what I'm telling you. Hang on, buddy. We'll be there in ten minutes."

· · ·

SCHNEIDER STUDIED their route with a sinking feeling, but it wasn't until they turned down Prospect that he knew just how colossally he'd screwed up. "I know where we're going," he said.

Franco looked genuinely disappointed. For the first time in their partnership he thought he was blazing a new trail, way ahead of Schneider. And now—

"Right there." Schneider pointed to an empty parking space in front of Kobo Coffee. He was out of the SUV before Franco could ask him how he knew the address. He bounded down the alley at the side of the coffee shop and stopped at the green door.

"Wait." Franco was out of breath, hands on knees. Body built for lifting heavy things not sprinting. Questioning for the first time his long-held scorn of cardio. "How do you—"

"It's Beth's studio." Schneider took out his gun and banged it against the door. Three taps. Not bothering to stand off to the side.

"What do you mean, *Beth's studio*? Beth who?"

Schneider leaned against the wall and dropped his head into his hands. The gun made a soft clink against his cheek. "She's the woman I've been dating."

Franco raised his great caterpillar eyebrows but said nothing. "Your girlfriend?"

"Yes." He couldn't begin to comprehend this level of betrayal. Jess was connected to Keven Danvers. And Danvers was connected to Beth, who he'd been having a relationship with. Shit, even Carter was involved.

"I don't understand," Franco said.

"Me neither." Schneider took a deep breath and tried to fortify himself for the next revelation. The door was too heavy to knock down, even for Franco. He took out a small leather case with a set of picks. Twenty seconds with the picks and they were in.

"Careful, Franco." Schneider flipped on the lights and

leveled his gun. Franco did the same. Together they covered the main studio and the back storage room. A small closet and even smaller bathroom.

"I don't get it," Franco repeated.

Schneider walked the perimeter, looking at the same pieces drying on the same shelves. In the center of the studio floor: an electric wheel and a butcher's block table with a hardcover copy of one of Bharanda's books, *Machinery of the Soul*. He opened the cover and read the inscription.

To Schneider, my love. I have tried to find a way for us to continue to be together. I've spun it a dozen different directions, but it always ends the same. Because you and I are alike. We put our work first, above our own happiness. I can accept this on the condition that you know I will always love you. No matter what comes next.

— Beth.

64

———

It was dark by the time Elizabeth made it back to the row house. She'd gotten confirmation from Keven, which was good. He was on his way with Jess. Less certain was Carter, who had been sounding increasingly nervous.

"Schneider discovered Keven's identity," he said on his holo. "Things went sideways. I wasn't able to bring him in."

"He will find his way here. He is resourceful."

"Then we're done?" Carter's tone changed. He sounded optimistic. "We're square?" Which was code, of course, for *can I have the rest of my money now?*

"No, we are not square." Elizabeth emphasized the last word. "You failed to do what I asked. That's as far from square as possible."

"I steered the case toward Stanovich, like you asked. That bought you an entire week." He felt emboldened and pressed on. "I even got Schneider suspended. Don't forget that."

"He accomplished the last part himself, but I agree; you've been of some service. And there's a new role for you to play to earn the rest of your money. I'm going to send you an address. Leave right away, because it will take some time to drive there."

"Why?"

"Can you do it without your partner knowing?"

"Yes, but what do you want—"

She ended the call. She went to the fridge and took out a plate of leftovers. Heated them in the microwave and set the plate on the hardwood.

Louis struggled to his feet. His breathing was labored. He made a slight wheezing sound as he limped to the food.

"I'm sorry I've been so busy lately," Elizabeth said.

Louis sniffed the food and took a bite.

She got herself a glass of wine and poured some in a bowl. She set the bowl next to the plate. "I'll be at the country house for the next few days, possibly longer. Would you like to come?"

Louis lapped up half of the wine, then lay down.

"You're sure? Keven installed a ramp for the back stairs."

He didn't answer and turned his attention to his food. He choked once while eating, but recovered and cleaned the plate.

Elizabeth retreated to her bedroom and packed a few things into an overnight bag. She made sure the pet door was functioning properly so Louis could access the fenced-in yard. He seldom ventured outside these days—aside from urinating and moving his bowels—but Elizabeth thought he should still have the option.

When she was ready to leave, she scratched him behind the ears. Slowly, painfully, he eased onto his back for a belly rub. She obliged and said, "You're sure you don't want to come? I hate the idea of you being alone for so long, eating kibble from an automatic feeder."

He kicked his leg reflexively and thumped his tail twice. His eyes were partially closed, giving him the half-crazy look that comes with extreme contentment. She scratched a few more times and then, when he rolled back over, she knelt to kiss the top of his head. "Goodbye, old boy. I'll see you soon."

65

K even was uncharacteristically nervous as he drove. He talked much more than usual, gesturing with his free hand. Never mind that it was too dark to see or that Jess was unable to respond. There was too much to explain! So much he wanted to share with her. And yet, the possibility loomed that she might not comprehend. Worse, she might understand but take a critical stance. She might call him crazy. He could withstand condemnation from the rest of the world but not from her.

"You see," he said, "It was a practical problem that drove us in this direction. IRB panels won't allow human trials, which is why Elizabeth and I had to test and refine the procedure in private."

Jess managed to roll her head toward the window. She couldn't stop her ears from hearing, but she could look in a different direction. The dark window was so much better than seeing his handsome crazy profile. How had she been so wrong? So easily misled?

"So much of what's been deemed impossible is more a function of the artificial limits imposed by others," Keven said.

"Like the idea that humans are stuck with their own biological hardware. Sure, there's transplants, but do you realize transplant technology is over a century old? And it relies on finding a viable donor and, of course, time. Which makes it available to only a select few and, even then, in times of emergency only. And the promise of 3D printed organs has never materialized."

Jess closed her eyes and focused on the feeling of the cold glass on her forehead. She watched the uniform shoulder of the highway give way to a water-filled ditch and the edge of a thick forest. They were now on a smaller country road, every minute getting farther away from the city.

"The Doctor and I have shattered the glass ceiling, Jess. Do you realize the implications? Humans can be maintained and even improved through the fabrication of organs and parts. But that's not even the most exciting aspect! We will be creating a hybrid race and you've got to see how that's the only way forward, Jess. Tribalism has dominated mankind since the beginning of time. How much blood has been spilled because of what God a person believed in, or their political affiliation, or the color of their skin, whether they're biologically human or synthetic? The only way to overcome this is to obliterate these distinctions.

"I know. You're probably thinking, 'that's just a clever justification,' but it's not, Jess. It's the truth. It holds up. All you have to do to see this is look back through time from the wars and genocides to the inquisitions and even the Children's crusade. The common thread? Killing those perceived as different."

They turned onto a private driveway that led deep into the woods. Jess looked into the blackness of the forest and wondered what Keven and Elizabeth were going to do to her, and how much longer she had left. She was going to miss her mother if not her mother's husband, Dwight. And her work. And, of course, her friends. But what surprised her most was the intensity of her regret about Schneider. She realized now it was *the* thing that had been missing from her life: her father. She'd wasted so much time being angry at him, time that could have been better spent *with him.*

"Part human and part synthetic," Keven droned on. "Hybrid. The best of both."

More than anything she wished she could go back to their last holo call. She wished she could have told him how much he meant to her. How much she still loved him.

Kevin continued talking. Blathering about the new world order and how it was going to arrive just in time. "The degradation of the environment has pushed the design of the biological human beyond its ability to cope, Jess. You see that, don't you?" He was practically vibrating with excitement. "Every major disease process shows that humans are trending toward redox imbalance. On a global scale, Jess, and it's already happening! Mitochondrial failure. Cellular collapse. Lifespan and health span decreasing and no one wants to deal with it."

But even more than that Jess wanted to forgive Schneider. She thought back to their last days together as a family, taking a tour of the house he was going to buy for them. The Craftsman with the little covered porch and the big yard. Walking up the gravel driveway holding her mom's hand, and Schneider's. She'd felt so happy and safe. Full. And she'd spent the last twenty years trying to have that feeling again. Maybe Schneider had, too.

She could see it now, how wrong she'd been about Schneider's motivations. He wasn't selfish. He'd been trying to protect her. Trying to keep her away from psychos like Keven. And he'd been willing to sacrifice his own wants and needs to accomplish it.

"Okay, I can see I'm getting a little far out, a little technical. Let me put it this way: the onset of chronic disease is occurring at a younger age each generation. Don't you see? Hybridization is the cure. It's what's needed. The future of the human race depends on it. As environmental degradation continues and our toxic load becomes unbearable we will not be able to survive. This is the only way."

Jess wanted to say to Schneider that she was sorry. She wanted to say the words out loud and make it real, even if he wasn't present to hear. But it didn't matter anyway because her face was thick. Immobile. The best she could do was think it and hope that somehow he would know.

66

Carter lay on the patio stones and rubbed his jaw, which screamed with pain and the gut-clenching feeling that something was seriously wrong, as in broken or dislocated wrong. He tried to bring his teeth together but as soon as his lower jaw came within a half-inch of the upper it began to tremble.

"Fuck." He muttered it quietly, unable to open fully enough to give the curse its proper volume. He looked around at the patio pavers littered with broken glass and a pair of shoes. Sneakers. Black Converse. He looked up from the shoes and saw his partner, Rubin. Rubin didn't say it, but his look conveyed the message that Carter had been dead wrong to go in alone.

"Schneider did this?" Rubin took out his set of tiny keys.

Carter nodded. As soon as his partner unfastened his cuffs, he rubbed his wrists and slowly got to his feet. He brushed off his cotton suit, but it was a mess. Yet another one ruined.

"It was actually Franco," Carter said. "I thought you were watching the street?"

Rubin looked around. "I was. He must have come through

one of the neighbor's yards. Pretty covert for a big fucker like him."

Carter limped toward the front of the house and their car. He eased himself slowly, painfully, into the passenger's seat and massaged his neck and jaw. "Drop me off at the precinct lot, will you?"

Rubin wasn't going anywhere, though.

"What?" Carter said.

"It's time to cut the shit, Derrick. What's going on, and don't give me any crap about a secret mission from the L.T. How long have we known each other?"

"Thirteen years."

"Which is long enough to know when one of us is lying."

"You're right. I haven't been telling the truth." Carter sighed and made a show of gathering himself for the effort of coming clean. He'd anticipated this moment because Rubin was smart. You could fool a guy like him for a little while but, eventually, he'd figure it out. Which is why Carter had cooked up a story in advance. A good story, one that was almost accurate. He forced another sigh and said, "Schneider and Franco are dirty." He made sure to say it like he wished it weren't true.

"What?"

"You heard me. They're on the take."

"How?"

"It's going to sound crazy. I had a hard time believing it myself. That's why I didn't tell you. I wanted to get enough evidence before—"

"Tell me why you think they're dirty, Carter. Just spill it."

"They took a bribe to steer the case in a certain direction."

"Yeah, what direction?" His words were thick with doubt. "And who bribed them?"

"Keven Danvers did. He owns this house. I'll explain the rest down to the smallest detail, but do you mind starting the car? I think my jaw might be dislocated. I need to get to the walk-in clinic."

Rubin considered, but he wasn't convinced. He'd never known Carter to hold back. That's why they were such a good team: they trusted each other and talked everything through. *Everything.* Even personal stuff, like when Rubin's wife, Gloria, had gotten breast cancer: they'd gone to the Golden Horseshoe and, over several rounds of beer—plus Buffalo wings and cheeseburger sliders—come with up a plan. Rubin took two months off under FMLA. And every night, after clocking out at the precinct, Carter came by with takeout food and flowers. Wouldn't take a penny for it either.

"This Danvers is the killer? That's who we've been looking for all this time?"

"Yeah."

"How long have you known?"

"Not until now. Schneider knew. Remember when I said he was holding something back?"

Rubin remembered. He'd dismissed it as Carter being dramatic.

"That's why we followed him here," Carter said. "I shouldn't have kept you in the dark, though. I see now that was wrong."

Rubin nodded, happy to have things back on even ground between them. "You're damned right."

"I'm sorry. I fucked up. There's more, but—" He winced and held his jaw. In truth, it was no longer feeling dislocated, but he didn't need to share that.

Rubin started the car. "Alright. You can tell me the rest on the way to the clinic. I'm convinced."

Carter shook his head. "Just take me back to the precinct for my car. After I get an X-ray I'm heading straight home."

Rubin pulled out and made a U-turn in the direction of the precinct, but the sour look remained on his face. Carter noted it and said, "You're still pissed I held out on you. I don't blame you for being mad. I was wrong."

"It's not that," Rubin said.

"What then?"

"I hate to hear about any cop turning dirty. It's bad for all of us."

"Amen," Carter said.

67

———————

Schneider locked the green metal door behind them. He hustled down the alley and pulled himself up and into the Mercedes's leather bucket seat. Ray Bans on and hat tilted low to hide the terror in his eyes.

"So what now?" Franco sat down heavily. He pushed the start button and listened to the electric whine of his seat and the steering column adjusting to his proportions.

"Head to Delancey. That's where her apartment is."

"Pricey neighborhood."

Schneider nodded. "She said she'd made her money investing in SynCorp. I didn't question it at the time."

"Why would you?"

"It's all connected. SynCorp, Jess and the SRA vote, Beth, Keven Danvers. I should have seen it."

They drove in silence, each lost in thought. Franco had half a dozen follow up questions he wanted to ask but decided to wait. Out of respect for Schneider, who he knew was mired in his own private hell. Worrying about Jess and whether they'd find her before she ended up like the others. Danielle and Steve Muncy.

"It's like we're following bread crumbs." Schneider said. "And they're leading us right into a trap. I don't know any other way to do it, though."

"Yeah."

"We need to jump ahead of the curve, Franco. You have any ideas?"

Franco shook his head but started to talk it through. "So, Keven Danvers abducts Rachel Montgomery and Paul Chafee. He puts them in a box, possibly alive, and loads them in his custom RV."

Schneider picked up the thread. "And he brings them back 21 hours later. Dead, without their arms."

It was Franco's turn. "We've linked Keven to Beth by a delivery to her art studio, where she's got a book by some big shot programmer guy who helped start SynCorp."

"Bharanda. And he didn't help start it. He *is* SynCorp."

"Whatever. We still don't know what the connection is between the two of them. How is she involved?"

"That's the question. Right up there." Schneider pointed at an empty parking space in front of Beth's townhouse. They looked around. The street was empty except for a blonde woman in a tracksuit walking a Yorkshire Terrier; she took one look at the metal detective and dragged her little dog away in the opposite direction.

Franco and Schneider headed to the front door. Up the stone stairs to the massive doors of quarter sawn oak and beveled, leaded glass. Schneider grimaced and said, "I've even got my own key." As if he were to blame for whatever Beth had conspired to do. He slipped the key. The bolt retracted with a subdued click.

"Now," Schneider said, and they went in, guns drawn, not sure if they were going to encounter armless synth bodies or empty rooms.

Schneider checked the basement while Franco guarded the door and stairs. It was spotless and almost empty, save for a high-tech furnace with an AC evaporator coil and stainless-steel restaurant shelves along the walls. Schneider gave a quick scan but they contained nothing of interest. Mostly cooking supplies: a pasta maker, heavy enameled pots and pans, and dozens of jars of canned tomatoes, beans, garlic, and olives.

He came back up to the foyer and they ascended the curving stairs to the second floor. They worked together, tossing every room, cabinet, and closet.

"It's clean." Franco had just emptied the kitchen drawers, which were usually filled with the detritus and minutia of regular life: bills, dry cleaning receipts, books of matches, etc.

They checked out the two upper levels, which were not in fact rented, as Beth had said. The third floor was locked. Schneider stared for a few seconds at a biometric sensor mounted on the door frame. That was at least encouraging.

"Look out." Franco brushed him aside and kicked the door in.

They entered a large open space filled with file boxes. Schneider took the lid off one and dumped it on its side. Thick books and bound manuscripts spilled onto the wooden floor. Subjects ranged from molecular biology and neuroim-munology to computer models of consciousness.

"What the fuck is this?" Franco squatted and picked up a manuscript titled *The Vagus Nerve (CN X) in Artificial Neural Net Configurations*. It was at least five inches thick.

"Heavy reading for someone who does pottery."

Franco scrolled the text with his finger, trying to make sense of it. "This was written by that SynCorp guy. E. Bharanda."

Schneider opened the next box, but it was the same. Books

and manuscripts. Lipidology. Skin matrix design. Sensory systems in A.I. "Bharanda means creator," he said.

"What's the connection?" Franco said. "How does Beth know Bharanda and Keven?"

Schneider squeezed the bridge of his nose. He didn't want to say it, but he had to. "Beth has been playing me. Whatever I thought I knew about her was a lie." He started up the final flight of stairs. "Come on. Let's finish up here. Maybe we'll get lucky."

The door leading to the fourth floor was unlocked. It opened to a room of the same dimensions but this one was mostly empty, save for a few pieces of furniture covered in sheets, and a dusty cobwebbed rowing machine.

Schneider descended the stairs two at a time to the second-floor kitchen. Compulsively, he pulled out his holo and dialed Jess's number. Straight to voice mail.

"Hey." Franco pointed his gun at the back door, which had a plastic panel inset at the bottom. An LED light at the top of the panel flashed green, and it retracted into the body of the door. A moment later, the salt and pepper muzzle of an ancient Labrador Retriever pushed through.

"His name's Louis," Schneider said.

"Yeah, well, Louis don't look so good," Franco said. "His back legs are shaking."

The dog studied the two men and then walked unsteadily to his bed, which was against the wall in the living room. Halfway there, his hind legs gave out and he fell onto his side. His entire body trembled.

"Jesus," Franco said. "It's having a seizure or something."

Schneider knelt beside Louis and put his palm over the dog's ribs. "His heart is hammering."

Louis turned his head and licked Schneider's hand. His breathing seemed to settle, and he struggled to get up.

Schneider helped him, pulling gently on his collar. Two heart-shaped tags at the bottom of the collar jingled.

"Hang on to him," Franco said. "He looks like he's going to fall over again."

Schneider scooped him up and carried him across the room to the bed. He lay him down on his side and examined the heart-shaped tags. One had rabies vaccination information, the other an address: 1132 Old Peruville Road. Schneider unfastened the collar and said, "Thank you, old boy."

The dog thumped his tail once and lay down his head.

68

———

By the time his partner dropped him off at the precinct lot, Carter was pretty sure his jaw was in fact dislocated. Or had been. The swelling had decreased enough to open and close, but it made a pronounced clicking sound and the hinge wasn't tracking smoothly. No way he was wasting time at the walk-in clinic, though. He drove straight home to raid his wife's secret stash of Vicodin—impossible to hide drugs from a husband who is a detective—and change out of his suit, which was not only soiled and torn but stained with blood. Apparently, he'd cut his palm on a shard of glass and smeared blood on the outer pocket.

"Christ." He parked behind his wife's sedan and went in the back door to hopefully avoid her. No such luck.

"What happened to you?" She was by the back stairs, lacing up her running shoes.

He blew through the kitchen and up the stairs, stripping off his jacket and shirt. In the bathroom he kicked off his shoes, socks, and pants. He went to the sink and washed his face with a soapy washcloth.

"I've got some bad news." His wife had followed him up. She watched from the doorway.

"Sure. Pile it on."

"Excuse me?" she said.

"Nothing." He squeezed past her and started working on a new outfit. "Just a bad day is all. What's your bad news? I'm listening."

"My car's making that noise again. You know, that springy suspension sound when I turn right. Last week it was just once in a while, but now it's every turn."

Carter stepped into a pair of slim black trousers. He shrugged on a charcoal shirt and worked the buttons. "I'll buy you a new one."

"Funny."

"I'm serious. You're due for a new car anyway. Think about what you'll want. We can go to the lot this weekend."

"You're serious?" She ducked around the corner and into the bathroom. He heard her open the medicine cabinet. She was going to get her floss, he knew. She was nuts about flossing. And her hair, and running, and yoga, and whatever other stuff she filled her days with while he was killing himself at work. It shouldn't have pissed him off, especially since she now had the body of a much younger woman. But recently she'd started needling him about it. *Why don't you join the gym? Don't you want to get back into shape?* He didn't. He couldn't. Because, unless he was missing something—and he was pretty sure he wasn't—someone had to work and pay the bills.

Carter coughed to cover up the noise of his wife's sock drawer opening. To the left, under her favorite pair of alpaca wool winter socks, he found the Vicodin bottle and twisted the top. He slid two out and popped them in his mouth. The effort made his jaw throb. He slid two more out and dropped them into his pocket. For later.

"What are you doing?" She was back, hands on her hips, watching.

Carter grabbed a pair of her black socks and unknotted them. Her feet were a couple sizes smaller than his but, still, it was plausible. "Mine are all dirty."

"You're going to stretch them out, Carter."

He stopped moving and sighed, for the moment forgetting about Schneider, his career, and the five million dollars hanging just out of reach. Twenty-two years of marriage and this is where they ended up: bitching over a pair of socks.

She felt it, too, the embarrassment of getting caught reading from someone else's script. She softened enough to say, "Take them. It's fine."

Carter didn't know why, but much of his frustration drained right out of him. In the past year his older brother had passed away unexpectedly and he'd responded by throwing himself deeply into his work. Now he could see that his wife had responded to his grief by throwing herself more deeply into running and yoga. Their lack of connection was a reflection of his withdrawal, not a lack of love on her part.

"I'm sorry I've been so distracted," he said.

She did not look at the bed but she wanted to. It had been a long time, so long that she'd begun to wonder if he was still interested in her.

"I'll make it up to you, I promise." He kissed her quickly on the cheek and bounded down the stairs, black blazer in one hand, stolen ball of socks in the other. He grabbed a pair of loafers by the front door and hopped barefoot into his car.

AT THE FIRST stoplight he struggled into his socks and shoes, then pulled up to a liquor store. He tied his laces and fastened his shoulder holster. Checked that his extra piece—a lighter weight S&W Model 37—was loaded with its capacity of five rounds. It was. If he needed anything beyond that, he'd call in a priest.

The liquor store was vast and industrial, a sea of dusky linoleum and triple-tiered shelves from an old grocery store. There were no other customers.

"Can I help you?" The clerk, a pear-shaped twenty-something year old, looked up from his work. He'd been constructing a black pyramid of Chivas Regal boxes on top of a display table.

Carter pointed to the whiskey section which, at first glance, was extensive. It was organized according to price with the best stuff on top. They were big bottles, though, which wouldn't meet his needs.

"Anything in particular you're looking for?" The clerk set the final box on the top of the structure. He stepped back and admired his work.

"What's the best small bottle of whiskey you carry?" Carter held his hands ten inches apart to show the size he wanted.

The attendant walked to the very end of the whiskey section and pulled a small blocky bottle from the top. "This is very special. It's a Japanese blend. We don't usually stock it."

"Nikka." It was the only word on the label he was able to read. "Any good?"

"It's aged in oak barrels long enough for the different blends to come together."

Carter grabbed it and headed for the register.

"It's one-sixty plus tax," the clerk said. When Carter didn't flinch, he rang it up and ran his card. "Enjoy," he said. "And let me know what you think next time you come by."

Carter unscrewed the cap on the way to his car and took a slug. It was good. He didn't know if it was a hundred-and-sixty-dollars-good, but so what? He was now a rich man. And soon he would be even richer. He tucked the bottle of Nikka between his legs and hit the highway, sipping liberally as he cruised in the right lane. Fifteen minutes later he crossed the steel bridge and looked at his holo, which was vibrating on the passenger's seat. It was Rubin.

"What's up, Javier?" he said, trying his best to sound like he hadn't just ingested two Vicodin pills and the sipping equivalent of four shots of whiskey.

"You seen a doctor yet?" Rubin said.

"No, the line was too long." Half true, since he had not seen a doctor. Casually, he wondered if this new ease with which he was able to lie to his partner meant he was changing. Crossing that proverbial line that was so often hinted at in cop shows.

"So you went to a bar instead."

"Funny." Funny how well Rubin knew him, only he'd gone to a liquor store instead of a bar. Still, pretty accurate.

"Nothing but overpriced single malt for my snobby partner, right?"

"You know that's right." Silence filled the cabin of the car. In it, Carter could feel a new tension between the two of them. He didn't like it, but there wasn't a hell of a lot he could do about it now. After today he'd fix his relationships. Home and at work. "What is it, Rubin? What's that relentless mind of yours working over?"

"I don't know. This stuff about Schneider. Something isn't right."

"It's hard to believe, I know." *Fuck*, Carter thought. He needed to play this exactly right, but how? His brain was mush and getting mushier. Stuck in whiskey-slow-down mode, not speed-up-and-fix-shit mode.

"You heard what happened between him and Dixon the other day, right?"

It took him a moment to remember. Something about a gun. Yes, Dixon's stupid ass had gone postal in front of the L.T.

"I heard, yeah, but what else is new? Dixon's always been riding that edge."

"What's new is Schneider covered for him."

"So?"

"So why would he do that? He had every reason to let Dixon hang himself."

"I don't know." Carter himself wouldn't have pissed on Dixon if the man were on fire. As far as he was concerned, suspension and early retirement was the only end befitting such a sad and undistinguished career. "But you can ask Schneider when we find him and bring him in."

"I already did. I ran into him in the break room right after it happened. I said, 'hey, not for nothing, but Dixon fucked up your car. Why'd you stick your neck out?'"

"What did he say?" Not caring, but obliged to ask. Rolling the window down a crack to let in the cool night air. Using his hand to catch and direct it, like he used to do when he was a kid riding in the back of his father's Lincoln. The stitched leather back seat that had been like an entire kingdom to a ten-year-old. A kingdom where he was the king and could pretend all kinds of things as his father, a functionally alcoholic detective himself, drove around to the cigar shop, the Shawmut Diner and, finally, the shooting range where little Derrick would stand at his father's side, waiting for the magic moment when no one was looking and his father would hand him the gun and let him squeeze out a few rounds.

"He said, and I quote, 'Dixon's an asshole, but he's still one of us. Which makes him *our* asshole.'"

"Huh." Carter shook his head to reorient himself, to keep his mind from reaching back in time to the expansive back seat of his childhood. Before his parents split and his father drank himself to an early death. Which was never going to happen to him. And not just because he was *not* his father; he was soon to be a rich man. He would have choices.

"I know," Rubin said. "How does a class act like Schneider get wrapped up in abduction and murder? It doesn't fit."

"People are complicated."

"You can say that again."

The warmth from the whiskey was building nicely and, with it, Carter's confidence. "Okay, partner. I hear what you're saying: it doesn't fit. How about we wait until tomorrow and reevaluate? Consider all the evidence before we say a word to anyone."

"That works for me."

"Good." Carter hung up, content that he'd bought a little more time, just enough to fulfill his obligations to the Doctor and be done with her dirty business forever. It was all going to be okay. Rubin would get his promotion. And he and his wife would get the money. He'd quit the force and they'd go far away. Someplace where they could live happily ever after.

69

———————

Keven parked Jess's car in the driveway of the country house. The drugs he'd given her had partially worn off. He was hoping he wouldn't have to administer more.

"Where are we?" she slurred.

Keven held her by the upper arm—gently—and led her toward the house. "This is where I work. I stay overnight several times a week, so you might call it my second home."

"I thought you worked in a research lab."

"I do. It's here. In the house."

She scrunched her face in doubt but it was okay. He'd show her. He'd explain. And in time, she'd come to understand.

Jess walked slowly, unsteadily, along a lighted path to the front steps. Keven helped her climb, letting go of her arm when they reached the door. He typed a code into a keypad. "Before we go in," he said, "I just want you to know I'm nervous. What you're about to see... I'm not sure how you're going to react but I'm willing to take the risk. From here on, no more secrets."

"Okay." Jess still didn't feel right, but she could at least comprehend what he was saying. Before, leaving the restaurant and in the car, she hadn't been able to follow the conversation much less formulate and speak her thoughts. She'd felt like an old person with dementia. Or a small child who needed to be told what do in simple steps. The weirdest thing was how compliant she'd been, like she'd lost the power to disagree or even question.

"All I ask is that you keep an open mind. Can you do that, Jess?"

"Yes." She was pleased to find that her speech had almost normalized. All that remained of the drug's effect was a slight drawl at the end of multisyllabic words. "I'll try. I promise."

He smiled and gave her a quick kiss on the cheek. She tried her best not to recoil. In the last few hours Keven had changed into a different person. Or was it he'd revealed his true self?

"Great." He turned the knob and pushed the door open. They were greeted by an attractive, elegant woman of indeterminate age. She might have been thirty-eight or a beautifully preserved sixty. Dark hair in a French braid, the tail of which hung over the shoulder of a white lab coat.

"Hello." The woman smiled warmly. "You must be Jessica."

"Jess," Keven corrected with a sideways look. "I want you to meet Dr. Elizabeth Bharanda."

Jess nearly choked.

"Won't you come in?" The Doctor stepped back and held the door wide.

Jess couldn't look away from her eyes, which were hazel and startlingly clear. They burned with intelligence. "You're Bharanda?"

"I am."

The phrase *knocked over by a feather* came to Jess's mind. This time she welcomed Keven's assistance as he led her inside to a chair and ottoman. It was in a little reading nook complete with a bay window and a sprawling Calico cat. Before her, a low walnut table that rested on a lush woven rug.

"Are you okay, dear?" The Doctor, or Bharanda, took the chair next to Jess.

"The money. That was you?"

"You say it like an accusation. But yes, I sent you a check. A donation." She turned to Keven. "Why don't you bring our guest a glass of water? She looks dehydrated."

Keven hesitated and then stalked off to the kitchen.

Dr. Bharanda leaned in close. "He's fond of you. I see why. Very beautiful, and you have both intelligence and kindness in your eyes. That's not as common as you might think."

"Thank you." Not sure how to take the compliment. She'd been too altered to follow everything Keven had said in the car, but one thing was clear: this woman was deeply involved, and likely the chief architect of some very bad things. To say she was not to be trusted was a colossal understatement.

When Keven returned, Jess accepted the glass but set it down on the rug. No way she was falling for that trick twice, and yet it seemed unwise to refuse outright. There was nothing threatening about the Doctor but, then again, Keven hadn't seemed dangerous either. And he'd drugged her in the middle of a date before going on an extended rant about taking over the world.

"I don't blame you," Dr. Bharanda said. "But the anticholinergic Keven gave you in the restaurant was just to get you here peacefully. There's no further need for drugs."

Jess looked at the glass but made no move.

"It doesn't matter." The Doctor rose and extended her hand. "Come with me, dear. There's too much to explain and not enough time. Better to show you."

Jess took her hand and stood.

Keven made to follow, but the Doctor stopped him with a

look. "I am expecting a visit from our mutual friend, Detective Carter. Would you stay and welcome him?"

Keven stood, blinking.

"Thank you."

70

Forty miles from the city and Carter was piss drunk.

"Approaching the destination," the GPS said.

He took a final sip from the bottle, screwed the cap tight, and tossed it on the back seat. His car swerved across the country two lane. The front right tire sank into the soft dirt shoulder then bounded back up onto the asphalt. He laughed.

"The destination is on the right." This time the GPS spoke with a little more urgency.

Carter slammed the brakes and skidded, coming to rest thirty feet past a hidden drive. 1132 Old Peruville Road. He turned around and pulled up to a massive wrought iron gate. He noted the camera lens atop a keypad and typed the code the Doctor had given. The gate swung open.

The driveway was more like a private road, narrow and winding. It seemed to go on for miles. He rolled the window all the way down and slapped his face to sober up.

"Come on, Carter," he said. "Keep it together. You're almost done."

When he reached the carriage house he saw Keven, the good-looking synthetic who was the Doctor's errand boy. Keven was dressed in faded jeans and a black V-neck tee, looking more like a model in an old Gap commercial than a killer. Carter wasn't fooled, though. He could see the cords standing out on his neck and the violence lurking behind the smile.

"Thanks for coming, Detective." Keven held the car door open. A true gentleman.

Carter hesitated. He'd forgotten his spare S&W in the glove box. Just a reach away. "Be out in the minute."

The bastard just stood there, watching him. Venal smile fixed to his insufferable square jaw. "Take your time."

Take your time. For a second Carter entertained the thought of wasting the synthetic on the spot. Two shots to the head or chest, go in the house and do the same with the Doctor. But it was too late for that. Even if he could frame the whole thing right—detective singlehandedly solves the big case, and without any backup!—the money trail led right to him. He'd be ruined no matter what.

Carter sighed and got out. He took a look around at the inside of the carriage house. The walls were done up in oiled cedar boards, tongue and groove, like what you'd find in a sauna. Must have cost a fortune to cover a space as large as this. Keven hit a remote button on a panel. The overhead door closed. "Elizabeth is waiting to see you, Detective."

"Let's go then." Carter waited for him to lead.

Keven stayed put. He handed Carter a plastic tube six inches long. "This is an auto injector. Stick it in your thigh. It won't hurt."

Carter turned it around in his palm. "What the hell—"

"It's a preloaded sedative. The needle will punch through clothing, just like an EpiPen." He made a motion with the bottom of his fist striking against his open palm. "Go on."

Understanding made its way through the boozy aura of Carter's mind. He shifted the pen into his left hand, and reached inside his jacket for his piece. Too slow.

"Wrong choice." Keven grabbed Carter's wrist with his right hand and punched him in the face with his left. Twice. The detective's eyes went out of focus. Keven had maintained his grasp on the wrist and used it to ease him down. He jabbed the pen into Carter's neck and watched the body go slack. Then he grabbed Carter's foot and dragged him across the smooth concrete floor toward the side door and beyond.

71

———

Jess took a seat at the kitchen table, opposite Elizabeth. Her vision kept narrowing—to focus on the point of threat, she assumed—but she forced herself to open up and look around. Notice everything, the way Schneider had taught her to, as a little girl. The room was dominated by a Massive Wolff stove and a porcelain farmhouse sink. Bianco tiled floor. Sub-Zero fridge with a door that matched the cabinets. All very classy, but nothing of potential use if, God forbid, she needed to force her way out.

You will, a voice deep inside her said.

"You must have questions." Elizabeth filled a kettle and put it on the range. She opened the fridge and took out a loaf of dark bread, a tray of butter, and a jar of preserves. "Ask away."

Jess had questions. Like, what the fuck was going on? Why had her boyfriend drugged her, and why was she in Bharanda's kitchen? But she got hold of the mix of anger and fear that had been simmering since the drug had worn off . "What should I call you? Doctor Bharanda?"

"Elizabeth is fine." She put two slices of the dark bread in a toaster, and sat down across from Jess.

"I'd like to go home now, Elizabeth."

"I'm sure. It's been an eventful day."

"Are you going to stop me if I try and leave?"

"You must be tired and more than a little confused."

"That's not an answer." Jess watched Elizabeth move about the kitchen gathering the toast, butter, jam, and three hand-made mugs. She'd had enough with the fake hostess routine. She stood up.

"Not yet, dear." Elizabeth handed Jess the ceramic mugs and said, "Bring these to the table. Your father will be joining us soon."

"What do you mean? My stepfather? Why would he come here?"

"Not your stepfather. The only real father you've known." Elizabeth sat down and gestured at the empty chair across from her. "You can pour your own tea. I'm sure you wouldn't trust me anyway. And I can't say that I blame you, though I have no intention of harming you."

Jess pressed her lips together. "Schneider? What's he got to do with any of this?"

"Take a bite of toast, please." When Jess responded with a cold stare, Elizabeth sighed and said, "The drug Keven dosed you with has left you dehydrated and hypoglycemic. If you want to be able talk and think, and understand what I'm about to tell you, eat this, and drink that."

Bharanda or not, Jess wanted to tell this woman to go fuck herself. But at the mention of eating and drinking her stomach growled. Her mouth salivated. Bitterly, she picked up a piece of toast and took a bite.

"Try some of this." Elizabeth unscrewed the lid of the jar of preserves and dipped a butter knife in it. "It's very good."

Jess wondered if she had the guts to grab the kettle and smash it into Elizabeth's face and run from the house, horror movie style. They were roughly the same size, but Elizabeth was so much more intimidating. She was all surface sweetness wrapped over a steel core. The kind of person who was used to controlling others and knew a million ways to do it. Jess spread a layer of jam or preserves or whatever it was on her toast. She said, "What's your connection to Schneider?"

"We're lovers."

She choked. "Bullshit."

Elizabeth poured herself a cup of tea and turned the kettle handle toward Jess. An open invitation to pour. "It's true, though I suspect his feelings have changed. For such an outwardly rebellious man he is quite traditional. A contradiction I find charming, by the way."

Beyond the kitchen, they heard an outside door opening and then closing. The sound of something heavy being dragged.

"Everything okay?" Elizabeth called out. She kept her eyes on Jess, the placid expression never leaving her face.

"Yes," Keven said. "Going to the lab."

More of the dragging sound followed by a soft elevator ding. Followed by quiet.

"Okay, fuck this. I'm out." Jess dropped her toast and pushed her chair back.

"Sit." Elizabeth thumped something heavy on the table. It got Jess's attention. Elizabeth held it up to show: a gun. It was small, but it looked real enough.

Jess stood defiant.

"I like you, but I will use this. If I have to. Do I?"

"I thought you were a scientist," Jess said. "A philanthropist."

"I am an agent of change. Like you. Now sit down."

Jess sat. "You want to influence the SRA vote. I get it. But you don't need me to do that. And you don't need Schneider."

"The SRA vote is a small piece of a bigger puzzle." She set the gun down on the table, but in such a way that the muzzle remained pointed at Jess. "Rights are important, but the process is too slow. I don't have the time or patience to change public opinion through conventional means. You should understand this better than anyone."

"I ran the ads," Jess said. "Just like you wanted. I did twenty-seven interviews in the last two weeks alone to hit the public opinion side of things. I went to the congressional subcommittee hearing—"

"You were a good little lobbyist, yes. And tomorrow, if Senator Talbot and Senator Muncy vote our way, the law will change. Which will be a big step forward."

None of this needed to be stated. They both knew it, but Jess decided to take the *our way* comment to mean that she was still on the team. Not that she wanted to be on the team, but if it meant Elizabeth didn't intend to kill her, that was good enough. She took another bite of toast—to show cooperation—and said, "But not a big enough step."

"Precisely. This is where you come in, Jess. Are you familiar with the open source movement in computer software development?"

Jess nodded. "Free software."

"Yes, but it's also a way of spreading ideas and technology quickly. We are going to open source my life's work. The technology of human-synthetic hybridization. All the information and instructions needed to push the human race into its next stage of evolution, sent out across the internet to the masses."

"We?"

"Yes, you want to know your role. I suppose it's time for that." She checked her watch and grabbed the gun. "Come. I'll show you the lab."

72

Franco kept the G Wagon at ninety the whole way. High beams on, other vehicles be damned. Not that there were many. He skidded through the curves, paying no attention to the signs warning him to reduce speed to 30 mph.

"Nine hundred feet." Schneider narrated instead of using the GPS voice. It gave him something to do instead of checking his messages every five seconds, hoping to see Jess's name appear on the screen. He'd gotten one text from Beth but it was little more than the address he already knew, followed by the cryptic line, "Take the elevator to the lab two levels down. We'll be waiting."

Franco slowed and cornered into the hidden drive. He stopped one car length from the gate and looked at Schneider for confirmation.

"Do it," Schneider said.

The G Wagon accelerated and punched through the gate with surprisingly little resistance. The iron was heavy, though. Half of it fell on the hood and shattered the windshield, sending a thousand diamonds of glass into the cabin. Franco hit the brakes and the piece of iron slid off, gouging the beautiful paint on its way down.

Franco accelerated and ran it over. Two thumps and then they were free, making quick work of the winding drive. When they got close to the house, Franco ignored the parking spaces and tore through the lush front lawn and into a bed of ferns studded with granite boulders. The front bumper cracked against the largest of the boulders and stopped the vehicle cold. He and Schneider jumped out and took the front steps two at a time.

"It's open." Schneider pushed on the door and they were in, sighting along the barrels of their guns as they went from room to room. It was a repeat of the Delancey apartment, only this time they quickly found what they were looking for: a copper-paneled pneumatic lift.

Franco pointed to a dark streak on the hardwood. The stain continued to the lift's sliding doors. "Blood."

Schneider pushed the down button. After a pause, they heard the electric whine of the lift coming up to greet them.

"This is a setup." Franco edged away from the doors like an animal sensing capture. "They know we're coming, which means we're walking right into a trap."

"Definitely." Schneider had ditched his hat and Ray Bans, but he still clutched his cane. "I'm going down, though. I have to. Can you find a back stairwell or some other point of entry?"

Franco thought about it. "Yeah. I'll find a way in."

A soft ding. The doors opened to reveal a six by eight hold. The lighting was soft, the walls covered in a rich mahogany veneer. Schneider held his breath when he stepped in.

"Good luck," Franco said. After the door closed, he added, "I'll see you in a few, buddy."

73

———

Carter felt coldness and nothing else. His toes were little nubs of ice. He suspected they were bare and, sure enough, when he tried to wiggle them there was no cottony restriction from socks, or the pressure and weight of a blanket.

"Hello, Detective." The Doctor stood over him. He was in some kind of a reclining chair. Like a dentist's chair. On his right were two more chairs, one empty, the other containing a young athletic-looking man who was sedated. "Thank you for coming over so quickly."

"Mmm." He tried to scratch his chin, but his arms were strapped down. Something about that triggered his fear center, the amygdala, but he couldn't make the connection. He felt floaty, which wasn't a word, but it fit. He was floating not above his body but very close to its boundary. He wanted to float higher but there was the pull of fear and the cold.

"You don't have to do this." A woman's voice. Not Elizabeth. Younger sounding. Carter rolled his eyes down and to the left. The room was unfamiliar, and he struggled to figure out how he'd gotten here. He remembered drinking from a little bottle of Japanese whiskey. And a garage of some kind. And, of course, that grinning synthetic bastard, Keven.

"Please. Don't." It was the younger woman again. The pitch of near-hysteria. Ready to cry, or scream.

Carter could see her now. Young and pretty, but terrified. Her hands were bound together with thick plastic ties and a longer one running through, attached to a steel rail on the wall.

"Why?" the young woman pleaded. "This goes against everything you've built. Everything you've written about in your books."

"Then you've misunderstood," the Doctor said. "Coexistence is not the result of bumper stickers or persuasive op-ed articles in *The Times*. It requires action. And sometimes great force. I created SynCorp to bring the third gen synthetics into existence. The world resisted. And now we are going to overcome that resistance."

Carter tried to piece it together, what she was frightened of. Her eyes were fixed on him. Was she afraid of him? He was okay. Keven knew how to throw a punch, sure, but he'd be okay. He'd live. He was going to tell her this but then he noticed something. Or, rather, the absence of something: his left arm. There was a hollow in his visual field where it should have been. That's what his fear center had been trying to tell him. "What—"

"Oh, I'm sorry, Derrick. It's not yet time to wake up." The Doctor hovered over him and turned a small valve or petcock on one of the many IV lines running into him. Or out of him. He couldn't tell the difference and it didn't matter because almost immediately he felt warm again. And sleepy. Floaty in that nice floaty way.

"You definitely do not want to be awake for this part."

Carter smiled with gratitude and closed his eyes.

A spray of blood as the other arm came off. Jess screamed.

"Quiet, please!" The Doctor stopped cutting and turned toward Jess. "You want him to survive, yes?"

"Yes." Jess felt her mind was on the edge of coming unhinged. She wasn't supposed to be here. She wasn't supposed to see something like this. No one was.

"Then don't distract me. Keven, dear, can you do something about her?"

But Keven was busy staring at a monitor. He stood by the elevator door cradling Elizabeth's gun. Watching. Waiting.

"I'll be quiet." Jess tried not to watch but it was fascinating, in a horrible gruesome way. The Doctor was using a laser cutter of some kind. It was attached to an articulating arm that itself was connected to a large wall-mounted machine. She guided the arm to focus a green beam of light on the line she'd drawn on Carter's skin. This time, without the distraction of Jess's screaming, there was no blood.

"That's better." The Doctor pushed the laser away and addressed Keven. "Where is the donor?"

"On his way down. As we speak." Keven stepped to the side of the elevator doors. As they opened, Jess understood: she'd been tied up at the far end of the room to serve as bait. As soon as Schneider saw her, he was helpless.

"Drop it." Keven pulled him out and jammed the barrel of his gun against the back of Schneider's skull.

Schneider dropped his piece and slowly put his arms up. "Let Jess go and I'll do whatever you want. She's got nothing to do with this."

"Hello, Schneider." She patted the empty surgical chair. "Please sit."

His eyes darted quickly, taking in Carter's condition—armless, his torso plugged with half a dozen I.V. lines—Jess at the far wall, and Beth's position between the two chairs. He felt the barrel of Keven's gun.

"I won't ask again," she said.

Schneider knew he'd made a mistake in coming down alone but he also knew he'd had no choice. And now he was unarmed, with no leverage over Beth and Keven. They held the cards, and the moment he got in that chair it would be all over. Any chance of helping Jess would disappear.

"Keven?" She shot him a glance that said, *will you deal with him?*

Keven rapped Schneider on the back of the skull with the butt of his gun. Schneider rubbed the sore spot. At the same time, he snapped his body to the right, leading with his right elbow. He expected to connect with Keven's face. Instead, a static sizzle filled the air. Schneider's entire body went rigid with pain and then he collapsed. Keven half-caught, half-shoved him into the empty surgical chair. He fastened heavy straps around Schneider's arms and then his legs. Schneider groaned.

"Old fashioned stun gun." Keven held the device up for him to see. "Highest setting, of course, because your titanium exo isn't very conductive."

Schneider coughed and then choked. It would be a minute before the muscles underneath the metal could relax enough for his diaphragm and lungs to resume their normal rhythm. He waited helplessly while Jess cried in the background.

"I had different plans for the two of us, you know," Beth said. "Lovely plans."

"It's not too late." Schneider's voice came out rough. "Let Jess go and you and I can ride off into the sunset. You can have my arms as a bonus. That's what you want, right?"

She laughed. "Arms, yes, but that's not the most important part. The most important part actually involves Jess. So I'm afraid she's in this until the end."

"What's the important part?" Schneider was stalling now. His only chance—and Jess's, and Carter's—lay with Franco. He doubted the Doctor and Keven were stupid enough to leave a blind entrance, but Franco was resourceful when he needed to be. Maybe he'd surprise them all.

She held up what looked like a slice of tissue half an inch thick. The cross section showed an outer layer of skin and an inner core of bone, surrounded by vascularized muscle. "This is what changes the world. The culmination of my life's work. It's grown from both human and synthetic stem cells. The intercellular space is filled with a bridging peptide."

"Sounds brilliant," Schneider said.

"I dare say it is. Do you know where the idea came from?"

Schneider shook his head.

"There are some very old stone walls in Mexico. The joints between the stones look invisible but they're not. Do you how the builders achieved such an effect?"

Schneider waited. She didn't need him anymore. Which was fine with him; the longer she talked, the better.

"They coated the joints in a kind of paste containing specific microorganisms. Over decades and centuries, the microorganisms ate away the rough edges of the stones."

"I get it," Schneider said. "And it is brilliant. Why don't you submit it to the academic journals? Or put it out through SynCorps? You could change the world without killing anyone."

"I'm not going to kill you," she said, "if that's what you're worried about. But to your question, Buckminster Fuller said it takes 25 years for a new idea to gain acceptance. I can't wait that long, Schneider."

"You can do whatever you want," he said. "You're the great Bharanda."

She smiled. "That's right. And after this, after today, the great Bharanda plans to retire."

"We call that prison," Schneider said.

"Funny." She began cutting away Schneider's clothing with a pair of surgical shears. She was surprisingly efficient. In just seconds she exposed the shining metal of his pec and deltoid plates and scrubbed them with antiseptic. "Do you think I take careless risks?"

"You're exposed now. I'd say that's a risk."

She marked the incision lines with a gentian violent marking pen. "Who do you think I am? Beth? Bharanda? Elizabeth? You have no idea, Schneider. No one does."

"It doesn't matter. My partner and supervisor know my location. Carter's partner, too."

"You're all pariahs." She extended the arm of the cutting laser. "You did exactly what pariah's do: cut themselves off from anyone who might help. Though I have to say, in your case it comes off as very admirable. It's what attracted me to you."

"Our patrol car is tracked by the dispatcher." Grasping at straws now, trying to keep her talking through any means possible.

She peeled off her gloves and coated her hands in antibacterial gel, then snapped on a new pair. "Except that you didn't take your patrol car. And neither did Carter." She powered up the machine. "Clock's ticking, Schneider. The peptide bridge works best within fifteen minutes of the recipient's amputation. We've got eight minutes and counting to get Carter some viable limbs."

The Doctor was distracted by the sound of the elevator doors sliding closed. Keven resumed his post by the monitor. "It's the partner," he said. "He's coming down."

74

The first thing Franco did after calling up the elevator was smash the video camera. The room had a vaulted ceiling, which had required him to go into the carriage house and find a pole saw. He snapped the blade off and extended the saw's handle and used it to disable the camera.

After that, he followed the lighted indicator above the elevator's doors. When it showed that the hold had reached the bottom floor, Franco pried open the control panel and started ripping out wires. He had no clue what he was doing but continued until the lighted indicator went out. Elevator disabled.

Down below, Keven switched the monitor to the camera at the back of the house. It was positioned over a set of steel hurricane doors leading to a double-thickness fire door in the equipment room of the lab. The equipment room was fitted with redundant systems including reverse osmosis water, generator, and air filtration. If needed, they could survive down there for a long time.

Franco smashed the second camera with his pole and then

took a tire iron from his wife's new car. He shoved the iron between the handles of the hurricane doors and wedged it as best he could.

"Tricky," Keven observed. Instead of trying to gain entry, Franco was locking them in. "Pointless," Keven concluded, "but still clever."

Behind him, Beth opened a refrigerated case containing the two meaty discs that would bridge human and synthetic tissue. She peeled the protective backing off one side of the discs and returned her attention to Schneider. "Anesthetic." She held up a needle, which she inserted into the shoulder capsule. "There's a thin flexible matrix between the metal. In case you're wondering."

Schneider felt the numbness spread through him in a single warm wave. He looked at Jess and said, "I'm sorry."

Beth turned on the cutting machine and guided it into position. "If you feel any pain, Schneider, let me know."

"Was any of it real, Beth?" It was his last chance.

"Oh, Schneider." She shoved the laser cutter away and took in a big breath. "You shouldn't have to ask."

"I'm asking. All the letters and emails. Dinner. That evening on Delancey Street." Stalling as best he could.

She smiled.

"That was some first rate acting," he said.

"I wasn't acting, Schneider."

In the background Keven paced around his monitor, cursing. "He's disabled the cameras."

Beth was about to respond, but Schneider caught her attention first. "Then how could you do this?" He heard some thumping above. He hoped it was Franco.

"We're all made up of parts, Schneider," she said. "You got to know the part of me that wanted to fall in love. And I'm grateful to you for that experience. Now you're getting to see the part of me that wants to change the world."

"You can have both," Schneider said. "You can have a relationship and change the world, just not this way."

Above, the ceiling shook. They all looked up.

"It's nothing." Keven abandoned his post by the monitor and set up a new position near the double door, in the equipment room. "He took the stairwell to the basement, but now that he's wrecked the lift this is the only way in or out. It works better for us. He did me a favor."

There was a crash from above. Someone dropping something very heavy.

The Doctor sighed. "I wish that were so, Schneider. But it's not. In this life, we may only get to be one thing. And this is what I am. This is the path I have chosen." She fired up the laser and, once again, moved the cutting head into position. "Here we go."

The green light shone on Schneider's metal plating and sliced through the first third of the cut like a piece of hot wire through an ice cube. Schneider watched, fascinated. A single puff of smoke rose up and disappeared.

The third crash shook the walls. A chunk of concrete dropped onto the floor.

"Damnit." Beth's cut wavered two millimeters from the line. "Keven!"

Another crash and Keven started unbolting the steel door. "I'm going up."

75

Franco's undershirt was soaked with sweat. His forearms were streaked with blood and dirt. The stone, which weighed a touch over two-hundred pounds, was red granite streaked with a dusky quartz. He'd found it in the flowerbed in the front yard, wedged under the bumper of the G Wagon. After backing up and dislodging it from the earth it had taken him three tries to lift it. By the time he carried it to the back door he was slick with sweat, his clothes torn to hell.

The biggest problem was finding a way to grasp the thing. It was smooth and egg-shaped. After several tries, he found that if he inverted it so the pointed end was on the bottom, he could wrap his arms around it and clasp his fingers. He hefted it and stagger-stepped toward the back of the house. The weight and pressure of the stone felt like it was going to tear the skin from the inside of his forearms. But he didn't let go. By the time he reached his destination, his muscles were shaking. He slipped once and dropped the stone on the concrete walkway, cracking it straight through.

Franco gave himself thirty seconds to rest, hands on knees, sweat dripping from the tip of his nose onto the stone. He struggled to lift it again and made it all the way into the house where he dropped it next to the stairwell. He let himself rest for three more breaths before pushing it down the stairs. The oak treads cracked and splintered and Franco followed, leaning heavily on the railing. His quads were cramping. If he slipped and threw out his back it would all be over.

"Hang on, Schneider," he said to no one in particular. "I'm coming."

At the bottom of the landing, he got on his hands and knees and pushed to extract the stone from its resting place. He wedged his boots against the adjoining wall for leverage and rolled it to the center of the basement floor. He wasn't sure about the construction of the place, but he'd spent several summers working for his uncle's contracting business and made his best guess. It was a basement, yes, but there was another level below. And judging by the age and design of the house, the subbasement was likely built on a concrete slab. But the floor beneath his feet would be made of standard construction materials—plywood sheathing, and ceramic tile—with the possibility of steel beams in place of studs, or composite trusses.

Putting it all together, unless he was standing directly over a beam he should be able to break through. He didn't have much of a plan beyond that, but that was okay. Franco knew he wasn't a thinker and he wasn't going to try and start now. With luck, he'd bring enough chaos on the heads of Beth and Keven to foul up their plans. He took three short power breaths, squatted low—ass to the grass as the guys in the gym liked to say—and hugged the stone. His body strained and shook with fatigue but he raised it, hip level. He stood straight for a moment, breathing more rapidly now. He bent his knees and hips slightly and then straightened powerfully, lifting the rock to the level of his chest. He held it for a count of three and then let it fall, taking care to step back and spare his toes from the hurtling mass of two-hundred pounds of granite ready to punch through layers of wood, fired clay, and pressed gypsum.

KEVEN HID behind the basement door, listening. He caught the rhythm of lifts and crashes and surmised that if he attacked at the apex, the detective would be helpless. Perhaps a poor word to describe a man who could repeatedly lift such a great weight, but the point still stood: with something like that in your arms, there was nothing else you could do.

As a rule, Keven disliked guns but this time he was glad he'd brought two: his own, a semi-automatic Sigg with ten rounds in the clip; and Schneider's service revolver, an S&W .38, which he'd tucked into the back waistband of his jeans. He wasn't sure how many slugs it would take to bring down a big man flooded with adrenaline and epinephrine, but he had more than enough.

Keven pushed open the fire door, catching Franco mid-smash. He looked down at the damage in the floor: a widening circle of broken tiles and splintered plywood. He couldn't see through to the subbasement, but the situation was clear. One more drop was all it would take. Worst of all, Franco's face and chest were obscured by the stone. No kill shot. He could take out his kneecaps, but the rock would drop and go right through. Maybe the detective would drop and go through as well. Another two-twenty to the total poundage.

"Listen carefully," Keven said. "Back up and I won't shoot."

Franco stayed put but turned slightly with the sound of Keven's footsteps. He managed to keep the stone between them, as a shield.

"Last chance." Keven paced the edge of the room, trying to get a bead on Franco. A shot from the side might propel him far enough back. But the detective continued to turn with him. He thought about doing it anyway, but Elizabeth's work was too delicate. Even if she had finished removing Schneider's arms, which was unlikely, the slightest disruption to the machinery or to recipient's body could prove disastrous. And Keven had worked too hard for that to happen.

"Back up and set it down slowly," he said.

"Fuck you," Franco said.

"You're a dead man no matter what. You realize that don't you?"

"Can't set it down." Franco grunted the words. His fingertips had split and were dripping blood. "Not enough strength left. I'm going to drop it."

"Set it down and I give you my word that I'll make it painless for you. That's the best I can offer."

"Okay. Sure." The skin on Franco's hands and inner forearms was about to tear off. He took a final quick breath and bent his knees, like he might actually do it, might put it down gently. Then he roared and thrust the rock up and out, to give it maximum height. Keven fired twice in quick succession.

76

Beth responded instinctively, pushing back her stool as the ceiling gave way in fist-sized chunks. One of the chunks—a piece of drywall attached to a splintered fragment from a 2x12, landed in her lap. A bent framing nail at the end of the 2x12 tore through her lab coat but failed to cause any physical damage. The rock itself destroyed the cutting laser and skimmed the edge of Schneider's chair, knocking it loose from its mooring.

Beth gasped as a tray of microsurgery tools clattered to the floor. She had been in the process of finishing the cut on Schneider's left arm; the laser shorted out just three centimeters shy.

"Damn it!" She looked up through the hole in the ceiling and saw movement. The shadow of a pair of legs. Who they belonged to she couldn't tell. Keven had clearly underestimated Schneider's partner. Still, she had faith in his ability. He was a fierce competitor who hated to lose. Unless he was already dead, he'd find a way to prevail.

Schneider looked down at his arm, which was hanging by a scrap of metal at the top of the shoulder cavity. He looked at

Jess with the intention of reassuring her that he was still okay, but something was wrong. She was having trouble holding up her head. Schneider looked around her and saw a piece of broken ceiling at her feet. When her head rolled forward, a trickle of blood ran down from her hairline.

"Jess!" He called out. She heard him, but was too confused to follow his voice.

Despite the chaos, Beth stayed focused on her work. She turned to a row of sliding steel drawers and rummaged through them until she found what she was looking for.

Schneider watched her closely as she withdrew what looked like a bone saw. "That's not going to work, Beth. The blade won't cut through."

She tested it to make sure the battery still held its charge. "Do you not trust me, Schneider?"

"Define trust?"

The hurricane door clanked open. Schneider held his breath, hanging his hope on the chance it might be Franco. It wasn't. A new layer of sadness descended on Schneider's soul when he envisioned his partner's wife, Tina, and their two daughters. He was grateful only for the fact that his own death would mean that he wouldn't have to face them. Someone else would have to deliver the news.

Keven came through the door and surveyed the damage. He went to Jess and examined her head. Wiped at the blood with his thumb.

"Get away from me," she said in a weak, unconvincing voice.

"How bad is the damage?" Keven said to Beth.

"Could be worse," she said. "Is his partner dead?"

Keven nodded and went to the sink in the corner to scrub up. By the time she fired up the bone saw and finished removing the first arm, Keven was at her side, ready to assist.

"I don't get it." Schneider fought off a wave of nausea. It was too morbid, too surreal to watch his severed limb being handled. "What purpose does it serve to make Carter into a—" He struggled to find the right word.

"A better version of himself," Beth said.

"It's proof of concept." Keven accepted the limb from the Doctor and laid it on a stainless table, next to one of the slices of tissue from the refrigerated case. He prepped the cut end of the limb with an orange-tinted solution and attached the slice with surgical staples spaced half a centimeter around the circumference. "Live human subject trials if you will."

"I won't."

She grinned at Schneider's effort and continued Keven's explanation. "We needed to show that it could work." She pushed her stool around to the right side of Schneider's chair. She traced the marked line of the next cut with a gloved fingertip. "Why pick random subjects when we could have the children of senators, and Nick Schneider, the famous synthetic detective who refused to wear his skin? It's very bold."

Schneider lifted his head, partly to look at her, partly to see if she was ready to resume cutting. "In case you didn't notice, people don't like me."

"Only stupid people," she said.

"Yeah, well, you might have picked a more sympathetic subject."

She toggled the saw's switch. Turned it off and set it in her lap. "You still don't get it, darling. When you were born, you and the others of your generation walked right out of the valley. Only you decided to return. It's incredible. Perhaps the greatest example of free will I am aware of."

"Except you got one thing wrong," Schneider said.

Elizabeth raised an eyebrow. "'What's that?"

"I wasn't born. I was manufactured."

She sighed, frustrated by his unwillingness to see it her way. At the flip of a switch, the saw buzzed to life.

Schneider held his breath. He wanted to be brave for Jess, but it was too much. He squeezed his eyes tight and hoped it would be over soon.

77

Rubin didn't buy a word of it. Not Carter's lie about going to the walk-in clinic or the story about Schneider turning dirty. He especially wasn't buying it about Schneider, because cops never turned all at once. It was a slow, one thing-leads-to-another kind of process. And when he'd asked his friend at Internal Affairs—she had personally conducted the interviews at the 14th after Schneider shot that kid—she'd shaken her head and said, "No question about it: he's straight."

"You're sure?" Rubin had said.

"As clean as a freshly scrubbed baby. Lavender scented. Pink skin that's just been towel dried."

"I get the point," Rubin had said.

The trouble was he didn't know why his partner was lying to him. Carter was having marriage troubles, sure, but that had been the case as long as they'd been working together. It had to do with his wife not being able to have kids. Carter didn't talk about it much, except once when he'd asked Rubin what he thought about adoption.

"I think it's a great idea," Rubin had said. "Why?"

"No reason." Only later, after a few beers at the Lucky Horseshoe, he'd filled in the details. His wife had made an appointment for them at an adoption agency. Carter had told her he wasn't sure he wanted to adopt; his wife had said she wasn't sure she wanted to stay married.

That had been years ago and they'd managed to stay together. Now Carter was acting squirrelly and telling lies. And Rubin was sitting in a Burger Boy parking lot tracking his partner's movements on his phone. He'd placed the bug on Carter's vehicle when he dropped him off at the precinct parking lot. In the intervening time, he'd watched the dot on the screen go to Carter's house, then Tower Liquor and, finally, an unknown address in the country. 1132 Old Peruville Road. Forty miles outside of New DC.

He waited fifteen minutes to make sure Carter wasn't on the move again. Just enough time to wolf down a Double Bacon Boy, a regular fry, and a large Dr. Pepper. In observance of the golden rule: When you've got a few minutes to eat, take it. Using the time to look up the Peruville Road address, which got him nothing other than it was owned outright by a nonprofit LLC called New Hope. He looked up New Hope and found they donated medical equipment to poor communities and third world countries.

Rubin finished the last fry, balled the wrappers into a paper bag, and hit the road. It was dusk when he crossed the dirty river. A group of kids were having a bonfire on the shitty stretch of beach next to the jetty. Soon after, he crossed the county line and headed north on an unlit two-lane, wondering how his partner was mixed up with New Hope. He remembered something Franco had said at the crime scene on the Dirty Boulevard. The cuts on the victim looked clinical. They'd all agreed the ideal suspect would have medical training. Carter had even said it: "I'm going with a disgraced doctor or surgical tech."

A pair of eyes glinted from the side of the road. Rubin

flashed his brights. A doe stared back at him, frozen in her movement. He lifted his foot off the gas and, sure enough, a pair of bucks bounded across ahead of him.

"Jesus." He swerved and locked the brakes, but it was too late. His left fender clipped the flank of the second buck. It spun out, hoofs clattering for purchase on the hard surface of the road. Rubin's car twisted in the same direction as the deer's hind legs slid out from under it. He stopped the car—sideways in the middle of the road—and almost as quickly the deer was back on its legs, bounding over the gulch that separated the road from the edge of the forest. A final leap and it was gone, the only trace of its presence a rustle of leaves in the dense undergrowth of the forest.

Rubin took it slow the rest of the way. It was a full five minutes before his heart rate returned to normal. His mind, however, stayed in hyperdrive, working through the various Carter scenarios. Scenario one: Carter was telling the truth. Schneider was dirty, and connected to this New Hope outfit. And for whatever reason, Carter was chasing it down himself. On a plausibility scale of one to ten, he gave it a two.

Scenario two: Carter himself was involved. He hated this possibility, but had to consider it fully. But involved with what? Murder-conspiracy? He gave that a rating of one. Involved in a peripheral way? He scratched his chin, deliberating. Carter was definitely lying, and keeping secrets. Did that mean he was disloyal? Fuck it. He gave this one a rating of seven, balled his fist and thumped the steering wheel.

"Just what are you up to, partner?" he said as he pulled in the hidden drive and idled past the ruined gate. He saw the G Wagon in the bed of ferns and an unfamiliar hatchback in the driveway, but no sign of Carter's Impala. He parked behind the hatchback and slunk back toward the carriage house. He peered in through a lite in the middle bay door. Too dark.

He focused his Maglight and saw it, parked in the third bay:

Carter's Impala. Which meant what? That Carter was up to no good and was being very sneaky about it. Well, Rubin could be sneaky, too. He shielded the light with his hand and traipsed around the carriage house. In the back, on an 8-square-foot concrete pad, he found a strange type of burn barrel. Upon closer examination he discovered it was more like an incinerator. The burn chamber had a thin dusting of ash and several metallic chunks. He picked up one of the chunks and was surprised to find it was nearly weightless. Aluminum? No, too light even for that. Titanium. He wasn't sure how he knew it, but he just did. Call it detective intuition.

For a moment he considered whether or not to call for backup. For some reason—possibly the last bit of his loyalty to his partner—he decided against it. He clicked off his Maglight and traversed back to his car, where he opened the trunk as quietly as possible and placed his jacket over the bulb on the side panel. He felt around for his department-issue duffel bag and unzipped it. Took out his Kevlar vest and throat collar, an extra semi-automatic, and a spare clip. He put on the jacket and collar and crossed the front yard, sticking to the shadows as much as possible. Weapon in his right hand, flashlight in his left. Back against the side of the house, craning his head to look in the living room. Lights on but no people. No Carter. And it was dead quiet.

He moved with his back against the siding to the next window, which opened to the kitchen. Same. Around the corner of the back of the house to the rear entrance. The screen was closed but the heavy oak door swung open. Below him, a crack in the walkway with freshly displaced concrete chips.

Rubin opened the screen door and went in.

78

———

Franco knew his injuries were bad, but he'd done it. He'd broken through. A crazy errant thought: he wanted to brag to James. Tell him he finally exceeded his deadlift goal, albeit in an unconventional way. Because even if he rounded the weight of the rock down to two hundred, he'd picked it up seven times for a combined weight of 1,400 pounds. He smiled, but the effort produced a pain that stabbed right through his body, front to back. Like he had a knife stuck in his upper right pec, and one in his lower abdomen. No, not knives. This was even more precise, like he'd been run through with a couple of hot wires. A skewering feeling more than a stabbing one.

After a few seconds of fumbling, he managed to find his phone and dialed Tina.

"Franco?"

He groaned. "Tina?"

She waited. When no more words came her voice took on a quick, panicked tone. "Franco, where are you? What's going on, baby? You're scaring me."

He smiled, but this time he gladly took the pain that came

along with it. Because he could hear it in her voice. She loved him.

"Franco!" She was making the commute from panicked to hysterical, her voice a brittle frequency keeping them connected, but for how much longer? Ten seconds, tops. "Tell me where you are, baby. I'll come get you."

"I love you, Tina." His voice was weak. Not much left. "And the girls. Tell them I love them. And I'm sorry. I should have done better."

"What are you talking about, baby? Where are you?"

He didn't need to say anything more. He knew how smart she was. She'd listen to the dead air for a little while, then switch over to the tracking program he'd reinstalled. She'd get his location and call it in. It would be too late, though. Probably too late for Schneider, too, but maybe Jess would have a chance.

He couldn't connect his thoughts any longer. Or maybe there were no more thoughts to connect. That was the totality of his life, what he'd just said to Tina. There was nothing more to think about. He closed his eyes and rested. He'd done all he could and now he was tired. Sleep was coming, but there was something else. A tapping. On his shoulder. And his cheek. No, it was a slap on the cheek. Someone was slapping him.

"Franco. Hey, are you okay?"

He recognized the voice but couldn't place it. He opened an eye and saw a pair of black Florshines. Old man shoes, which seemed funny, but he didn't have the energy to laugh. Brown polyester cuffs over black nylon socks. It had to be Rubin.

"Stay with me, man." Rubin called it in on his phone. It would all be over by the time help arrived, but maybe Franco would make it. Rubin rolled him over to take a look. "Oh, that's not good." He folded up a handkerchief and put it in Franco's hand, pressed it over the gut wound. "Hold this here." Franco seemed to understand but lacked the strength to apply any real pressure. If anything he was catching the blood as it pumped out, changing the color of the cloth from a soft cream to spilled wine.

Rubin leaned close. "Where's Schneider?"

Eyes closed now. Shallow breathing.

"How about Carter? Where's Carter?"

Reluctantly, Franco opened his eyes. With great effort, he rolled them up and over, casting his gaze toward the hole.

Rubin got down on his knees and crawled to the jagged edge. The hole itself was small, no greater then eighteen inches in diameter. But the damage to the floor around it extended three feet. The space between the floor and ceiling was very thick. There was the edge of a steel beam and panels of rigid insulation. Soundproofing. But the thickness concerned him most, because it made the angle of vision to the space below too acute. His field was narrowed to a square of long metal lockers.

He crept closer and listened. A woman's voice followed by an electric buzzing. He looked over the rim of the hole, which he knew was risky. So easy for someone to aim up and shoot him in his face. But no bullets came. The voices were a little louder; they didn't seem aware of him, presumably because Franco was too close to death to be a threat. It took a moment for his eyes to focus but when they did, he saw the glint of a metal forearm. It looked like Schneider's arm except it wasn't attached.

A piece of plywood gave way under his hand with a sharp snap. The voices grew silent. He kicked off his shoes and crawled as quietly as possible back to where Franco lay.

"Hang in there," he whispered.

Franco said nothing.

"I'm going down."

79

"I'm sorry," Schneider said.

"Don't be silly," Beth said. "You haven't done anything wrong."

"Not you." He looked past her toward the wall, where Jess was tied. Her head had stopped bleeding but she looked confused. Possibly concussed. "I never should have left you, Jess. I'm sorry."

She covered her face with her bound hands. When she took them away, her eyes were clear. "Schneider."

He shook his head. "I need to say it. I made a terrible mistake leaving you and your mom. I'm sorry, Jess. I didn't mean to cause you pain."

"Schneider, look at me." When he did, she gestured with her head and eyes to the door.

Beth stopped cutting and pushed Schneider's head back. "Do you want me to mess this up and accidentally kill you?"

"Accidentally, on purpose, what's the difference?"

"Don't be so dramatic. But do stay still."

Keven paced the surgical floor until he found what he needed: a laptop and a folding chair. He carried them to the far end of the room by Jess and sat down. Balancing the laptop on his knees, he said, "I need the code, Jess."

She shook her head. "The code to what? I don't know what you're talking about."

"The access code to your agency's secure site."

"Why? What does that have to do with any of this?"

"You and Brendan are the only ones authorized to post. The message I'm going to send must come from you." He pulled it up on the screen and handed it to her.

She stared back. "You can hybridize humans and synthetics but you need me to type in my password? You've got to be fucking kidding me."

"Password, no. Print and retinal scan, yes."

"We can do it without your consent," Beth said. "I doubt you'd like that."

Jess sighed and focused on the handle of the hurricane door. From her position tied to the wall she could see it turning, just a quarter of an inch. It creaked a little, but the screeching of the saw covered it.

She sighed and took the laptop, making sure to fumble it in her bound hands. It clattered to the floor. "I can't do this with my hands tied up."

"No," Beth said over the buzzing.

Keven picked up the laptop and held it for her. He had hacked into her organization's website. The user authentication window popped open. She hesitated until he gave her a *now* look. She put her finger on the print pad.

"Now your eye." Keven waited for the prompt and lifted it higher, so the camera could scan Jess's right eye. She complied. As soon as it was finished, she returned her attention to the hurricane door. It jolted but didn't open. Although the door was designed to swing in from the outside—presumably in the event of an emergency—Keven had welded a heavy sliding bolt. Unless he chose to open it, no one was getting in. The door jarred again.

"What now?" Beth stopped the saw. She'd cut across Schneider's pec-deltoid juncture, but there was much more to go. The oscillating blade only reached an inch and a half deep, which meant she needed to go all the way around the joint. Each pass would penetrate the titanium alloy outer shell and an inch or so of vascularized tissue. This would leave the bone and surrounding tissue intact; she hadn't yet figured how to deal with that, but she would. Maybe a handheld laser, if she could adjust the depth-of-cut setting.

Keven was busy typing, attaching the data file containing his and the Beth's work, which would soon be open sourced to the world. "Uploading," he said.

"I thought his partner was dead," Beth said.

"He is, and the files are all uploaded. It's done." Keven snapped the laptop shut.

"Doesn't sound like he's dead," Schneider chimed in, trying to rattle Keven.

"I shot him twice. Chest and stomach."

"It would take more than two slugs to put Franco down. He's a lot bigger and stronger than you."

Keven pulled his gun from his back waistband. He stalked to the hurricane door. He racked the slide and posted at the side of the doorframe. He opened the bolt and waited.

80

A flurry of shots and then it was quiet.

Rubin had timed it as best he could but, in the end, it was a blind rush. He'd heard the bolt slide open and knew what that meant. The shooter would be well positioned, back against the wall, weapon aimed at the widening crack in the hurricane door and whoever might come through it. It was a weird thing to engage in a shootout with a complete stranger. A nameless, faceless person on the other side of a door. In his twenty years with the police he'd never fired his weapon. Or been fired at. He knew it was more common than most civilians knew, but still, weird.

His plan was to go in facing the shooter, positioning the front of the Kevlar as a kind of shield. Because Rubin was going to get hit, no question about that. The mysterious stranger on the other side had the advantage of the door swinging in. Meaning that, when it opened, Rubin would have to walk straight into the kill zone. His only chance of surviving was the vest. If he could use it to absorb two or three rounds, he might get to see his wife at the end of a very long night. That was the best he could hope for.

Right.

He thumped his fist twice on his padded chest, made the sign of the cross, and went in. A flicker of indecision as he crossed the threshold, followed by three concussions of close-fired rounds. Too close.

A halo of smoke and pieces of shell casings, mid-air.

The vest punched into his ribs like he'd been hit with a baseball bat. No, like he'd been hit by a baseball bat swung by Mark McGwire. Not that he'd ever seen McGwire play. That was way before his time. But he'd read somewhere that McGwire's swing had generated well over 4,500 pounds of force. That's what it felt like, 4500 pounds of force spinning him around and driving him back against the wall.

He managed to spray off a few rounds but he wasn't sure how many or what, if anything, they'd hit. He'd aimed at the muzzle flashes from the shooter, who had been exactly where Rubin had thought he'd be—plastered against the wall like a sneaky bastard, just waiting to pick him off. But contrary to Rubin's expectations he was crouched low. On one knee. Even sneakier.

Smart, Rubin thought. He'd been compressing his profile. Minimizing his chances of being hit.

Rubin dropped the angle of his gun and squeezed off two, taking one more in exchange. It ripped through his left thigh, nicking the bone and the femoral artery. He didn't know it at the time nor did he know the slug exited the back of his leg and lodged in the wall. His only awareness was of his knee buckling. He staggered back, his finger still flexed over the trigger, and painted the wall and ceiling with the rest of the rounds in his magazine.

"Jess!" Schneider strained against the heavy strap that pinned his chest to the chair. The room was acrid with smoke. It took a second to clear enough so he could make out her shape at the far end of the room. She wasn't moving.

Rubin touched his neck, which felt heavy and swollen. If he'd taken one in the throat it was all over. But his fingers touched fabric and he realized it was just his collar. The same one his partner had ribbed him about several times. "Statistically," Carter had said in his dry, know-it-all way, "throats get cut by knives, not shot with bullets."

Rubin tugged on the collar and scratched his neck. His hand came back streaked with blood. He smiled with satisfaction, eager to find Carter and tell him just how full of shit he'd been. He even knew how he'd say it: "Statistically, asshole, you were wrong."

He searched the room for his partner but there was too much smoke. And his blood pressure was dropping quickly. He slid to the floor wondering what was going on with his body. Seven feet away, facing him, the shooter squatted against his own wall. His eyes were open but he was very still. Staring back at Rubin, blinking slowly.

"Jess!" Schneider thrashed against his restraints, seemingly unaware of his missing left arm and the gaping wound in his right that continued to ooze dark oily blood despite Beth's cauterizing tool. The heavy nylon webbing had initially been cinched over his chest and both arms. Now, with one limb gone, there was a bit of slack. He continued thrashing and was able to wrest his right arm from the webbing. It hurt like hell, but the Doctor's modified bone saw hadn't yet cut through any tendons and, after several fumbling attempts, he released the ratcheting mechanism.

Beth emerged from her hiding spot under Carter's chair. She stood and surveyed the damage, waving her gun at Schneider. "I've made a mess of you, haven't I?"

"You're going to shoot me?" Schneider sneered. "It won't matter, you know. You've gone too far. And for what? Your deranged vision of progress."

"It seems paradoxical, I know."

"You can't outrun this, Beth."

She tucked the gun in pocket of her lab coat. "We'll see, my dear." She blew him a kiss and drifted away, toward the gurney where Carter lay.

Schneider tore at his leg restraints with his right hand. The restraints on his legs were heavier and harder to access. The hardware was meant to be tightened and released from a completely different position. He persisted, though, and gained a quarter of an inch of slack. It was still too tight.

"Oh, dear." Elizabeth had turned her attention now to Carter's monitor, which was making a flatlining noise. She hovered over his anesthetized body and touched the side of his neck with two fingers. Made a tsk sound and ran her fingers up to a small hole just above his ear.

Schneider pushed on the ratchet but it still wouldn't budge. He tried pulling himself higher on the chair to increase his leverage, but his torn arm had little strength. He looked around frantically, and reached for a scalpel on a stainless tray next to his chair. He touched the handle of the scalpel but knocked the entire tray to the floor.

"Damnit!"

He dragged his torso off the edge of the chair. The blood rushed to his head and he groped with his one hand, counting on the leg restraints to keep him from pitching onto the floor. He pinched the scalpel between his thumb and second finger and, with tremendous effort, pulled himself back up onto the chair. Three slashes at the webbing and he was free. When at last he made it to his feet he was overcome by a wave of dizziness.

Beth looked ready to abandon the scene completely. She was near the hurricane door kneeling beside Keven, speaking to him in hushed tones.

Schneider swayed and lurched toward her.

"Don't." Beth pulled the gun from her pocket and waved it

loosely at Jess, should he try and stop her. "Tough choice, Schneider. Try and stop me or save the girl."

Schneider felt more solid on his legs now. The scalpel twitched in his hand.

"What will it be, justice or family?" She gave him a knowing smile. Watched for a brief moment as Schneider knelt and worked the scalpel between the plastic zip ties and the pale skin of Jess's wrists. Beth had already slung Keven's arm over her shoulder and was pulling him up. A second later and they passed through the threshold of the hurricane door and were gone.

81

Of all the restaurants in the world Franco insisted on the Shawmut Diner. Two touch-and-go surgeries and all he wanted was to go to the crappy old cop diner and order a Belgian waffle with whipped cream, syrup, and a side of bacon. The doctor—who told him he was fortunate to be alive, and extremely lucky to have escaped without nerve damage or paralysis—gave strict orders for two weeks in a wheelchair, participation in water aerobics for soft tissue rehab, and a strict Mediterranean diet. Franco said he'd try the chair for a week, but the rest was horseshit.

Schneider and Jess arrived early and secured the coveted corner booth. They watched Tina push her husband across the narrow center aisle. After a few feet, Franco gripped the wheels and tried to take over. He rolled a full three feet before his wife regained the handles and jerked the chair to a stop.

"Dammit, Franco," Tina said. "You're supposed to take it easy."

"I am taking it easy." But then, surprise of all surprises, he self-corrected and said, "I'm sorry, honey. You're right." He even let her push him the rest of the way and waited semi-patiently as she folded the foot plates and helped him stand and transition to the vinyl booth.

After the obligatory not-so-small talk—in this case about Schneider's arm, which had been successfully reattached, and Jess's concussion, from which she'd almost completely recovered—they settled into private conversations. Tina poured cream into Jess's coffee and said, "How excited are you? I watched the whole thing with my girls on C-Span last night. Amazing."

Jess smiled. "It's a big moment but bittersweet, you know? I'm always going to connect the passing of the Synthetic Rights Amendment with your husband getting shot, and what happened to my father." She reached for Schneider's hand and gave it a squeeze.

Schneider squeezed back. He'd never have admitted it, but he'd waited his whole life to hear those two words. He was grateful he was still wearing his Ray Bans. To stave off the tears, he cleared his throat and addressed his partner. "Listen, Franco. I don't know how to—"

Franco waved his hands to cut him off. "You don't have to say anything."

"I do."

"We're partners. It's what partners do."

"You saved my life and Jess's. You put yourself on the line and nearly died. Thank you, Franco."

"And you taught him how to dress," Tina said. "Let's call it even."

After the waitress delivered their food, they talked and ate. And drank more coffee. A few cops and detectives stopped by to pay their respects; Schneider slipped away to take a call on his holo. He was not at all surprised to hear her voice.

"You're well, I presume?" It was Beth. Elizabeth. Bharanda.

"Well enough," Schneider said. "No thanks to you."

"You know what they say. Nothing is personal and, at the same time, it's all personal."

"No one says that." Schneider checked the number. It was a Boston area code, but he knew she could just as easily be in Bombay. "Where are you?"

"Why? Would you like to start dating again?"

"Sure. Tell me where to meet and we can have a few drinks. I'll show you my scars."

She laughed. It was a nice laugh, uninhibited. Genuine.

"What do you want, Beth?"

"Just to hear your voice. I was thinking we could talk about—"

He swiped off his holo and returned to the booth, to the people to whom he belonged.

ACKNOWLEDGMENTS

Thank you for reading this book. I hope you enjoyed it and will consider leaving a review wherever you purchased this copy.

Additional thanks to the wonderful friends and family who helped with this book. This includes Paul Griffin for his endless encouragement. Allen Zadoff and Kathy McCullough for sharing their publishing knowledge. Poppy and Jennifer Goodman for reading and editing. And Ella, Mara, Rich, and Carole for entertaining my thinly-veiled attempts to talk about sci-fi at the wrong times. Too much is said about the difficulties of writing and not enough about the challenges of being related to one.

ABOUT THE AUTHOR

Shawn Goodman is an award-winning novelist and nonfiction writer who draws from his work as a psychologist to craft stories that challenge our understanding of humanity and the future.

You can find out more about Shawn at www.shawngoodmanbooks.com. He reads every message and will do his best to respond.

ALSO BY SHAWN GOODMAN

Kindness For Weakness

How To Survive Your Parents: A Teen's Guide to Thriving in a Difficult
Family

Something Like Hope

This Way Home

www.ingramcontent.com/pod-product-compliance
Lightning Source LLC
Chambersburg PA
CBHW022006310726
48972CB00006B/1547